PLETHORA OF GITS

Steve Walker

Hodder & Stoughton

Copyright © 1995 by Steve Walker
First published in 1995 by Hodder and Stoughton
A division of Hodder Headline PLC

The right of Steve Walker to be identified as the Author of
the Work has been asserted by him in accordance with the
Copyright, Designs and Patents Act 1988.

10 9 8 7 6 5 4 3 2 1

All rights reserved. No part of this publication may be reproduced,
stored in a retrieval system, or transmitted, in any form or by any
means without the prior written permission of the publisher, nor
be otherwise circulated in any form of binding or cover other than
that in which it is published and without a similar condition being
imposed on the subsequent purchaser.

All characters in this publication are fictitious and any resemblance
to real persons, living or dead, is purely coincidental.

British Library Cataloguing in Publication Data

Walker, Steve
Plethora of Gits
I. Title
823.914 [F]

ISBN 0-340-62494-9

Typeset by Phoenix Typesetting, Ilkley, West Yorkshire
Printed and bound in Great Britain by
Mackays of Chatham PLC, Chatham, Kent

Hodder and Stoughton
A Division of Hodder Headline PLC
338 Euston Road
London NW1 3BH

PLETHORA OF GITS

Also by Steve Walker

21st Century Blues

CONTENTS

The Goose Under the Arm	7
Haddock	21
Does a Man in a Fur Coat Eat Pork Pies?	37
Out Into the Light	59
The International Incident	67
Betty and George	95
A Psychological Need to Police ...	113
Zulus on a Ridge	141
Time	147
Cumber	169
Seventeen Thousand Custard Pies	201

THE GOOSE UNDER THE ARM

There was a pile-up on the westbound carriageway of the M4 that morning. The jam it caused soon stretched from Heathrow back to London.

Chief Superintendent Windscale was in his usual transport, a plain navy-blue paddywaggon, grilles on the windows, reinforced to take his 47-stone bulk. His seat was a huge burst chair, stuffed with foam balls and screwings of newspaper. He was making its burstness worse that morning, bored in the jam, by unwrapping the screwings to see what they were about – one of his old cases, maybe. He found a list of BBC-1 early-evening programmes from 1977, the bottom half of League Division 4 from the same year and several parts of an article on cystic fibrosis.

Thoughtlessly keen to find the rest of the article, his arm was stuck deep into the chair when Sergeant Petherwick stopped swearing about the traffic and said: 'Anyway, even if he is lying at the bottom of his swimming pool, it has to be sayed, he was a bloody awful comedian.'

'Uerghhhhhhhhh,' woofed the small mouth in the flabby head. His anus made a similar noise, basso to his gob's tenor. Flesh wobbled about under his shirt as he extricated his hand from the chair's innards and readjusted himself in the irregular arrangement of safety-belts and parachute harnesses that held him in place. He unravelled the screwing of paper he'd found. Not cystic fibrosis. On one side was the letter *Q*, all by itself, on the other more TV listings: *7.30: THE FRANKIE MOSS SHOW.*

'To be fair, he used to be a good enough belly-laugh's worth . . . years ago, mind,' said the sergeant.

'That's the generally held view, is it?'

'What?'

'That his career was in decline.'

'Dunno. Suppose. One day he just weren't funny to nobody nomore. Lots of them gets so they tisn't funny nomore.'

'Mehermehermerrr,' mumbled Windscale, his all-purpose conversation starter and stopper.

He was miffed. London was full of juicy murders, with clues becoming colder by the minute, and he was wasting his time on the murder of some rotten comedian. Plus: he was feeling vomity. He'd had the contents of a whole fish-and-chip shop for breakfast and it felt like some of the fish had come back to life, shoals of them wandering in his gut with a grievance. Usually, when he felt sick, he stayed in bed and solved murders over the phone. Nine times out of eleven he could do it that way. Even if he got it wrong, who cared? They all got what they deserved. Everybody was guilty of something.

Windscale's mouth turned down till he looked like one of the wronged cod trying to swim up his stream. He was having a rare moment of introspection: could it be that a lifetime of murders and blubberosity had turned him into a grim humourless figure? After all, he had not, to his recollection, laughed at a comedian, or even a joke, since . . . no, never, hardly once. 'I suppose you think you're funny!' was what he often said to sarcastic villains before committing police brutality on them. But he always laughed when he kicked the swine, didn't he? Yeah, he had a sense of humour. Of course he did. It was everybody else that didn't. Them rotten comedians especially, in their sleep-inducing TV shows, or they'd have made him laugh at least once, wouldn't they? Yeah.

He held the unravelled screwing in a sweaty hand: 'Was he funny in 1977?'

'Who?'

'Frankie Moss.'

'Urhhhm. Naw. Way before that. He was on *Crackerjack*. I used to watch him when I came in from school on a Friday.'

'Very funny, was he?'

'Cor, yeah. Every time he came in with that goose under his arm . . .' Sergeant Petherwick erupted into a cocofanny of girlish laughter. She lurched the van forward six feet then had to stop again. 'Bugger this!' she shouted.

Windscale opened a box of Rice Krispies and began eating them in dry handfuls. Some spilled from his fingers to be lost in the baggy enrapture that was his clothing, perhaps to remain there for days before making a tiny crunch at a jerky moment, or slipping to one of the monstrous policeman's sweaty regions where they'd dampen and dissolve like last summer's freckles.

'I wonder if he still has the goose,' said Sergeant Petherwick.

'What . . . khrunch-kwunch . . . goose . . . kwunch . . . was . . . khrunch . . . that . . . kwruknch?'

'The one he always had in his act. Yerh must have seen it.'

'He was a ventytrilumquister?'

'Hell, no. It was a real, bona fide, died-in-the-wool, fully-paid-up goose.'

'Not a dummy goose? With his hand up its back passage?'

'Naw. It used to bite him. Wasn't part of the act, either. Off its own bat, it did. Funniest thing of all, when the goose bit him. It hated his guts, I suppose. Hey, maybe the goose should be our chief suspect! Or somebody rooting for the goose!'

This was a serious allegation. Windscale took out his notebook and with a hand pustulant with sticking Krispies poised his pencil. 'What was the goose's name?'

'Herman . . . or Norman . . . No, it were Herman, for sure.'

'Just Herman or Herman Goose?'

'Errrrgh . . .'

'Or Herman the Goose?'

'Herman Goose. But I wouldn't swear. Bugger this! Likelihood is it's been dead for years. Unless . . .' she flicked her tongue across her lipstuck lips, broadcasting the smell of crushed strawberry throughout the van. Windscale sniffed with sweet-toothed hungrilyness. 'Unless,' she said, 'there were a number of gooses, a succession of the buggers down the years. There were a number of Rin-Tin-Tins, yerh know.'

Windscale nodded thoughtfully. His chins bounced down his lapels like an avalanche of flesh-covered tennis balls fluming down the south face of the Eiger. 'There were a number of Charlie Chans,' he added, and with sinister import: 'One of whom was Swedish.'

'Mehermerherhmerrr,' copied Petherwick, but femininely.

Frankie Moss's £800,000 mansion, as that morning's Press described it, was in the verdant tedium of the Berkshire countryside between Windsor and Basingstoke. A number of eminent comedians, apparently, lived in the district. Some had turned up, along with the police and reporters, to the aforementioned mansion, and were milling about, biting back their wisecracks lest they end up in everyone else's act, but commenting drily on the eye-plastering tastelessness of the decor.

Windscale's van pulled up at 10.31, by which time the local filth had done everything except pull the deceased out of his pool.

A detective unknown to Windscale was waiting at the gate with a goose under his arm.

'We've bin expecting yerhs,' he said, a mite astonished at the impossible pudding he saw climbing out of a relieved van.

'I arrest you in the name of the law,' said Windscale casually.

'Erm, Borrowgroves,' explained the detective. 'Thames Valley CID. Honest!'

'I arrest you on suspicion of involvement in the murder of Francis Aloysius Moss and warn you that anything you may say will be taken down and used in evidence.'

'Beepityhonk,' went the goose. It was obviously suffering the beginnings of a profound emotional shock.

Windscale pulled out his cuffs and flung them at Borrowgroves. 'Find a way of putting these on, lad. Make it pronto.'

'It's a phoney rap!' yelled Borrowgroves. 'I was in Slough grilling a bigamist until the early hours.'

'Not you, yer idiot!' This was Sergeant Petherwick speaking, she with the body of Aphrodite but the face of a bull mastiff. 'He's arresting the goose!'

'The goose? Of course! Brilliant! The obvious suspect!' He cuffed its waddlesome feet with relief.

Windscale took charge of the emotionally drained waterfowl, dragging it by the neck, and stomped moodily up to the house.

The open-plan living-room was full of chatting comedians all giving their encomiums of Frankie Moss to a sofaful of dandruffy reporters. They were all well-known faces: Jerry Muckle, Harry Scouse, Jackey Mills, Jimmy Forrest, Bib & Tucker, Livid & Woebegone, Manny Narna, Stan Leekie, and Roy Dibbs. Windscale slapped the goose on the wall to shut them up.

'What a plethora of gits!' he growled.

A small wizened man with a corrupt noseless face came up to him and poked him in the belly (his finger was completely lost in the poke). 'Weren't we ugly sisters together in Darlington? 1962.'

PLETHORA OF GITS

Windscale hardly moved, but somehow, with a twitch of a muscle in the deep interior of his colonosphere, he slopped himself sideways and pinned the wizened man to the wall. Photos of Frankie Moss playing golf with various notables fell to be caught by the deep-pile carpet.

'Who are you?'

'Jackey Mills, of course. It's terrible when sisters lose contact, isn't it, dear?'

Windscale flexed his belly again, pulling Jackey Mills up the wall. 'I know you.'

Mills was flattered. He expected to be asked for his autograph next.

But Windscale fixed him with an Old Testament eye and said: 'Yerh a villain.'

'Me? No, I told you. I'm Jackey Mills. Eeeeeeeeesn't it a wonderment.'

'What?'

'My catchphrase.'

'What is?'

'Eeeeeeeesn't it a wonderment. People usually laugh when I say it.'

'Look at this, sergeant, and you'll learn something.'

'Yes, Chief.'

'See the eye.'

'Villain's eye, Chief.'

'See the nose.'

'What nose, Chief?'

'Exactly.'

'Villain's nose, Chief.'

'But, I swear, I've never done anything wrong in my entire life. I still owe a landlady 4/6 for b-&-b at the Mosley Hotel, Blackpool for Whit Weekend 1957. That's all. Promise.'

'Yerh a murderer, a smash-'n'-grabber! No, no . . . please excuse my truncheon: I am misinterpreting my Lombroso, therewith doing yerh an heinous injustice. Yerh never killed nobody, never smashed-'n'-grabbed nuffink. Yerh a pickpocket! Sergeant?'

'Definite pickpocket type, Chief.'

'Even if yerh've not yet ridden the Underground wearing a pair of false arms, the day will surely come. Even if yer've never worked the

Cup Final crowds, bumping into all and sundryness . . . yer surely will.'

'Will I?'

'Won't be able to stop yerself, mush. Know what my advice is?'

'No.'

'Save Her Majesty the trouble. Do yourself in. If you want to know how to do it without mess, see me later and I'll be happy to tell yerh. It's the advice I gives to all villains.'

Up came Borrowgroves with happy news, only to be received by . . .

Windscale: 'And you!'

'What?'

'Crooked copper, you are.'

'Me? Never.'

'Get away, lad. It's written all over yerh.'

Sergeant Petherwick looked at Borrowgroves scathingly. 'The Chief is never wrong.'

'Errrm, okay. I'll kill myself later. But first, can I show you what I've found. A tape. I reckon the victim was telling jokes into it when he was surprised by the killer.'

'Good work, Borrowgroves. Sorry to lose you.'

'Me too, sir.'

Before Borrowgroves set the tape rolling there was a happy back-stage chattering from Frankie Moss's fellow comedians and golfing partners. But when the dead man's happy-dappy voice came booming its weak jokes through the stereo, several of those present burst into wailing sobs. They cried out of one eye and eyed out of the other eye, seeing if their grief looked more convincing than everyone else's.

Windscale had the tape stopped. He stood on the foot of one of the wailers. 'You think my sergeant here is attractive?'

Petherwick's cruellest face loomed over him. 'She is, yes, very.'

'Cum, cum – you don't think she's attractive at all, do you?'

'Yeah. I do. I really do.'

'Would you like to sleep with her?'

'Yeah. I suppose. Given the chance, who wouldn't?'

'I don't believe you, lad. Don't believe a word. And I'll tell you why, shall I? Because you're a nancy-boy, that's why.'

PLETHORA OF GITS

'No, I'm not,' he said. It was the worst lie heard in the British Isles that morning.

'Then why are you behaving like one?'

'I never touched no one's nothing,' he said.

'Only nancy-boys cry like nancy-boys. Isn't that true, sergeant?'

'Check, Chief.' She scratched her nose with her lower lip. She looked like she'd hanged more men than she'd slept with.

Windscale boomed to the room: 'Any of you nancy-boys sobs just once more, they'll have to have sexual intercourse with my sergeant.'

When the tape was started up again there wasn't a sob to be heard.

FRANKIE MOSS: '*Man goes into a psychiatrist's and says doctor I keep thinking I'm a dog, psychiatrist says go lie down on the couch, man says I'm not allowed on the couch. Man goes into a psychiatrist's, says doctor, doctor this morning I thought I was a wigwam, yesterday I thought I was a tepee. I know your trouble, the Doctor said, you're two tents . . .*'

Windscale ate all the apples in the fruitbowl while he glumly listened. The final crack went: '*Whatta you do if you wanna wake up in the morning with a nice white smile on your face – sleep with a plate in your mouth overnight . . .*' Then there was a strange sound, like a croak.

The tape ran on in silence for twelve minutes, Windscale hanging over it like an explosion in a slaughterhouse, shapeless in his dark-blue suit. No one in the room breathed, the leather sofa barely squeaked. The tape came to the end of itself and stopped with a pa-cloonk.

'The murderer,' announced Windscale as the pa-cloonk was dying in the ears of the assemblage, 'entered through this door.'

'How you know that?'

Using the goose as a hook, Windscale nabbed the questioner (Bib of Bib & Tucker) and plonked him in the deceased's chair. 'Because, Mr Moss was seated here facing the sliding windows, with his back to that door. It is the only way the murderer could have entered without being noticed.'

Bib tried to get up but Windscale slapped him back with the now barely conscious goose. 'Then he grabbed Mr Moss from behind, like this, placing his mit over the epiglottis, so . . .'

Bib croaked.

'Hear that?' Windscale asked his audience.

They didn't. He tried again.

'I heard it,' said Jackey Mills.

'Didn't hear a dickiebird,' said Tucker of Bib & Tucker (they'd never got on).

They gathered closely around.

'Once more,' said Windscale. He gave Bib's epiglottis a knock. There it was! A croak, like a waiter horrified at the size of his tip.

'Wasn't as good as the one on the tape,' humphed Borrowgroves.

Windscale gave the epiglottis another whack. This time it was a good loud crack-croak, like a toad announcing a military coup.

'With the victim thus incapacitated,' continued Windscale (Bib was spitting bubbles of pink saliva in his sleep), 'the killer then took him by the ears thus . . .'

'We'll have to put this in the act,' grinned Tucker.

'. . . and gave the head a neat twist, thus . . .'

The sound of the bones grating in Bib's neck evoked a horrified *ooooooooooooooooooo* from the room, a more concerned one from Tucker.

'Hey! Me'n'him's doing the Palladium tonight.'

'He then dragged the victim, thus . . .'

Out they all went through the sliding doors, Windscale leading, dragging Bib, with the comedians following in reverse order of stardom, Jerry Muckle coming last because he'd top any bill he was on. Petherwick and Borrowgroves came last, continually kicking Jerry Muckle down the bill.

'On reaching the poolside,' demonstrated the massive detective, 'the killer took the victim, thus, and lifted him over his head.'

'He was a big bloke, then, like yourself.'

'Not necessarily,' said Windscale, standing gingerly on the goose's neck to prevent its escape. 'We are looking for a lunatic. The strength of a lunatic is often out of proportion to his size. He then twirled the victim like this – they can never resist a twirl, murderers can't – and tossed him, so, into the middle of the water.'

Bib disappeared under his splash. By the time the ripples calmed themselves he had sunk down deep beside the original victim.

'Hadn't we better get him out, Chief?' queried Petherwick.

PLETHORA OF GITS

Windscale watched the water for a while, deep in thought. At last he gave a big sniff and said: 'Better had.'

Sergeant Petherwick snapped her fingers and several constables removed their trousers. They jumped in to save Bib. Windscale took no notice. He was discussing the case with himself in his notebook. It had a photo of the Home Secretary sellotaped to the cover. Windscale was a great admirer of the Home Secretary, perhaps the greatest admirer of that much-admired personage.

Up came Jimmy Forrest, the chubby cockney cheekie jack-the-lad whose persona hadn't changed in 40 years.

'Oojar, John?' he said.

'Pardon?'

'Oojar, John? People usually laughs when I says oojar John.'

'I thought you said "Eeeeeeeeesn't it a wonderment?"'

'That's Jackey Mills, "Eeeeeeeesn't it a wonderment" is. I'm "Oojar John?" Oojar, John?'

'Humph.'

'I'm not really fat, you know. Nar, I'm not fat. I'm two fellas living in the same suit. Oojar, John? Oojar, oojar . . . oojar, John!'

Windscale observed the suit. Its loud checks were the sort favoured by bookmakers between the wars.

'Really, you know, it's great for the act. Full of gags, like, being a fatty is. But the chickamedoodlers don't like it and me winkle's a stranger. Have any trouble yourself, dad, being fat?'

Windscale looked at him with the eyes of a kamikaze pilot moments before the crash. 'I'm not fat.'

'Nar. Just had a big breakfast, that's what I tells 'em. Oojar, John?'

Windscale rendered him unconscious with a flick on the nose. It was a trick taught him by a veterinary surgeon, a fellow member of the *BRING BACK HANGING CAMPAIGN*, whose meetings he attended religiously every Sunday.

'Mehermerherhmerrr!' called Windscale, summoning his sergeant from giving the kiss-of-life to Bib, who, despite a broken neck, awoke with new life in all his organs.

'Help me undress, sergeant. I'm going in.'

'In, Chief? For a dip?'

'There might be clues, girl, on the bottom, among the fluff and drowned hedgehogs.'

He produced a snorkel-mask from a pocket and put it on while Sergeant Petherwick unlaced his shoes and detwanged his braces. His trousers dropped like a heart-shot buffalo, weighed down by pockets huge with confiscated weaponry and cold boxes of Kentucky Fried Chicken. He stepped out of them with a stripteaser's ease, though he needed Petherwick's head to rest on. Next, he thrust his arms back to have his jacket pulled off. This the patient sergeant did, catching the stray notes and obsolete clues that frothed porridgelike from the side-pockets. The removal of the shirt, which Petherwick undid with her first-ever coy smile, revealed an expanse of scabrous mole-strewn lepery-white puce-rashed torso, looking like a police-box splattered with the accumulated flesh of a century of Labour politicians, scraped off their bones on their deathbeds. The nipples were red and sore as if chewed by sleepwalking gurkhas. They shone bulbishly in a shapeless trough of congealed semolina.

Windscale was naked except for the stained shorts of a bachelor. He was unembarrassed, proud even, of his extra-nude display and wasn't even slightly insulted when several of those present retched off to vomit elevenses behind a rhododendron bush.

But when they began straggling back to rinse their sadclown faces in the pool they were, with obvious exceptions, given the gift of the stiffest erections they had ever maintained. Sergeant Petherwick was also undressing, to assist her chief in his underwater adventure.

Windscale, looking like Moby Dick having let himself run to fat following the demise of Captain Ahab, and after a deep breath which exploded his lumpy chest like God inflating a disgusting planet with a single puff, sank immediately towards the detritus which might contain a sodden clue. Sergeant Petherwick, whose bra and pants became immediately see-through, had some trouble getting her bosoms under the water. They twirled tantalizingly on the surface, slapping her dog's face, becoming enmeshed by the luscious seaweed that was her chestnut hair, like something Moses had requested in a wicked moment. It didn't help that the displacement caused by Windscale's hippoish bulk was shlapping the water out on to the lawn and washing away the various police, comedians and hardened journalists there assembled.

'Burlooooopa-dlooooop,' said Windscale.

'Phlaphooooop,' said she.

PLETHORA OF GITS

They were fingering about the corpse of Frankie Moss, whose face wore the smile of his last gag, a happy smile waiting for a laughter and applause that would never come. But in his watersplashed eyes was a downflung realization never expressed on the variety stage, seen in fact only in the bleakest moments of a dull life, in mirrors or when strangers are observed alone.

Windscale slowly filled his fist full of interesting toenails, bloody elastoplasts, knots of hair, collecting this by a delicate stuffing-in with one finger, reminiscent of a conjuror hiding away plain-coloured handkerchiefs before pulling them out all spotted and be-flagged. He even, somehow, as he'd predicted, found a hedgehog, not a dead one either . . . it didn't half struggle!

On the surface the goose swam in circles and honked. How far away that honking sounded. And on looking up, Windscale lost all sense of place. The goose's orange feet wagged. Ripples came and went and met each other. Wet Rice Krispies floated out of his armpits and past his eyes. It was a wet night, that was it, an averaging-out of all the wet nights he'd known. He was waiting for a bus near the White City. He was on his way home from school, looking forward to one of his mother's suppers. Chestnut hair was flying around the street – a barber's shop must've left its door open, he thought.

Very probably Chief Superintendent Windscale would have drowned, but while talking to some imaginary people in a bus queue in the London of 1958 he managed to swallow five feet of the pool water. His eyes were suddenly above the water, being lapped at. The goose was circling him. He came out of his rapture and sucked in a zeppelin's portion of air.

Sergeant Petherwick was sitting on the grass wearing nothing but a pained expression. 'Find any clues, Chief?'

'Fourteen toenails, six elastoplasts, 608 strands of variously-coloured hair . . . and a hedgehog.' He opened his fist and it all sprang to life, a peculiar alien landscape after rain. 'Hey, tissent a hedgehog after all. It's someone's toupee. Funny, cos it put up quite a struggle.'

'That isn't no toupee, Chief.'

'Tissent?' He noticed that she was nursing her groin bravely. 'Buggering tish! Sorry, sergeant.'

'Easy mistake to make, sir.'

'Errrr . . . stick it back on somehow, could we?'

'Don't trouble yourself, sir. They grow back.'

Windscale's clothes were sodden from the displaced poolwater, but, with Petherwick's cross-legged help, he managed to swathe himself in the dripping cloth, shroud fashion. He gave up on the jacket, flinging it over his arm when its arms proved to outnumber his own. He carefully filed away his clues and the sergeant's amputated thatch in a trouser pocket, whistling an embarrassed snatch of *A Policeman's Lot is Not a Happy One* while doing so. He also coughed up three goldfishes.

'AH, HA!' yelled Windscale.

He'd seen Harry Scouse stroking the goose.

He dripped straight up to him. 'AH, HA!' he yelled again.

'Somephink the matter, wak?'

'You are, are you not, stroking that goose?'

'Errrrrr . . . like . . . errrrrr . . . It's upset.'

'Have you, and I must be blunt at a time like this . . .'

'Aye.'

'So you admit it.'

'What?'

'Have you been seeing this goose?'

'Errrrrrrr, like . . . when it's there, like, in front of me eyes, like.'

'And privately?'

'Pri . . . vately?'

'I think yerh knows what I mean. Cum, cum, man, spit it out.'

'Wha?!'

'Is yerh having an affair with this goose?'

'?'

'Sergeant! Arrest this man! He is our killer!'

Such detection! The assembled giggleation of comedians gave Windscale a belt of applause. He didn't acknowledge it, but stepped into their midst to explain his logic in his best country house manner. The accused, meanwhile, was being dragged away by numerous constables, protesting his innocence and swiping at their hats. Journalists scooped past to phone their editors.

'In looking for a motive,' began Windscale, 'I jumped upon a chance remark of my colleague, Sergeant Petherwick.'

The sergeant blushed in all her places to be so credited.

'The goose was the motive. The murderer wanted it for himself, to bolster up his flagging career. But he couldn't have it, not with the victim still alive. His first move, of course, was to seduce the goose, make it insane promises of yachts and jewellery. Then, when everything was hunkydory with the goose, he struck down an innocent man!'

'Shame! Shame!' yelled the assemblage.

Windscale then discreetly distributed wet copies of the Home Secretary's treatise on hanging and took Jackey Mills aside to advise him on how to kill himself, before grabbing the goose by the neck and squishing away across the recently mowed lawn.

'A brilliant man,' said Borrowgroves.

'Yes,' sighed Sergeant Petherwick, in a heart-melted way that suggested Windscale would be her ideal man if he were 34 stone lighter.

'Where's he taking that goose, then?'

'Evidence.'

'He's going to eat it, isn't he?'

Petherwick lowered her eyes and admitted quietly. 'I expect so.'

HADDOCK

There were those, a pathetic miserable few, who had lived their whole lives claiming that Eddie Haddock wasn't funny at all. True, he didn't tell jokes, he didn't do sketches, he didn't sing comic songs, juggle, do tricks, or even fall over. Americans, especially, didn't know what was so hilarious about him. But the British – aristos in their draughty halls, City whizkids, grubby unfortunates begging chips as the shops close on a wintry night, University professors, zoo keepers, taxi drivers, Page 3 girls – laughed at him more than they ever laughed at anyone else. He was the most popular comedian ever, loved, a national treasure. He was mentioned from time to time in political speeches, had become in recent years a symbol of Britishness more potent than any other, was more cherished because everyone knew that you had to be British to laugh at him.

The sight of Haddock was enough. Six foot seven, bony and starved . . . starved because of the years he had supposedly spent in a Japanese P.O.W. Camp. His endless talks – and they were 'talks' that he did, not routines – would often drift back to the Fall of Singapore, but it was a Singapore of Manchester back streets and kippers. His usual garb was a red pullover, a jacket from a demob suit with the sleeves ripped off, a pair of baggy khaki shorts (one leg longer than the other), and bare feet. His face was carthorse-long, with morose lines cutting down it from the small blue worried eyes, and boxing in his Hitler moustache. Since the days of the Beatles he'd worn a Beatle haircut. He usually had a kipper hanging around his neck on a string.

When this peculiar beast appeared on stage the audience laughed for five minutes before he said anything. They slapped their knees and guffawed as he walked from the wings to the mike. If, on the way, he turned his head towards some particular squeal of laughter, he brought the house down. His third Royal Variety Show was famous: he came on stage and observed the audience through binoculars. He said nothing. He just looked, up, down, across. His every weeniemost movement increased the laughter and when, at last, he shyly turned his sights on the Royal Box, the laughter was accompanied by a frenzied standing ovation.

Whenever he did actually reach the mike he invariably began with one of his many catchphrases. '*Are you under the Doctor? I'm under the Doctor.*' was perhaps the favourite. Then he'd look sadly and suspiciously towards the wings and point angrily: 'Sez who? Sez me!' This had become part of the language, yelled in tiffs, rows and hooplas from Abergavenny to Palma Nova. When the audience was calm – he somehow calmed them, mysteriously creating a titter far to the left if he wanted time to decide exactly what he was going to say – then off he went, off the cuff, on some queer tale about his life at home with his mother. These tales, which could go on for half an hour, weren't funny if seen written down (except that after a line or two you could hear Haddock's voice saying them, that monotonous voice with its flat vowels and trailing offs). He never smiled, he never cracked anything like a joke in these rambling storytelling talks. Most of the time it was as if he were talking to himself.

'When my brother were alive,' he'd say. Howls from the audience, who knew this tedious never-named brother of old. 'Ooooh, eee were a curmudgeon – it were eees curly hair that did it.' This gentle soul was Haddock's twin but was somehow three years younger, had run a tripe shop, had been a Brigadier-General, a close friend of Baldwin's, a dentist, had lived most of his life in a coal scuttle, and had died by various methods, but rarely violently, sometime in the recent past.

Haddock also had a rabbit, also recently deceased, who had been good at picking winners but always rejected the affection he wished to lavish on it. His mother, always spoken of with profound devotion, was forever having trouble with tradesmen, went into trances . . . 'There she were staring at the mantelpiece again. There'll be no tea tonight, our brother sayed.'

And, of course, there was the Bulgarian Consul, first mentioned at Sunderland Empire in 1961. This entity, together with next door's cat and anything to do with Wigan, was the centre of evil on the planet. At Christmas time the Bulgarian Consul followed Santa around in a disguised Lamborghini, stealing all the presents as soon as they were put out. He vandalized bus stops but was never caught in the act. One time he went around hiding prawns in people's wellingtons.

PLETHORA OF GITS

Apparently, at the beginning of his famous binoculars act Haddock was supposed to have said: 'He's in tonight? Is he in? He's in.', referring to the Bulgarian Consul, but he never bothered to say it and didn't make a catchphrase of it till years later.

The greatest thing about Haddock's talks was that they were always different. He never told the same story twice. An audience knew that if they saw him on stage, on TV, in the clubs, they'd be hearing a unique story, never to be repeated. No other comic could touch that. Haddock was the greatest.

His success on television was the strangest thing of all. Right through the '50s producers were reluctant to give him his own show. He couldn't do sketches, he couldn't do a variety show or a sit-com because he couldn't *'interchange'*, as they put it, with guests or actors. All he could do was stand and natter. He'd be as entertaining as a bandleader without a band. Indeed, at first, when THE HADDOCK SHOW was encumbered with the interruptions of dancers and crooners, it was not successful. It was only later, when Haddock was left alone to talk to the camera, that he could become the master of the medium. Every twitch, every onset of wryness was sent through the air into the living-rooms of England. It was generally agreed, despite breaking all the rules, rules which still applied to everyone else, his show was one of the greatest achievements of television.

After thirty years as a national institution Haddock was becoming taken for granted. But, in 1983 in the middle of the General Election, his mother died. It was headlines in all the tabloids: *MA HADDOCK DEAD*. The display of public affection and concern was quite amazing, annoying to those miserable few who weren't admirers.

When the 60-year-old orphan next appeared on stage, that very night at Her Majesty's Theatre in a bill with Wesley Ukfield and the Nolan Sisters, he did not walk on to the usual laughter but a tremendous ovation of claps and whistles. When it died down Haddock's first line was . . . 'When me mother were alive.' More applause. Then he launched into a brief account of how the Bulgarian Consul had done away with her. The audience were confused, there was plenty of applause but the laughter, when it came, was polite.

For a while after that the great comedian didn't concentrate on his talks. He came on to stage in different get-ups, as a legionnaire, a traffic warden. The punters still laughed, but not as hard. Haddock was slipping at last. He had a go in movies (he'd done walk-ons for decades and one biggish part in a Carry On) and made *GIMPY*, a mawkish tale of a deranged vicar trying to save the world. It flopped badly. But, meantime, the bad moment passed. A Royal Variety, his fifteenth appearance, pepped him back up to the top. Across the stage was a big banner saying HADDOCK – KING OF COMEDY, and he came on dressed as a King, to greater laughter than any other comic could hope for. 'Let them eat cake.' he said. 'Sez who? Sez moi.' and walked off to his biggest success in years.

After that he returned to his traditional talks, yakking incessantly about when his mother, his brother and his rabbit were alive. 'Since the old woman died I've eaten nowt but the sleep in me eyes. That's why I needs me kip, for it to collect in nice big lumps.'

A new catchphrase: he'd stand pathetically at the mike, scratch his bare feet on the stage and say: 'Eeee, if she could see me now!' Sometimes he burst into tears, gripping the mike for comfort, sobbing and howling. The audience loved it. The more he wailed the more they creased themselves. Best of all was during Haddock's TV show: he broke down just before the commercials and was entwining the mike when Part Two came up. He spent the rest of the show in tears. The laughter in the audience never let up, but at home it looked real. People were worried. Only at the end, when Geoff Capes, the strongest man in the world, walked on dressed as a rabbit and carried the thumb-sucking comedian away, was there any reassurance.

A month of two later there was a profile of Haddock in the *Daily Mail*. It went right back to when he was a stooge for Big Boots Jack, insisted that he had never in all his life said more than Good Morning to anyone except his mother, that he was a virgin, an alcoholic and an idiot. The truth was getting out.

When asked about the story on a talk show Haddock tut-tutted: 'Eeee, the things that people say.' When the host pressed further Haddock pointed his finger and put it right on the end of his inquisitor's nose. 'I'm going ter tell you sommink I've never telled to no one.' There was a moment of acute tension in the studio, then Haddock exploded all the rumours about himself by admitting that not only was he Bulgarian but that he himself was the Bulgarian Consul. It was a famous moment of television. Clips from the interview were shown again and again in the following weeks.

* * *

PLETHORA OF GITS

Solly opened the door to Haddock's bedroom. 'We ain't got long, Eddie. You wanna sandwich?'

Haddock nodded.

'A cheese sandwich?'

Haddock pouted. He wasn't sure.

'A cheese and pickle sandwich?'

He nodded an unsure nod. Cheese and pickle would do. He sat back in his chair and continued talking. This was a talk just like the ones he did on stage, just as unique, just as funny, except that there was nobody there to listen. He did this all the time now. Never stopped. On and on and on. Walking in the countryside with Solly, from Pennine to Pennine, he'd drone on about his usual subjects. Sometimes Solly was in the mood for laughter. Sometimes they were just as glum as each other. Solly slept downstairs on the put-me-up. He didn't sleep too well because of his bladder, so all night he lay there, ears unable to stop straining, hearing the sound of Haddock's talk floating on the air like the smell of gravy.

'I don't think he ever sleeps,' Solly was on the phone to Mr Myerson, Haddock's new agent (Ma Haddock had done business for him till the day she dropped). 'He lies there nattering to himself all night. Don't do nothing but that all day is bad enough. But all night, oy!'

'What about the drink?'

'So he drinks. We all drinks – you drinks, I drinks, the Bulgarian Console, I was hearing only the other night, drinks like a porpoise. It's normal to drink. But when a man sleeps he goes away to dream, not to yakkity-yak till morning.'

'How you know tisn't just talking in his sleep? Mrs Myerson, she talks in her sleep. Plans for the extensions, a new fridge-freezer, maybe.'

'I seen him. I seen him lying there all stretched out with his eyes open with one fist on his chest for a microphone. What to do! Oy! Oy! You's supposed to be a clever man. You tell me.'

After so long at the top Haddock was easily a millionaire. It was all put away somewhere gaining interest. But he still lived in the same house he'd lived in with his mother since 1948, nor had the decor changed much in that time. This was in Ashton-under-Lyne, an outer bit of Manchester. All of Ashton is dingy and depressed, but Haddock lived in the worst part. A set of blood-red terraces, on one side the railway tracks, on the other a steaming factory always under the threat of closure. Some of the houses in Kitchener Terrace were kept gleamingly clean, in the old working-class tradition. Some were a mess. Haddock's was a mess. Purple cloth was fastened close to the downstairs windows. You couldn't see in however hard you tried.

Solly, who'd only lived-in with Haddock for a year, knew all the locals to talk to, what their daughters were doing, what their various ailments were. But Haddock had gone unseen for the 38 years he'd lived there. One old bat had a story about him. Once upon a time there'd been an advertising hoarding opposite his house. For years there was a poster of a girl with a big white grin jumping for a ball at Blackpool. Seemed like it'd been there forever: getting grubbier and grubbier. Then one day, late Sixties this was, a man came and scraped it off, put up an ad for washing powder instead. Haddock came out into the street in his dressing-gown shouting 'Bugger off!' over and over again, or it may have been 'Bulgar off!' like he said in his act. He kicked the man's bucket of paste over and would have done the same for the man if his mother hadn't taken him in.

Haddock wasn't talking when Mr Myerson arrived and peeped into the bedroom. He was eating a cheese-and-pickle sandwich and turning the pages of a twenty-year-old *Radio Times*. He had a pile under the bed. They were his only reading.

'He looks okay to me.'

'Okay? He's eating a sandwich. Adolf Hitler, may he burn in Hell forever, would look okay eating a sandwich.'

'Naw, he's okay.'

They stepped into Ma Haddock's room to be more private. Everything was left as it had been in her lifetime. Pretty pink bed. Glossy photos of bodybuilders pinned to the walls. Mr Myerson looked at these uncomprehendingly, puffing his cigar. As the smoke cleared, bare buttocks were the first things he saw. None of the bodybuilders were facing front. Mr Myerson wobbled his cigar at them, hoping Solly might enlighten him as to their purpose. Solly waved them away. It was a wave full of uncommunicatable knowledge.

'So, this is where he lives?'

'This is where he lives. In that room next door he lives. He comes out for the toilet, to bath once a week, to go for walks maybe. A prison cell is what it is.'

'The damp, Solly. I haven't smelled damp like this since my days in the Mile End Road. Can't be good for him. He's past sixty.'
'So, who isn't?'
'Why doesn't he move?'
'Maybe he likes it here.'
'Not a racing man, is he?'
'Him? Never.'
'His rabbit was.'
'What rabbit?'
'The rabbit he talks about in his act.'
'Oy, that rabbit.'
'So, he's a wealthy man. He should move. To a nice house. The country. A room for you, Solly. A housekeeper, maybe. I know a nice woman – I was at her husband's funeral. How much he pay you, Solly?'
'Solly? Pay Solly? He don't never pay Solly. Not a three-pond-note does he give to Solly. Never does he say "Solly, you've worn the same shirt since last winter, here's a wad, Solly, get yerself a new outfit maybe".'
Myerson took out his wallet and found a £50 note sleeping there among friends. He gave it to Solly. Both their faces were lost in cigar smoke when the note changed hands.
'What about the food, the upkeep of this shit-hole, how do you manage . . .?'
'I forges his mother's signature. Once a week at Lloyds.'
Myerson snatched the £50 note away from the fingers that had been enjoying the feel of it.
'Hey, boss, what's that for?'
'You've been robbing my boy! You!'
'Solly ain't no thief! I take just enough for Eddie and me, a night on the town now and then for Solly maybe. So what's the harm? I earned it.'
'You've been bleeding the poor bugger dry.'
Solly went a little mad. 'Look! Where's the gold watch? Where's the chorus girls?' He started a queer search around the room for either or both. 'Where's the sun tan? Where's the fast cars? Look! Look!' He pulled up his shirt. 'Where's the restaurant? See any restaurant?'
Without saying anything, just by moving his eyes and shuffling his feet, Myerson took back his accusation of thievery. 'Tisn't good

business practice, Solly. We'll have to fix up something proper for you.'

Solly's head sank down its neck. He was suddenly frightened of Mr Myerson. He wished he'd never told him that owt was wrong, then he'd have stayed in London collecting his 10% and left him and Eddie alone forever. Naw, he had to say what he had stored up to say. It had to be said. For Eddie's sake. For the sake of the future of Eddie's act.

'Mr Myerson . . .'

'Yeah, Solly.'

'He's our boy. Ain't he, yours and mine?'

'Sure, Solly.'

'There's something I must tell you about him. Something important.'

Myerson puffed his cigar. 'Go on.'

'He's doo-lally. For sure. Never was there anyone more doo-lally. His mother, maybe, may she rest in peace, but no one else.'

Myerson was confident. 'He's okay, Solly. He's not just a turn, you know, he's a creative artist. He's bound to appear strange to the likes of us. They're all peculiar. I could tell you stories. Stories I could tell!'

'He's doo-lally.'

'Naw.'

'He can't go on the way he is, for sure. It's not right.'

'He's fine. Fine. I just seen him. He's the same as ever he was. Better. Last week's show. Great.'

'He wets the bed.'

'So, he's a problem! Every time I see my accountant I have an apoplexy. So what!'

'Wets the bed, I tell you! Every night. What am I, a nurse, to be hanging out the sheets every morning.'

'He's upset, after his mother passing over, that's all.'

'Phoo! You won't be so sure when he says in the act some of the things I've heard him say in his room at night.'

'What things?'

'Dirty things.'

'So, maybe a bit smut in the act, who could it hurt. Mary Whitehouse maybe.'

'About his mother, may she rest in peace.'

'His mother?'

PLETHORA OF GITS

'What she did for him. To relieve him. Oy! And more, much more. I'm an old man, older than you even. Solly has seen it all. I worked the Windmill. Never have I heard such things! One night, for sure, they'll come out in front of 20 million people. Then you'll be sorry.'

Myerson shrugged. 'So maybe I'll retire.'

The door creaked a bit, then wafted wide open. Eddie Haddock was standing in the doorway, long and pale, in the same daft outfit he wore on stage. Like a lapsed prefect caught smoking behind the bike sheds Myerson waved away his smoke and hid the cigar behind his back.

'I heard voices,' said Eddie.

'It's Mr Myerson, Eddie. Come up special to see yer.'

Eddie didn't step forward. He'd never been in his mother's room. 38 years in the house but never into that room.

'It were you then, the voices.'

'Me and Mr Myerson, who else yer think?'

'I thought maybe the bodybuilders.'

Myerson rolled his eyes at Solly.

'They're in here of a night, I knows. Sometimes I hears them compliment each other on the size of their penguins. It's a muscle in the chest, tha knows, a penguin.'

Solly poked Myerson in the ribs. Eddie was being funny. They laughed at him.

'But most of the time they just sits about all sweaty and heavy flexing themselves like murder. They makes no noise. But I knows they're here. Sez who? Sez me! Me ma sent them, for ter look after her kid with her gone. Nice of her.'

Myerson was laughing so hard the ash fell off his cigar. 'How's yer rabbit, Eddie?' he asked, eyes streaming.

Eddie stared at him blankly. The more he stared, the more Myerson laughed.

'Course,' continued Eddie, 'when me ma were alive I used ter bonk them, over the head like, when I found them out here on the landing of a night. Some mornings they'd be, oooooh, fifty or sixty bodybuilders lying in a heap at bottom of stairs. T' this day I've three drawers full of jock-straps.'

'Enjoy yer sandwich, Eddie?'

A rare smile. 'Yer'll find the puke behind me door, sliding down the standard lamp.'

Solly gave Myerson the funny elbow. 'Such lies he always worries Solly with!' But before going downstairs Solly had a quick butchers behind Eddie's door just to be sure.

The living-room was the three-ducks-up-the-wall type. The furniture was all the same colour, a sort of mortician's hat-band off-green. The carpet was the same. Most of the ornaments dated from jubilees, coronations and Royal Weddings. A cheap painting of a clown hung over the fireplace. On the back of the kitchen door was an old poster showing EDDIE HADDOCK top of the bill at the Palladium, 1960.

The taxi arrived to take Eddie to the TV studio. 'There's plenty of time yet,' said Myerson. 'Tell it to wait. Look at this place, Eddie. Excuse me for saying, but it's a shit-hole. A nice house somewhere, cottage maybe, a garden for your old age, swimming-pool even, full of girls if you're so inclined. So why not? I have friends in the property business. I can fix it up for you, very reasonable.'

Eddie gazed glumly around. 'This is the paper the Haddock is wrapped in.'

'And the chip,' chipped in Solly.

'You work hard, boy. You deserve better.' But Myerson didn't push the point further. Eddie's line 'the paper the Haddock is wrapped in' had gotten through. Maybe Eddie wouldn't be so funny anymore if he lived somewhere swankingly comfortable.

They stood about drinking whisky out of paper cups, the way Eddie always drank it.

Myerson was quickly pixilated with the drink. 'A white orse walks into a bar, see,' he tells Eddie, head hanging right back to look up at Eddie's face. 'White orse, got it, into bar. White orse says "I'd like a whisky." Barman says: "What sort you want?" Orse says: "What sort ya got?" Barman says: "Well, there's Bells, Teachers, and then there's one named after you." Orse says: "What, Eric?"'

Myerson's laughter wasn't the same as the laughter he laughed when he laughed at Eddie. But he laughed a good deal at his joke, filling up his paper cup and giving his cigar little kisses. It was a while before he realized that Eddie wasn't laughing. 'Get it, eh? Get it?'

'What's an orse?' was Eddie's line. This nearly killed Myerson. He had to sit down. What's an orse! And the way he said it, so grave, so funny, it gave Myerson the image of Eddie standing on stage and an orse walks on and Eddie says 'What you be?' It says 'I's an orse.' and he says 'What's an . . .?'

Solly came back from seeing to the taxi driver.

'The boy's in great form, Solly. What you worried about? Never better. What's an orse! Wheeeeeeeeeeeeeee! Great show tonight, Eddie. Great.'

He had a few more whiskys. Eddie kept filling him up while trying out expressions in the mirror (the one set at his height, level with the ceiling. There was another at his mother's and Solly's height, way down the wall). Myerson dropped off to sleep, a slosh still left in his cup. It was all over his shirt when a grief-stricken Solly woke him up with the news two hours later.

Manchester was on its way home. Bus queues. Last minute shoppers. Sore feet clipping the pavements. A million bad days heading for Stretford or Glossop or some such place that isn't Monte Carlo. Tired, fractious faces, all but their misery blanked out by harsh electric light that was yellow where it started but white when it drenched their doggy faces. A week or so ago it had been light at this hour, now it was almost dark. Winter coming: more reason for misery. Eyes kept rolling up, expecting rain.

The taxi with Eddie Haddock and Solly Norman in the back sat in long lines of traffic on its way to the BBC studios in Oxford Road. Solly was happy from the whisky, was nattering to himself about making a comeback, doing a summer season or a quiz show maybe. Eddie was watching the street, rapt like a visitor from the 13th Century. Perhaps some odd thing he saw during the drive – a couple arguing outside a shop, a jeweller taking his rings out of the window, a Pakistani under arrest – would be the trigger for tonight's act. Three-quarters into the drive he sat back, more glum than ever, and wept. The driver had been watching him in the mirror all the way, chuckling – he nearly hit a bus due to chuckling – now he was worried.

'You okay, Mr Haddock? He's errrrrr, cryin.'

'Watch the road, why don't you!' wuffed Solly. 'Mr Haddock is rehearsing for tonight's show.'

'He can cry just off his head, like, can he? Bloody fantastic, that is, like. Doesn't they say that that's the suprememost test of genius, like, thems that can turn it on when they like, like.'

'Shut yer mouth,' said Solly.
'Sez who?'
'Sez me!!!'

Haddock was still weeping in his dressing-room, dry tears now. A bubbling sob would suddenly hatch out and his eyes fill with tears, but no tears dropped, they drained away and waited for the next sob to hatch. Good job none dropped, cos he was doing his make-up. A make-up girl was there in case he needed her – she was creasing herself at Haddock's antics – but, as usual, he preferred to do his own face. Sometimes whichever girl was in attendance made a suggestion, only ever one suggestion, to show she was creative. This one was too creased to bother.

Solly came in with the Producer. They were both smoking cigars which Solly had flinched from the pocket of the inebriated Mr Myerson.

Eddie turned to them with the most tragic face ever. 'Is he out there? Him. He's in, isn't he? He's out there, in, in and out there.'

Hilarity all round. The Producer nearly lost his upper set through an open-mouthed haw-haw laugh adopted in his toothsome days.

'I wonder what disguise he'll be in tonight,' grinned Solly. 'I should maybe machine-gun to death the whole audience, God forgive me, then we'd be sure of getting him.'

The Producer's laughter died down. 'How'd we know which was him? Cos it'd be an ace disguise.'

'Oy! Like everybody, he makes mistakes. Inside his suit, for sure, in curly writing, "*Made in Bulgaria*" it'll say.'

They went away with the make-up girl, leaving Eddie alone looking into his mirror, clipping stray hairs from his Beatle cut and his Hitler tache with a tiny pair of scissors, pulling dourer and dourer faces, contemplating Bulgaria. Eddie didn't go to school, hardly even a day of it, had no idea of geography. To him Bulgaria was a massively enormous place taking up all the World that wasn't England, Ireland or America. It was full of teeming cities where every second man carried a Christmas pudding with BOMB written on it.

As usual, he began that night's performance in his dressing-room, talking about some far ago time when his brother brought a werewolf home and how it upset the rabbit. When Solly came to fetch him he was already ten minutes into the talk, but this, in the end, made the whole thing more effective for the audience. They hooted like a party in a loopy house when they saw him walk on talking to himself, more so because the floor manager was frantically waving him back – the titles were still rolling, he was too soon, too soon! He put his talk on pause and gave the floor manager one of his looks. The floor manager broke up. The studio was uncontrollable.

The show had been on air for ten minutes before Haddock could begin the proper part of his act, still having to cast stares at the regular hugely-loud shriekers. Without any explanation he continued the narrative he'd begun all alone in his dressing-room: 'So there it were, in the yard, arl dark and snarlin and starin at the moon comin out from behind clouds. Wer couldn't see where it were crouchin except every nineteenth second, cos me ma's washing flapped, flap, flap, flap, in eees way and all wer could see were the inside of socks . . .' He waited nineteen seconds and said 'Flap.' Nineteen seconds after that he said it again, more bored. Nineteen seconds later, too bored to say it, he waggled one leg of his khaki shorts.

Not knowing what he was on about made the act far more effective. It kept them guessing. Some knew as soon as the moon was mentioned that it was a werewolf, most just stayed in giggling confusion till Haddock actually said the word: 'Our ma sayed to our brother: "If you bring another of them werewolves in here I'll give yer yer head in yer hands and yer brains ter play with." Sez who? – Me ma sayed, that's who. Ooooo, he were a curmudgeon . . .'

The story continued with the werewolf being rescued by animal lovers, shaving twelve times an hour, having its teeth removed by a friendly dentist, and for some obtusely evil reason standing for Parliament, this with the sinister backing of the Bulgarian Consul. Though unable to speak on the hustings for longer than a minute, due to the continual sprouting of its hair, it was duly elected. Haddock's brother, meanwhile, having fallen into a vat of peanut butter, had gone to London in order to have his skin removed. Dodging imaginary doodlebugs on his way to Harley Street he recognized the werewolf coming out of a bespoke tailor's . . .

The story was reaching a climax, which Haddock's talks rarely did, when he suddenly went quiet. He stood in complete silence for the last seven minutes of the show. All this while the camera was close on his face. The audience back home could see the tears welling up in his eyes. Turn the sound down so that the bursts of laughter from the studio audience couldn't be heard and what you saw wasn't the slightest bit funny. It was terrifying.

The floor manager gave Haddock the wind-up and he said what he'd been waiting seven minutes to say: 'He's in, isn't he?' A huge round of applause. Cheers. Endtitles rolled over a miseryguts face.

Some newly-appointed BBC bigwig he'd never seen before was brought up to him in the corridor. 'Brilliant show tonight, Eddie. You've always something extra to give, haven't you?' He then blew a raspberry. It was his attempt at being funny.

Solly took this person off for drinks somewhere and Eddie returned to his poky dressing-room where he sat on his ownee-o, continuing the werewolf story. Suddenly, just like in tonight's show, he stopped. His eyes were fixed on a pair of shoes peeping out from behind a rack of Victorian costumes. There were almost imperceptible movements in those shoes, the movements of itchy toes wiggling. Yep. Bulges in the leather: toes scrunching up.

'Hi-di-whoo there. Halloooooooo.'

No answer.

Haddock sat forward to look more closely. The kipper he always wore on a string around his neck swang out like a broken hand on a clock that knows the time but won't tell.

Haddock's long fingers made a parting in the costumes. Toes cracked. Whoever was there took a step back, bumped against the wall, knocked over a pile of top hats. He'd given himself away. He could do nothing but step out.

Eddie stared at him for a long time, a longer stare even than the stare on tonight's show. It was very quiet in there. In the third minute two girls walked along the corridor outside, making what seemed a tremendous racket.

'Eeeeeee, I've never laughed so much in arl me life. I nearly wet meself, I did. I did!'

'Wheeeeeeeeeeeeee! Wheeeeeeeeeeeee! Wheeeeeeeeee!' went the other one.

In the seventh minute a man ran heavily down the corridor shouting: 'Dennis! Dennis! Have you seen Dennis?' This Dennis was destined to be a red herring in Chief Superintendent Windscale's

PLETHORA OF GITS

investigation. He was eventually found in bed with three schoolboys in Scarborough.

Haddock, at last, broke yet another of his long silences. 'So you've come, then.'

'Come?' said the man.

'I've been waiting.'

'Waiting?'

'Aye.'

'For me?'

'For you.'

'But you don't know me from Adam.'

'Sez who?'

The man was perturbed. 'We've never met. Not as such.'

Eddie flopped back with a pathetic sigh. Tears fell fast and free from his eyes. 'Why couldn't yer have taken me first, that's the real cruelty of it? Why kill an innocent old woman?'

The man was rubbing his hands together, more confident now. 'I don't never kill old women. I only ever kills comedians.'

Eddie didn't seem to hear. One hand held a sore head. He patted it, trying to stop a buzzing in there, a buzzing like the sound of all the talks he'd ever given playing at once.

He had a question. 'Do they tell you what to do . . . ?'

'Who?'

'Them . . . the Ministers of the King of Bulgaria. Or does yer do it all off yer own bat?'

'What?'

'You know.'

'Know what?'

'What you do.'

DOES A MAN IN A FUR COAT EAT PORK PIES?

Windscale was too huge for the couch. He'd broken its legs off on a previous visit. So today he was lying on the floor of his psychoanalyst's consulting room, eating two Mars bars at once. At the same time he was relating a tedious incident from his adolescence.

'Were you overweight at the time?' asked Doctor Beckenbaur.

What a curious question! 'I've never been overweight.'

'No?'

'Bloody no.'

'Humph!' went the Doctor, who wasn't exactly a sylph himself.

But the most striking thing about him was that he was dressed as a German Field-Marshal. Windscale had once asked him, as all his other patients did eventually: 'Excuse me, but why are yerh dressed like Hermann Goering?'

'Who?'

'You.'

'Me, what?'

'Dressed like that.'

'Like what?'

'Like Hermann Goering.'

'But I am dressed perfectly casually.'

'Errrr . . . what about them epaulettes, and the medals.'

'What epaulettes? What medals?'

'Them, there, those ones.'

'A common enough delusion.'

'No, I'm sure.'

'Cheese for lunch?'

'Three balls of Edam.'

'There you have it, then.'

Thus Doctor Beckenbaur convinced all his patients, nay the whole World as it passed by, that he wasn't dressed as Hermann Goering.

Meanwhile, the cheese question was one Windscale took very seriously – he never ate cheese again, lest it impair his judgement. And if a witness smelt cheesy he would ignore its evidence.

'I tell you I seen him shoot her. He was right there. I was right here.'

'Been eating cheese, have we, sir?'

'Eeeeer, yeah, actually.'

'Huh!'

After a while of a cheeseless diet Windscale did dare ask, this was at the previous appointment to this one, why the Doctor was still appearing to be in his epaulettes and medals. Answer: possibly Windscale was eating cheese in his sleep. No! No! Impossible! In that case it was the very thought of cheese that brought on the delusion. Big fright, that! If it got worse maybe he'd see whole streets of Goerings, Hitlers and Lord Mountbattens. Everyone he met would be in pompous uniforms, a constant reminder of cheese, making the delusion ever more powerful and the uniforms in a state of constant promotion before his beringed eyes. He'd have to live out his days in a nudist camp.

'Today,' said Doctor Beckenbaur, gently picking his nose with his swagger stick, 'perhaps we can be bold enough to move on to your first sexual experience. You were how old? fourteen?'

'Errrrrrrrrrrrr . . .'

'Fifteen?'

'Errrrrrrrrrrrr . . .'

'Sixteen? Seventeen? Eighteen?'

'Um . . .'

'Nineteen? Twenty? Twenty-two?'

'You missed out twenty-one.'

'Ah! 21, then.'

'Errrrrrrrrrrrrrrrrr . . .'

The good Doctor advanced through the policeman's apparently sexless twenties. Windscale meanwhile, wore a fixed grin, teeth brown and viscous with Mars bars. By the time thirty was reached he'd broken out in a tropical sweat. He fished into his pocket for a mop and fetched out Sergeant Petherwick's pubic hair, which made do.

'Ahhhhhhhh!' screamed the shrink. 'You are a pubic hair collector also!' He pulled open the doors of a bureau to reveal a hairy display

PLETHORA OF GITS

that was his own collection. Windscale was trying to work out what foodstuff could be bringing on this new delusion, when the telephone buzzed.

It was for Windscale. Commissioner Claeverlock at Scotland Yard. The Doctor stroked his collection while the prone Windscale kept saying 'Yes, sir,' down the line.

'I am afraid I shall have to curtail today's session, Doctor. I must leave for Manchester immediately. Eddie Haddock, the comedian, has been murdered.'

'He was my favourite,' said the Doc, saluting Haddock's memory amid a pubic landscape.

It was one of Windscale's uncomfortable days. His body was pulling him downwards all the time. But it was also one of the proudest, perhaps *the* proudest, days of his life. The Home Secretary himself had asked for Scotland Yard's best man to be sent up to advise on the Haddock case. And Windscale, due to his recent success with the murder of that lesser comedian, Freddie Moss, was the filth immediately plumped for. The pride was greatest because his idol, the man whose autographed photograph he always carried by his heart, would now know that he existed.

Haddock had been a national institution, one of the most readily recognized faces in English life. It was vital, the Home Secretary had told Commissioner Claeverlock, to tell Windscale that the murderer should be apprehended as quickly as possible and with the minimum of fuss.

Windscale lay in the back of the zooming van prostrate like a whale waiting to be made into soap-bars, counting in his sleep between snores. Now and then the Home Secretary appeared in his dreaming, giving him a medal and kissing him in the French manner.

Petherwick was at the wheel. She'd been at a pop concert at the Hammersmith Odeon with her latest fiancé when she was bleeped. No time to change. She was bare-armed, bare-legged, wearing giraffe-spotted pants and a tight black leather waistcoat set off nicely by a pair of epaulettes from every tassle of which hung a tiny silver skull. Her Neanderthal face, looking at the best of times like that of a morose Arapaho, was painted the colours of the Tonton Macoute ice-hockey team. Her shaved eyebrows, meanwhile, were drawn back on in a series of 999s, enough for 43 emergencies. Windscale would have berated her for this getup but he dismissed it as a cheese-inspired delusion.

Not much traffic at that time of night. They'd have made Manchester in under three hours if Windscale hadn't insisted they stop at every service-station for yet another supper. In the end they screeched into an empty brightly-lit city just as the clocks were striking midnight. Windscale hadn't been to Manchester since 1964 when he'd gone there to see his sister in a wrestling bout.

A commissionaire dressed, so Windscale guessed, in the uniform of a Belgian Air Commodore, met them with a 'We've been expecting you, sir' and led them across deserted cable-tripping floors and similar quiet dark bits before pushing open swing doors on to the glob of noisy activity that was the vicinity of the murder.

Windscale only just fitted into the corridor. He scraped off nostalgic portraits of grinning sports presenters and trod on 41 constables before he got where he was going. Eddie Haddock was spreadeagled on the floor of his dressing-room with a large plastic kipper stuck down his throat.

Lots of people, all very upset, were milling about in the corridor. Solly Norman, inconsolable, kept fainting into the arms of a policewoman, then coming to and, as an expression of his grief, pulling buttons off his clothing. When at last he was dishevelledly buttonless he started yanking off the policewoman's. Various BBC staff were spilling out of the other dressing-rooms, all making statements. A number of senior policemen were getting to their feet, having been bumped into the twilight zone as Windscale stuck his head in to view the body. Among these was the Chief Constable of Lancashire himself.

'Hoi! You! Giant Haystacks!'

Windscale gave him a glance. Cheese, he thought. Hell, he was looking at an ordinary copper and took him to be the Chief Constable. Getting serious this.

'Bugger off, sonny,' said Windscale. 'You're getting in the way of my sniff.'

'What the . . . ?'

Petherwick stepped forward. 'His sniff, sir. Chief Superintendent Windscale is sniffing the scene of the crime.'

PLETHORA OF GITS

In all the excitement one of Sergeant Petherwick's bosoms had come out of her leather waistcoat. For some reason it frightened the Chief Constable. He backed away from it and hid for several hours in a prop basket. When he dared come out again he found Windscale in charge of everything, sitting on a desk with a dawn-filled window behind him, eating some hamburgers and reading through a heap of statements.

'Ahhhhhhhhhhh!' Yelled Windscale, his maw full of half chewed junk. 'Bugger this, Petherwick! I said no bloody cheese in the burgers!'

'Look here,' said the Chief Constable.

'Shut up, you! I'm busy solving a murder.'

'Who the bloody hell . . .!'

'Not another word from you unless you take your clothes off.'

'My clothes off?'

'You heard.'

'But . . .'

'Get em off, lad!'

'Bloody won't!'

'Then bloody sod off!'

Windscale gave the Chief Constable a look more murderous than any he'd seen in 34 years of policing. He had no alternative. Red with anger, he took his clothes off.

Hands cupped over his genitalia, he was about to insist that Windscale tell him what the hell he thought he was doing bursting in on Lancashire Police business, when Sergeant Petherwick breezed in saying: 'What bloody cheese! I checked in each one myself when I squirted the marty sauce on for yer.' Then she screamed. 'Yeeeeeeeeeeeeeee!' The denuded Chief Constable had a policeman's helmet tattooed in the middle of each buttock. In the moment of seeing these Petherwick imagined them to be the eyes of some ravenous moon-faced beast enticed into the room by the reek of hamburgers. The shortest moment later she realized what she was really looking at: a naked man. So, as she always did when confronted with a naked man out of context: she smacked him unconscious.

'A flasher, Chief.'

'Where?'

'Lying under those filing cabinets.'

'Oh, yeah. I see. Good work, Petherwick. Have him charged.'

'Dirty buggers, men. All dirty buggers,' she said, dragging the Chief Constable out from under the filing cabinet by the hairs of his scrotum.

Windscale bumped away the queue with his belly and loomed over the counter of the fish-and-chippy. He threw a plastic bucket into the hands of the boss-eyed proprietor.

'Fill this with chips!'

The man did so.

'And wrap me up a dozen haddock.'

The mention of 'haddock' caused several people in the reassembled queue to burst into tears.

It was a surprisingly nice day. Big white clouds, warmth from the sun if you looked at it full in the face. Windscale stepped out into the streets of Ashton-under-Lyne, pockets full of haddock, stuffing his face with chips from his bucket.

'I think I'll walk,' he said to Petherwick.

She followed in the van, in a lurching first gear, window wound down, enjoying the looks of shock and fear her monstrous superior inspired, her mastiff's expression complicated by a tense concern: Windscale rarely walked far.

Windscale wasn't exactly, to be accurate, walking. He was shuffling, stuck to the pavement like a Dalek in need of a service. Every ten steps or so one of his knees buckled, and for an instant it looked as if something as disastrous as the fall of the Roman Empire was about to occur and overturn the tea-table of the World, but he just bounced forward slightly and let out a belch that blew him upright.

As he turned off Oldham Road into Katherine Street a small boy skipped into his path.

'Gis a chip, mister!'

Windscale walked into him and over him. The boy came to consciousness several weeks later, watching Blue Peter in a neck brace.

A while was spent washing down his haddock and chips in the Dog & Partridge. Petherwick played *Hey Jude* on the juke box.

'What you do in the Sixties, chief?'

'Catch villains.'

'Nothing else?'

'I ate plenty, never stopped. Should've eaten more.'

PLETHORA OF GITS

At last, after several more snacks and meals, including 721 Maltesers, Windscale frapped an aggressive policeman's knock on the front door of the late Eddie Haddock. He'd come to look over the premises for anything that might give him a lead.

A certain Curly Nott, a very bad comedian, answered the door. He was there looking after the grief-stricken Solly Norman.

Windscale put his finger on the end of the man's nose. 'Who the Hell are you?'

'I'm Curly Nott.'

'Let me see your passport.'

'Errrr . . . don't have it with me.'

'How do I know your not an illegal immigrant?'

'I'm not black.'

'How do I know you're not black?'

Nott was stuck for an answer. He told this joke instead: MAN: If you are really a policeman, then why on earth are you wearing a red and yellow patterned suit? POLICEMAN: Just a routine check, sir.

Windscale didn't laugh. He belched in the comic's face and commenced his entry into the premises – commenced, not just stepped in, because he was too fat for the doorway and it took a quarter of an hour to get him in. Curly Nott, Solly Norman and Haddock's agent Mr Myerson all pulled at Windscale's braces. Petherwick pushed from behind. It was useless! Then she had the idea of using the van. She drove it up the pavement and nudged him through with that. Windscale popped neatly into the living-room, bouncing only once. Nott, Norman and Myerson, still holding the braces, twanged into the back yard, then all the way up to the Dog & Partridge, then into the back yard again, then as far as the end of the street, then crashed into a condiment cupboard in the kitchen, before dropping in a tangle at Windscale's feet. Nott then found himself taken upstairs to have the white scrubbed off him by Sergeant Petherwick: Windscale was convinced he was an illegal immigrant.

In the end, Nott found it a not unpleasant experience to be denuded and scrubbed by a bosomy policewoman, even if her face was uglier than Churchill's deathmask. But it was against his taste to have his erection battered into limpness with a toilet brush. (Some of Windscale's bullish philosophy had gotten through to Ms Petherwick: I AM THEREFORE I SMASHANDGRAB-AND RAPE AND MURDER AND TRY TO BRING DOWN THE-GOVERNMENT. Her footnote to his Principia was that the penis was the root of all evil and should be hit, kicked and chopped off at every reasonable opportunity.)

Solly brought tea and biscuits in for Windscale, then collapsed in a miserable heap. 'Oy! Oy! Oy! Such pleasure he brought to everyone. A saint! A saint!'

Windscale dunked a biscuit. 'Don't you worry, sir. We'll get the bastard.' He turned the pages of a scrapbook.

'Eddie never bothered for himself. A humble man. A saint! His mother kept his clippings for him. I have continued her good work. Here, see. Him and me on the same bill, Sheffield Empire, 1957.'

'He is top of the bill.'

'Thirty years. Packed them in. He was the greatest.'

'And this is you, is it, here at the bottom? After Wozwo the wonder seal.'

'I was doing my shaving routine back then.'

Windscale looked at himself in the mirror set at Haddock's height. He was just tall enough for it. He practised a terrifying grimace there, just as Haddock had practised his gurns from 1948 till the almost present. Then he turned the grimace on Solly, who backed away against the posters with HADDOCK splashed prominently across them.

'You were jealous of him, weren't you? Him a big star, you right down at the bottom of the list after a trained seal. All these years you've had that jealousy gnawing away inside. And at last, at last, it came out! Admit it, man. You killed him! You killed Eddie Haddock, your friend, your mentor! Confess! Confess!'

'No! No!'

'It was easy, wasn't it? Because he trusted you, the poor fool. I've a jolly idea for a joke, you said. You can start your performance with a kipper down your throat. Here, I'll help you get it in. And you rammed it in and held it there till he choked. Didn't you?! Didn't you?!'

'I loved the man!' squealed Solly.

Windscale fingered a photograph in his inside pocket. He too loved a man: the Home Secretary. He held Solly to his bosom. The little man wept quietly away while Windscale poked about the room.

PLETHORA OF GITS

'Fraid I can't get down to any black, Chief,' said Petherwick, kicking Curly Nott into the room ahead of her. He was glowing red from nose to toe.

Windscale pulled the man's nipples together with thumb and forefinger. Red? Red. Red all over. 'He must be one of them Red Indians.'

Petherwick shrugged. Why not?

'We'll stop at a post office later and post him back to New Delhi.'

The search of the premises continued. Windscale opened a cupboard and found a budgie cage with the skeleton of a budgie lying on the bottom on an old page of the *Manchester Guardian*.

'It reminded Eddie of his boyhood,' explained Solly. 'Sometimes he mentioned it in his act. Maybe you remember.'

'I am not an aficionardo.'

Upstairs, Windscale spent a long while in the victim's bedroom while the others waited on the landing. They all figured he was up to some terribly subtle detective work. Fact was, he was asleep. Several times he poked his head out with a yawn into which Sergeant Petherwick kindly threw a few Maltesers.

Windscale might have slept on Haddock's bed all day, but the rat-tat-tat of his own flatulence woke him up. His head swivelled around and caught sight of itself in the dressing-table mirror. Old blurry photos of Haddock's mother were tucked into the corners. Windscale's face rose up larger and larger, ballooning in the middle of them. His jowls were heavier than usual due to a mush of unswallowed food lying along his gums. They pulled down his cheeks so that a crescent of wet scarlet was visible under each yellow eye, eyes that were suddenly wide with a discovery. In white letters on red plastic tape was a curious . . . motto? message? question? Windscale plucked away a couple of photos so that he could read it all:

DOES A MAN IN A FUR COAT EAT PORK PIES?

'Sergeant!!!!!!'

She came in double-quick, her small severe fringe still a-fly when she caught Windscale's triumphant pout.

'We have found our killer, Petherwick. It is a man in a fur coat who may or may not be in the vicinity of a pie shop.'

'Brilliant, Chief!'

Solly, Myerson and Nott were quizzed on the landing. Solly claimed he'd never seen the message before. Myerson wrote down a list of people he knew who boasted fur coats. Nott said: 'There's a funny thing, now there's a funny thing. Man goes into a pub, asks for a pork pie, puts it on his head, goes out. Next day same man comes into the pub, asks for a pork pie, puts it on his head, goes out. Next day, ditto: man comes into the pub, pork pie, on his head, goes out. Next day comes in, asks for a pork pie, no pork pies, so he asks for a packet of crisps, puts it on his head, about to go out when the bartender says: "Why you got that packet of crisps on yer head?" Man says: "Didn't have any pork pies, did yer?"'

Windscale kicked him down the stairs.

Where were Windscale and Petherwick when the shooting started?

Windscale had been in the lavatory for three-quarters of an hour. His visits always involved a succession of flushings and a six-pack of toilet paper. When he came out he announced he wished to complete his search of the house. Solly opened a door and said with the deepest possible reverence: 'This was his mother's room.'

Windscale sucked in his belly. Petherwick pushed it in further for him, her arms disappearing up to the elbows. They both popped into the room and the door creaked shut behind them. That's where they were when the shooting started, alone, together, in a frilly bedroom.

'Ooooooh, what a luvly bed,' said Petherwick. She took off her macintosh and stretched out on the bed, legs spread wide, so wide that the threads were straining on the seam of her giraffe-spotted pants. This was an excellent opportunity for deepening her relationship with the Superintendent. Surely the sight of her quivering on the bed would enflame him?

Windscale was looking at photos on the wall, of bodybuilders mostly.

'You don't get proper men, anymore,' said Petherwick in a deep voice.

'Naw,' said Windscale, strumming the lapel under which lay a photo of the finest man who ever lived: the current Home Secretary.

'All bloody villains these days. Look at this lot. Villains. Puffs and villains. Villains and puffs.'

One of her fingernails started drawing circles on Windscale's thigh. He thought it was an itch. He scratched it. But no, it went on. He looked down in considerable confusion at his half-naked sergeant and her circling finger.

'Even policemen aren't what they used to be,' she said, voice even deeper.

'Bloody dwarfs these days,' he said, suddenly sodden with sweat, then started counting. '31, 32, 33, 34, 35, 35½, 36 . . . heard of a copper t'other day, missed out on a nab cos his feet were too short to reach the pedals in his panda, kept slipping off the driving-seat and crashing into Belisha beacons. The public can't respect a copper under six-foot-eight. Coppers should be properly big.'

'Big. In every way,' said Petherwick. 'Like you, Chief.'

'Errr, like me, aye.'

'Big.'

'Big.'

'Substantial.'

'Check, substantial.'

'Even big men these days, Wilf – can I call you, Wilf, Wilf, seeing as we're alone? . . .'

'Errrrrrrr . . .'

'Even big men these days are small men inside. But there's an even bigger man inside you, isn't there, Wilf?'

She wiggled her legs, threads snapped in her pants, all the boils on the fat that bulged at the back of Windscale's neck burst in unison.

Just about then the shooting started. At first Windscale thought it was his boils bursting, then that he was passing a noisy flatus. He paid no attention. Very puce in the face, he was nervously daring himself to hold Sergeant Petherwick's hand. Not looking, he quiveringly reached out for it, like a blind man reaching for a doorknob that isn't there. He had to look. Petherwick's legs were together again, she was sniffing the air. He sniffed it too. Wasn't something of his? So what was it, then?

Ping! A windowpane cracked in four with a hole in the middle of it. Bugger! They were smelling gunsmoke! They were under fire!

Windscale sidled up to the window and had a butcher's. The street outside was full of jam sandwiches surrounded by gun-toting filth, growling policehounds, the lot. Police marksmen were hugging the chimneypots of the terrace across the road. Ping! Ping! Ping! Ma Haddock's room, untouched since her demise, was noisy with rickosheas, criss-crossing the gaze between Windscale and Petherwick, plugging themselves into the wallpaper from which dropped dribbles of fine plaster, like something coming out of a pop singer's nostril after a sneeze.

Ping! Ping! Ping! and then no more pinging. The windows were smashed glassless. Out on the landing Solly and the others all screaming 'Oy!' over and over again, running around and around like a demonstration of clockwork mice.

The shooting stopped. All quiet for a minute, just shot-up bits of this and that falling over everywhere in the house.

Windscale put his head bravely at the window. 'What's bloody going on?'

A phufft on the roof opposite resulted in a teargas cannister hitting Windscale on the bonce. He lost his temper, but his foul language was lost in the gas mask he took from his deep pockets and pulled furiously over his head. He found another for Petherwick.

A megaphone spoke. It was the Chief Constable. 'ONE, TWO, THREE, TESTING. I'VE GOT YOU NOW, YOU FAT BASTARD! WHAAAAAAA-HA-HA! WHAAAAAAA-HA-HA! I'LL BLOODY SHOW YOU WHAT'S WHAT. I'LL BUGGER YOU UP GOOD AND PROPER.'

'He is undoubtedly insane,' said Windscale to the creature in the gas mask crouched beside him. She was much prettier in the gas mask. Good Lord! Sometime during the fracas they had taken each other by the hand. They were holding hands! Tears pooled in the scarlet crescents under Windscale's eyes. Real tears, not gas tears. Normally he'd have held them in, but he was safe behind his rubber mask.

He pulled out his own megaphone and stuck it at the end of his filter: 'DO NOT FIRE! DO NOT FIRE! THIS IS CHIEF SUPERINTENDENT WINDSCALE OF SCOTLAND YARD SPEAKING!'

'OPEN FIRE! OPEN FIRE! SHOOT THE FAT BASTARD TO BITS!' shrieked the other megaphone.

PLETHORA OF GITS

'BARMY BUGGER!' yelled Windscale's megaphone, already with three bullet holes in it. The room was full of angry zinging insects.

'WHO YOU CALLING A BARMY BUGGER, BARMY BUGGER!!!'

'YOU'RE THE BARMY BUGGER! A GLUE-SNIFFING BARMY BUGGER!'

Windscale had more invective to unleash but the megaphone was shot out of his hand with a crackle. The room was so fogged with gas he couldn't see where it had gone to, or anything at all, couldn't even make out the shape of the windows where the bullets were pzzzzzinnng in.

'You all right?' he shouted to Petherwick.

'Uh-huh,' she said through her mask.

He didn't know if that meant yes or no. Perhaps she was shot, groaning and injured. He squeezed her hand but she didn't squeeze back. Then he felt weightless (quite something if you've been 47 stone for twenty years) and wondered if he himself had been shot. Was he perhaps deaded and floating in a miasma towards an eternal episode of *Dixon of Dock Green*, where he and Jack Warner would exchange eternal anecdotes plodding a villainless beat . . .? But there was Petherwick gripping his thumb as hard as she could and pulling him down from his miasma. He brought a brilliant idea with him, one that undoubtedly saved their lives.

He took out his photo of the Home Secretary and held it at the window. Gas billowed around it, but the coppers outside could see what it was.

'It's signed, too,' said one.

'Cor!' said another.

The shooting stopped.

'FIRE! FIRE! SHOOT THE BASTARD!' ordered the Chief Constable.

But they did not.

He let off a couple of shots from his Luger, one of which clipped the right moustache off the Home Secretary. When he saw what he'd done he slumped on his feet and hung his head in shame.

Windscale and Petherwick lifted their masks at the same moment. 'Brilliant, Chief,' she sighed.

He let go of her hand and looked away.

'Don't you fancy me, Chief?'
'I fancy a Chinese,' he said.

It was amazing the number of men in fur coats who congregated in the vicinity of pie shops. A chilly night had perhaps contributed to their appearance in such a garb. 452 were arrested that first night in the Manchester area alone! Paddy-waggons screeched into Strangeways to decant long lines of fur, as if bears were being arrested for some obscure theological reason.

So a long hard night for Windscale and Petherwick! And they hadn't had a proper kip since the day before yesterday. Windscale's yawns grew wider and wider, more and more Maltesers, Mars Bars and Crunchies being flung in to give him energy. Normally they'd have been put up by the local force, but Windscale still suspected that the Chief Constable harboured ambitions to assassinate him. Otherwise, they might've checked into an hotel, but whenever Windscale stayed in an hotel he was knocked awake to attend to a suicide, murder or gunpowder plot in progress down the corridor. He'd never had more than eleven minutes sleep in an hotel. So they made do and parked the van in the street and arranged themselves for slumber. Conveniently, they were just outside the railings of the municipal cemetery where Haddock was due to be planted the following morning.

Sergeant Petherwick hoped that perhaps 'something might happen', that Windscale would be inflamed by being boxed in with her bodily odours. She denuded herself on the clammy front seat and lay waiting for Windscale's portly mug to rise up from the back. She listened carefully to the intimate noises of his undressing, the creaks of bone, the smacks of flesh as his spare tyres shuffled themselves. She closed her eyes, truly expecting that when she opened them she'd see that great face where she was expecting to see it. She opened her eyes. Nothing. Eyes closed again. A minute more. Eyes open. Nothing. Try again. Eyes closed.

What was without doubt the voice of the Home Secretary saying WHAT THIS COUNTRY NEEDS . . . over and over again at the Conservative Party Conference reached Petherwick's ears. She peeped over the seat. Windscale was lulling himself to sleep with its reassuring tones, sleepily masticating a pork pie.

'Comfortable, Chief?'

PLETHORA OF GITS

'Uh?'

'You going to be able to drop off?'

'I usually have my police dog beside me.'

'Reggie? I thought he was dead.'

'I had him stuffed. He's a great comfort to me.'

After a nervous pause Petherwick bravely said: 'I could be your police dog for you.'

Windscale gulped and belched before daring a reply. 'All right, sergeant.'

So she lay at his feet all night, stark naked and shivering, hoping that the fat sod would 'do something'. But he daren't. Fifty times he had himself worked up to sneak a foot from under his blanket and knead Petherwick's bosoms with it. Fifty times Petherwick opened her mouth in preparation of sucking the end of the big toe (she wasn't, it must be admitted, of the opinion that it was a big toe) that periodically protruded from under Windscale's blanket. But just when her suck was ready it retreated from whence it came.

The exhausted pair didn't get a wink of sleep. They lay tense and wondering, their chests fizzing with a tingle of sexual apprehension, vaguely listening to the repeats of the Home Secretary's speech. Petherwick even applauded once or twice, hoping it might start a conversation that would lead 'to other things'. But Windscale was too terrified to respond to her prompting.

At 4.32 she said: 'Comfortable, Chief?'

'Uh-uh,' he said.

At 5.17 she went so far as: 'Need another pillow, Wilf?'

'No, no. Quite all right, thank you . . .' and after a painful wait he managed to blurt: 'Stephanie.'

Being called Stephanie gave the desperate young woman as many orgasms as there were pork pies dissolving in Windscale's gut. She drummed the floor with her heels, hands clasped over the spiky garden wherein her pubic hair was regrowing. Stephanie! Stephanie! He'd called her Stephanie! This was all the more exciting to her because she was really called Cheryl.

The van's windows turned from black to blue. Suddenly there was a moment when they became white. Inside the van was then a quite different place. Windscale sat up. Petherwick was at his feet, a length of hair held coquettishly in her mouth.

'Good morning, sergeant.'

'Morning, Chief Superintendent.'

The atmosphere of sex was gone. Petherwick dressed hurriedly in her macintosh and boots. She squeaked a hole in the condensation on the back window, wherein immediately appeared a milkcart.

'A pinta, Chief?'

'Get some eggs, too. They has eggs these days, milkmen does.'

Petherwick kicked open the doors and stepped out into the drizzle. Her first yawn of the morning closed on her police whistle, which caused the milkman to pull up to do business. Leaves from the graveyard trees floated down around them while they transacted.

Back in the van Windscale was emptying himself of the wind his gut had manufactured during the sleepless night. It came out in a long hiss, like a zeppelin being let down after an unsuccessful war, punctuated by a noisy ack-ack of flatulations which rocked the van to and fro.

'Find any, then?' asked the milkman.

'What?'

'You's on surveillance, isn't yer? After grave-robbers.'

'Attend to your milk, you pathetic excuse for a man!' said Petherwick.

Sneezing from her long nude passionate night, Petherwick set up a portable stove by the roadside and cooked Windscale a twelve-egg omelette, enlivened by some horse chestnuts she found lying on the pavement. He had just started stuffing his face with it when Haddock's funeral turned slowly into the road.

'Sod this for a lark! I haven't finished my breakfast!' said Windscale. So he found the bits of his rifle in his pockets, assembled it between yawns, and shot the front tyres of the leading deathwagon. By the time they'd got the tyres changed Windscale had polished off his horse chestnut omelette, six pints of milk, and a furry Malteser from his pocket.

It turned out that the Archbishop of Canterbury had been a great fan of Haddock's, had in fact been inspired to take the cloth at a performance of the great comedian's at the Rotherham Regent way back in 1949. He was conducting the funeral service.

Because of his hat he couldn't sit in one of the cars, so was following along behind the mourners sitting on the roof-rack of a

PLETHORA OF GITS

Ford Cortina. He was helped down by a number of Boy Scouts, of one of whom he seemed inordinately fond.

'Blessings on you all, my children,' he said.

'Bugger me!' burped Windscale, yanking off his trilby. 'It's the Pope.'

Most of the mourners were Haddock's fellow entertainers, dozens of them household names or one-time household names. Most of Britain's comedians were there, all with glum faces, a long line of darkly-dressed funnymen trying not to look at each other in case they were set off giggling.

Jerry Muckle, eager as ever to top the bill, wearing dark glasses to emphasize his grief, nudged his way towards the front. He stopped at Huey Penzer and said: 'Did you hear about the young couple who didn't know the difference between putty and vaseline? Their windows fell out.' Then two steps forward to be beside Norrie O'Hanlon: 'What's red outside, grey inside and crowded? A bus full of elephants.'

'I know. I know,' said O'Hanlon sadly.

Muckle's next victim was his fellow cockney Fred Beeves: 'Corblimeyluvaduck,' he said, 'Whatya call a Scouse in a suit and tie? The Accused.'

A few more old gags and he was at the head of the line of mourners, having displaced Curly Nott in comforting the sobbing Solly Norman. He stopped the procession for a full twenty minutes to give his eulogy to a breakfast television crew, managing a few tears from under his dark glasses and not forgetting to mention that his show was on ITV, all regions, at 8.30 every Saturday. Len Engels kept the other mourners entertained with card tricks.

The little chapel of rest was crammed full when Windscale and Petherwick filed in.

'D'yer think one of this lot is the murderer?' whispered Petherwick.

'Mebbee,' nodded Windscale, looking at the backs of their heads for a sign only he would recognize. (When a young detective he'd written an exhaustive report on the relationship between crime and baldness, proving that 89.2% of murderers over the age of 27 are bald.)

Throats were cleared. A sheet of paper describing the service was distributed. The assemblage settled down. Then a cadaverous organist played a tedious wheezy preamble before hitting one long note during which the Archbishop of Canterbury arose in his seat saying: 'We will now sing "Oh, I do like to be beside the seaside."'

This, Haddock's favourite song, was not sung with its usual jauntiness. Taking their lead from the slow dolorous organ-music, the congregation sang it like a 45 record played at 33. It was the most miserable rendition of any song in the history of the World and made everyone thoroughly gloomladen as they looked from the words on their sheet up at the lone kipper laid atop Haddock's coffin.

The Archbishop patted a Boy Scout before stepping up to the pulpit to give his address: 'Man that is born of woman hath but a short time to live, and is full of misery . . .'

He hadn't been going long before the delicate atmosphere of reverent depression he was trying to create was ruined by some idiot giving a political speech. It was Windscale's tape-recorder. He'd set it off while ruffling through his pockets for a toffee. 'WHAT THIS COUNTY NEEDS IS DISCIPLINE, DISCIPLINE AND MORE DISCIPLINE. HANGING SHOULD BE IMMEDIATELY REINSTATED FOR EVEN THE MOST MINOR OFFENCES, THUS IN THE PROCESS OF TIME WEEDING OUT ALL SOCIAL MISFITS . . .'

A good number of the congregation were gently applauding these sentiments. But those nearest the front could hear the Archbishop when he protested: 'That isn't me! That isn't me!'

When Windscale, with Petherwick's help, finally shut the tape-machine up, the Archbishop refused to recommence his address: he was sure he'd just heard the voice of God. Devastating for him, because he'd never in real seriousness thought that there ACTUALLY WAS a God! He climbed up his crozier and wouldn't come down.

The fussy exertion of switching the speech off finally exhausted Windscale and Petherwick. It was, after all, two days since they'd seen their respective beds. Windscale leaned heavily on the tomb of an unknown soldier, fighting to keep his peepers open. Some crafty thing inside his thinking convinced him to give up the fight and he flopped back making a sound like blancmange falling from a great height. Petherwick stood vigil over him till halfway through *All Things Bright and Beautiful.* She then succumbed and laid her hairy pink cheek against the cold stone of the church. She had a dream in which she was kicking Maltesers on a beach and her fiancé, Herbert, came sailing to shore on a barnacled wine gum.

PLETHORA OF GITS

When he ran up the beach to her, still in his usual pin-striped suit, a gigantic Mars Bar dropped from the sky – they watched it coming down for ages – and planted itself heavily in the sand between them. The meaning of the dream was obvious.

Windscale gave a sudden snort and woke both himself and Petherwick. The church was empty, dark except for the stained-glass. Windscale sat up and stared. Several minutes passed and he was still staring.

'Chief! Chief!' yapped Petherwick.

He looked at her but did not recognize her.

'Chief! Chief!'

His eyes followed motes of dust down into the pews.

'Chief!'

'Uh? Where'd everybody go?'

'We dropped off, the both of us. It's gone 11.30.'

When they went outside the first thing they saw was the Archbishop of Canterbury retching into his hat.

'Something the matter, your Holiness?'

'Blurrrrrrrrrrgghhhhhhhhhhhhhhhhhh!' he went. The hat overflowed and spoilt a Boy Scout.

'He needs something to settle his stomach,' said Windscale, who considered himself an expert in medical matters concerning the digestive tract.

He found a tube of Alka-Seltzer in his pocket and poured the lot down the eminent cleric. The resultant fizzing caused Windscale's patient to fling his arms around like someone waving down fourteen aeroplanes at once. He spent several minutes wiping the a-fizz froth from his mouth, desperate to speak but coming over like a radio being fiddled with late at night. While he struggled, distraught comedians came down the path in twos and threes, wiping soil from their suits, some holding sore heads.

'Has something happened?' Petherwick asked a couple. They hurried away in tears.

His lower lip pouting anxiously, Windscale blimped up the path against the tide. He bellied comics out of his way as he progressed, bouncing some right up into the leafless starkness of the trees.

A constable with a be-soiled uniform was busy at the graveside, helping people out of the grave.

'What's bloody going on?' yelled Windscale.

55

The constable took out his notebook, cleared his throat and addressed an imaginary courtroom: 'As I was proceeding about my duties at this here graveside wot I am now standing at, a large hand perpretrated me from where I was then standing right into yon grave here, whence I landed on me bonce, thud, on top of the deceased, that is to say, the original deceased, him what was deaded then before thems what is deaded now. Whereupon, as I was proceeding out again I was knocked back in to where I'd first been knocked by a tumble of screaming comedians. Has yer got me so far, Chief Super?'

'Errrrrrrr . . .'

'There we all was then, in the grave, thrashing about like: myself, approximately 40 comedians and variety-based entertainers, twelve Boy Scouts and the Archbishop of Canterbury. Being the first to drop in I found meself on the bottom of the melage. I attempted, and with no consideration of me own safety, to get out me whistle, this whistle here.' He held up his whistle as evidence. 'Unfortunately, in such a confined space it remained inoperative as some geezer had his proboscis jammed in its ole. I made strenuous attempts to get meself out from under but being wholly unsuccessful I continued my enquiries from where I was and ascertained that all these gentlemen had likewise been perpretrated into where they was by that aforementioned hand which had perpretrated meself. While making these inquiries I discerned an increased screaming from thems at the top of the heap and in pokin an eye through a gap I observed that they were been repeatedly struck about their persons by a curly-ended gold object, some eight feet long and decorated with visions of Saint Benedict catching a cherub. This I took to be an Archbishop's crozier. I at no time saw the fizog of the assailant as he was at the other end of the murder weapon.'

It was a dumbfounded Windscale who leaned over to look into the grave. Lying with their legs and arms all over the place, heads bloodily caved in, on top of Haddock's smashed coffin, were four murdered comedians: Jerry Muckle, Solly Norman, Fred Beeves and Chalky Dookan. (Dookan, in fact, had no headwound, just a slight bloated appearance. The autopsy later revealed that he'd swallowed a Boy Scout.)

The constable continued: 'Presently, the whacking stopped and what with a lot of them others being unconscious like, I managed to force me way, and with no consideration of me own safety, to the top of the melage. Whereupon, stood standing here, I looked about for a bit but could see no sign of the assailant or the murder weapon. I therefore busied meself helping the survivors out from this here ole, this ole what I am now pointing at.'

He was still diligently pointing at the ole when Petherwick arrived at the scene.

Windscale had walked off among the graves, gross and glum, gut thrust forward, hands deep in pockets, slowly sinking into the soft earth. It was the worst moment of his life. He had failed the Home Secretary. If he hadn't been away snoozing in the church, none of this would have happened. Four people would still be alive (five including the Boy Scout) and the murderer would have been apprehended.

Petherwick left him alone with his thoughts and got busy with the investigation of the crime, which mostly consisted of searching the grass for pork pie crumbs or hairs that may have dropped from a fur coat. The rain came down heavily, its droplets big and pink on the foreheads of the deceased, droplets which all of a sudden were full of the reflections of the Chief Constable and his men, hanging over the oblong, come to attend to the mess.

OUT INTO THE LIGHT

Someone told them it was the best Chinese restaurant thereabouts. The entrance to CHEZ WANG was up a dirty alley full of dustbins. But this didn't mean it was a stinkhole: it was a temporary entrance. The real entrance, worthy of the Peking Odeon, was under renovation after a fire.

Windscale was in a bloody awful mood. He'd been on the phone half the afternoon getting a bollocking off Commissioner Claeverlock. He kicked dustbins down the alley, skittling a number of Chinese waiters who were down the far end for a smoke.

Inside, the restaurant was all red plush and bamboo. Lost of empty tables. Paper lanterns. A frieze of Hong Kong harbour ringing the room. Smoke from the aforementioned fire still lingered around the ceiling. Scorch marks made hypnotizing patterns on the furniture, tablecloths and on the waiters themselves, sitting playing dominoes in a faraway corner. One came over, smiled with a discoloured set of double blanks, and said: 'Hugh hready to horder?'

'Errrrrgh . . . I'll have numbers 1, 2, 3, 4, 5 sounds nice, 6, 7, 8 . . .' Windscale's counting suddenly dried up in his throat . . . He was back in his shrink's again, not daring to admit a terrible truth about himself. He looked at the bare shoulders and plunging cleavage of his dinner-companion. 'Erm, just bring me a plate of everything. Oh, and a funnel. I'm bloody hungry.'

Having taken Petherwick's more modest order, the waiter struck a match on his teeth and lit a candle. Petherwick sighed. At last, a romantic dinner!

Windscale was attempting to take his mind elsewhere. He laid out documents on the table and commenced making notes in his tiny policeman's notebook. Strange that so huge a man, with fingers like the just-gone-limp penises of a gang-bang of police horses, had such miniscule handwriting. In the middle ages some monastery might've employed him to copy out the Bible inside the eyelids of the especially devout; thereby enabling them to read scriptures backwards with their eyes shut when facing a strong light.

Petherwick sat bored, her wiles stumped, eyeing dead fish floating in a long tank of green water. This was ridiculous! She gathered her seductive powers together and pulled her chair around beside Windscale's.

'Can I help?' she said.

'Ugh,' said Windscale, trying not to look at her, smell her, sense her presence in any way. It wouldn't have been difficult for him if she hadn't been so excellent a policewoman, so honest and perfect a citizen, so bereft of the slightest stain of villainy which tainted everyone he could think of except himself and the Home Secretary.

Petherwick had an excellent seduction technique. Every time she leaned over in search of a document she made sure one of her bosoms slid out, flapping right under Windscale's nose. 'Oooops!' she said and scooped it back in.

When the first few plates of food came she made herself useful by holding the funnel steady with one hand and scraping the gunge into the funnel with the other. In that way Windscale was able to continue his pretence of paperwork while the cuisine slipped down his neck. Now and then he burped and spatted the ceiling with prawn-balls. Petherwick found this rather endearing.

'Murmphdrrumpish . . . slervendrurble . . . Mmmm . . . floughumdummm,' said Windscale.

His mouth was so full he could have been saying anything short of confessing to these recent murders himself, but Petherwick heard what she wanted to hear.

'Oooooh, of course, Wilf. We'll have the bridal suite, shall we?'

'Murpheldrumph!!'

'With a nice big bed where we can stretch out good and proper.'

'Dghf!'

'It's a pity I don't have my uniform with me. Would you like me better in uniform?'

'!'

In his distress Windscale somehow let the rim of the funnel slip behind his lips and it took several waiters, prizing his lips back with dessert spoons, to get it out.

'I usually use a bigger funnel,' he explained, handing over a

PLETHORA OF GITS

selection of confiscated Barclaycards with which to pay for the meal. His pockets were full of such things.

Petherwick was a little shocked. 'You shouldn't do that, Chief. It's illegal.'

'Illegal? I can't do nothing illegal. I'm the police.'

'Of course. Sorry.'

'Errrrrrrrrrrrm, the bridal suite, please.'

'May I congratulate Sir and Madam?'

'What for?'

'On your nuptials, of course.'

'Oh, oh, that. Aye. Bloody get on with it.'

'If Sir will just sign our book.'

Windscale made up a name: MR & MRS COPPER. He put it in the book in his tiny handwriting.

'Ah, yes, Mr. . . urrrrrrmmmm . . . Copper. The bridal suite is on our top floor. Lowther will help you with your bags.'

Petherwick handed over a suitcase oozing with prawn balls. 'Excuse me a moment, Sir.' The reception personage called them back. 'Stop me if I'm being impertinent, but are you perhaps, I mean to say, from the look of you, are you perhaps one of our boys in blue?'

'Who, me?'

'Cos, sometimes you know how things are, sir, if there's a little trouble during the night, and there's a lot of funny people about nowadays, it would be reassuring to know that we had someone who could deal . . .'

'I'm not a policeman!' blurted Windscale. 'Am I, sergeant? . . . errr, dearest one?'

'Him? A policeman? Never. He's a . . . He's a . . .'

'I'm a psychoanalyst.'

'Oh, really, how interesting,' said the man, and desperately suppressed a twitch until the lift doors had managed to close on Windscale's gut, after which he clucked for some minutes and banged his head repeatedly on his bell.

It was a long, wide room with a low ceiling and an enormous bed. The porter began demonstrating the television set.

'Bugger off,' said Windscale.

He buggered off.

Yet again Windscale and Petherwick were alone in a confined space. But this time it was going to be different! Petherwick gave him a Giaconda smile that turned his insides to goo (more goo it would've been hard to find in one place) and went into the bathroom to prepare herself. Windscale nervously scoffed a few prawn balls and looked out the window at the depressing vista of satanic mills and glaringly-lit roads. His ears picked up the *whissst* of tapwater, the *wharrrrrrrrisssssss* of toilet flushing, the *hga-hga-haagagagagagagagag* of gargling. Then Petherwick started humming the theme from *Z-Cars*. Windscale guessed he was in for a wait. So he did to the television what the porter had done and it came on.

It was himself he saw, filling the screen at Haddock's funeral, tweaking a reporter's nose on the BBC-2 news. The shock took the blood from his head. Police dogs ran barking on the whites of his eyes, sucked one by one into a black hole that was at the centre of each eye. When the last dog had yelped its way down, Windscale returned to consciousness. He was on the bed, on his back, a stark naked Sergeant Petherwick sunk up to her patellas in his belly flesh. She was undoing his trousers, not without difficulty cos every time Windscale breathed out she bonked her head on the ceiling. This didn't bother her, it made her more keen for the other sort of bonking she had in mind.

The trousers, in the end, came off quite easily, revealing legs about the size and shape of a brace of shaved corgis. She'd seen him this nude before, when he'd gone in the pool to inspect the corpse of Freddie Moss. Just the shorts to go! Difficult to start with, then Windscale obligingly let off a windy poop which blew both Petherwick and the shorts into a fitted wardrobe at the other end of the room. Mad with passion she dived back into Windscale's belly flesh and rolled about there like a frisky mermaid on a deep-sea sponge. Windscale tried to join in the sexiness by making a grab for her neck (it was how he grabbed criminals, hitherto his only physical contact with anybody) but his arms were too short to reach the part of his belly where she was cavorting. All his snatches came away with were handfuls of Maltesers, which came from God knew where!

Petherwick hauled herself out of the quicksand of Windscale's belly by yanking on his chest hairs, then crawled up his chest and lay across his face. He was suddenly terrified. He didn't know what to do. He'd never had anyone lie on his face before. Cats, he knew, were apt to

PLETHORA OF GITS

do it and suffocate you to death if you slept in a room with one, which was why he'd always killed any cat he happened to stumble into in the vicinity of his flat in London. Cummon! his brain yelled at him: BLOODY DO SOMETHING!!!!! He was going to lick out her belly-button, but he bit her leg instead.

'Arrrooooooooooooooooo!' went Petherwick. It was a squeal approaching delight, like that of a young miss who though hit on the head by a safe knows at the same time she can keep the money inside. 'You like it rough, ay, Chief?'

'Errrrrrmmm . . .'

He was still deliberating when she smashed a teasmaid over his forehead.

Then their first kiss! Petherwick drummed her stiff feet on his chest while doing so. Materializing chocolates of diverse and exciting flavours, coffee-creams, rum marzipans, apricot parfaits, walnut truffles, passed stickily between their locked slobbering bouches.

'Mmmmmmmmmmmmmmmmmmmmmmmmmmmmmm,' went Petherwick, her lips and cheeks all brown.

'Mmmmmmmmmmmmmmmmmmmmmmmmmmmmmm,' went Windscale. All his birthdays had come at once. There was a rippling excitement in every part of him.

'Want me to pretend you're arresting me for the Great Train Robbery? . . . Anything that I say will be taken down . . .'

'Naw. Naw. I tell you what, you couldn't pretend you're the Home Secretary, could you?'

In a pouting, panting voice Petherwick began: 'WHAT THIS COUNTRY NEEDS IS DISCIPLINE, DISCIPLINE AND MORE DISCIPLINE . . .' And every time she said discipline she punched him on the nose.

'More! More! That's it! More!' wheezed the Chief Superintendent.

As Petherwick about-turned and crawled back up his belly again, knees digging in deep, the prostrate Windscale got a view of her behind that shocked, disgusted, bewildered him with its strangeness. So many of those in the World! Petherwick's, with its pencilled on pubic hairs, was the first he'd seen outside of the magazines in the Vice Squad room.

Soon she was out of view, sliding down the other side of his belly into the folds, tyres and sweaty crevasses that made up his nether-regions. Several minutes' silence followed.

'Hullo!' called Windscale.

More silence.

'You there, Petherwick?'

'Errr, I can't seem to find your love truncheon, Chief.'

'My what? Oh!'

She carried on looking among the troughs and sags.

'It is there. I promise,' said Windscale shyly. 'I saw it only the other day, in my tooth-mirror.'

She delved in deep, lost herself altogether in a dank tunnel. Something was spitting at her. Help! For a moment she was saying catechisms! Maybe she'd gotten inside him somehow, was Jonahed in his labyrinthine colon, about to be melted by his gastric juices. No . . . She lifted fat and there was the Open University on the television, and there, lit by its flickering light, was a sore carroty sort of thing: Windscale's penis. She dragged it spitting and twanging out into the light.

Triumphant: 'FOUNDDDDDDD ITTTTTTTTT!'

Getting the thing put where she wanted it put would not be easy. Queer diagrams being shown on the Open University might've been of some help. Presently, upside down, her hair in her eyes, her toes gripping on tight to a useful pair of warts somewhere on the descent of Windscale's paunch, she was ready to pull herself onto the penis . . .

There was a frantic knocking on the door.

'Bugger off!' panted Petherwick.

'Bugger off!' yelled Windscale, three-quarters cherryless.

It was the man from reception. 'Mr Copper! Mr Copper! Please, we need your help! We need the help of a psychothingmywotsit! There's a man on the roof who says he's the Duke of Edinburgh. He's threatening to jump!'

'Let the bugger!'

'Please, sir! Please!'

His penis was pressing into Petherwick now, with her squealing like a police car warp-speeding up the M1.

'Please, sir! You must come. He'll throw himself off at any minute.'

Windscale ignored him, licked the salt off his lips, had an egg sandwich, and concentrated on losing his elderly cherry.

Desperately, the receptionist yelled: 'WHAT IF IT REALLY IS THE DUKE OF EDINBURGH?'

PLETHORA OF GITS

Windscale knew his duty. He rolled off the bed, bowed his legs to let Petherwick slide off his penis. WHUMP! She hit the floor with a splash of sweat.

'I have to attend to a little matter... Stephanie.' (How she groaned when he called her that!) 'I won't be a tock.'

'I'll be waiting, big boy,' she said.

There was indeed, as the receptionist had said, a man on the roof saying he was the Duke of Edinburgh. He was in full Admiral's uniform and smelt strongly, even from a safe distance, of taramasalata. He said he couldn't face the future without his weekly fix of THE EDDIE HADDOCK SHOW. Windscale suggested with, for him, the minimum of irritation, that there was always repeats. The man wasn't consoled. He teetered and nearly went off.

'Tell you what,' said Windscale. He fetched some old transcripts of Haddock's talks from his coat pocket, the top few from a huge pile the BBC had given him, and commenced reading aloud in a stolid policeman's voice but with a twinge of passion left over from his recent excesses. The Duke of Edinburgh was rapt.

'Sez who? Sez me!' said Windscale, as the rain drizzled on to the words he was reading in the spotlight provided by the receptionist sitting on his head with a torch. 'Eeeeeee, he were a curmudgeon. He says ter travel agent, he wants for ter go somewhere sunny like, not Blackpool this year, no, cos landladies, yer know, very partial to a bit of curmudgeon on side, always gets hissel in bother, so he says like he wants somewhere sunny like but where landladies'll find him pug-ugly like. So travel agent says how's bout Pazardzhik, it's near Plovdiv, not far from Panagyurishite. Women there only takes a shine ter yer if yers got yersel a moustache and he hasn't got hissel a moustach so ees alright isn't e . . .'

Windscale turned the pages, making notes as he went. This was it! As he read on and his detective brain became more and more interested, his voice became less and less clear. In order to hear what he was saying the Duke of Edinburgh was forced to come down from his edge and nestle nearby. They all sat together on some chimneys and Windscale read out the rest.

It turned out that Haddock's curmudgeon brother went on holiday to a resort named Pazardzhik which it turns out is in Bulgaria, which the travel agent didn't tell him because the travel agent was in the pay (like almost everybody) of the Bulgarian Consul. So he's there for his first week and forgets to shave, grows a moustache and is pursued through the narrow streets of Pazardzhik by rampant peasant women, 'lips stained crimson with a lifetime's beetroot', and ends up in a dungeon being cruelly tortured by guards while the Bulgarian Consul (who's still in London) listens to his screams over the phone. But he escapes: 'So there he were like, in this dark room wi' no exits and only a table in't. So he shouts and shouts until he got hissel a saw throat, he took the saw, sawed table in half, two halfs make a hole, so he escaped through hole and took him so long ter walk home that Rotherham were back in First Division. But e were never same again. Sez who? . . .'

While Windscale was away Petherwick had kept herself amused with his truncheon. Then she fell asleep.

'Sergeant! Sergeant!'

It was Windscale shaking her, not loverboyish any more, all rozzerish.

She jumped to attention with the sheet wrapped tantalizingly around most of her. 'REPORTING FOR DUTY, SIR!' she barked.

'I've found our murderer, sergeant.'

'Brilliant, Chief!'

'It's all in here. Whole thing's a bloody bastard bulgaring conspiracy! Bit of a sod, too, mind. International incident if we're not careful. Sez who?'

'Sez you, sir!'

THE INTERNATIONAL INCIDENT

Windscale and Petherwick drove to London that same night, Windscale composing a letter to the Home Secretary as they bounced along.

The next morning Sir Cyril Passey-Wix entered the Home Office, as he did every morning, at precisely 7.32. He was humming the great Act I aria from Gluck's *Alceste*. At the end of his sleek black quiff were two waves which made the quiff look like a chesty figurehead on a ship. Together with a hipswaying walk not unlike that of the late Mae West, it gave him the appearance of some small corsair heavily laden with cardigans scudding through waters that would everymore be British.

He sat primly at his desk and cleaned his spectacles while Loveridge brought in the breakfast trolley. His eyes fell upon a small brown envelope leaning on his ink-stand. BLOODY URGENT! FOR THE EYES OF THE HOME SECRETARY ONLY. It was in miniscule, jagged writing, of a kind autobiographers might write in their last moments, during a plane crash or while being strangled by their relatives. Sir Cyril was fascinated by it, but it was his rule not to look at anything till he'd finished his breakfast and done *The Times* crossword.

Loveridge poured warm milk over his Weetabix, and so eager was the Minister to see the letter that he stuck his spoon in the object before the milk had finished pouring. Loveridge, meanwhile, held the jug in the way of the spoon for an inordinately long time: he was keen not to let a drip which was clinging to the jug's lip drop on to the sleeve of Sir Cyril. When the thing wouldn't budge and the situation was becoming an embarrassment he gave the jug a little shake, a shake not unlike he might have given to his member in any of the several gentleman's lavatories he was known to frequent. The similarity was not lost on himself or, unfortunately, on the Home Secretary, whose spectacles glinted at him with an irritation so intense that the aforementioned drip was enabled to fall unnoticed on to his sleeve.

All through his breakfast Sir Cyril kept looking at the letter. Something exciting, had to be! Better had. Dull of late. Not a riot for weeks! Finally, after one bite of his second piece of toast (he always had three), he had to ask: 'Urrrrrum. Yon letter, Loveridge . . .'

'Yes, sir.'

'Not an appeal for clemency from that five-year-old mass murderer who garrotted the entire contents of an old people's home in Bridgend?'

'I don't believe so, sir.'

'Thought I recognized the writing.'

Sir Cyril hamstered down the second piece of toast and, beaten by his curiosity, abandoned the third. He snatched the letter and slit it open with a fingernail unusually long for a man.

Loveridge was astonished, had never been more astonished, dropped *The Times* turned to the crossword page. He could barely speak. 'Your third piece of toast, sir. Your third piece of toast!'

'Feed it to a pigeon of your choice, Loveridge,' said the Home Secretary. His eyes had already jumped into the letter, in the way someone might leap in search of news of an inheritance or an exam result.

Windscale had poured all his heart and intellect into the letter. In the tiniest writing The Home Secretary had ever seen, the letter read thus:

Dear Esteemed Paragon,

It's the bloody sodding Bulgarians wot done it! Got a pile of evidence, O Great One. In Mr Haddock's monologues it sez again and again about how the Bulgarian Consul is after him, how the bugger killed his mother, brother, his rabbit even.

Motive: bloody villainous foreigners, that's what. Gitty puffs and goat-pokers trying to undermine our British way of life. Hang the buggering greasy lot, what yer say, sir?

May I take this opportunity of expressing my deepest affection and loyalty, sir. You are what this country needs! You are a shining example to the youth of today . . .

At that point Petherwick had turned off the motorway and

PLETHORA OF GITS

Windscale's scrawl went uncharacteristically huge, skating off the page and back, saying something very like *I'VE A GLAND THAT KEEPS THWONKING OUT CHOCOLATE*, before returning to its usual disturbed neatness with:

> ... *makes my water bubble to think that your handsome grey eyes will read these humble words wot I here have wrote.*
> *Awaiting your faultless instructions.*
>
> *Yours in profoundest admiration.*
>
> *Detective Chief Superintendent Wilfred E. Windscale.*

Petherwick was at home, a dingy flat at the top of a high-rise in south London. She was enjoying a well-earned soak. Her fiancé, Herbert, was mewling through the bathroom door, trying to get her to name the day, at the same time phoning his office to check on the stock prices. They'd be happy forever, he assured her, between ruining a gusset company and accumulating enough wheat to hide Belgium. He'd made £613,000 since she locked the door on him, he insisted! ... Oh! The voice on the phone told him he'd just lost it again. Never mind, he'd make some more this afternoon.

Petherwick wasn't listening to him. Her mind was far away in a Lancashire hotel-room. But then Herbert drummed the door like a weak Gestapo officer.

'April the Fourth!' she shouted to shut him up.

There was a little squeal of pleasure, then the drumming started up again. She jumped athletically out of the bath, dressed from nose to twinkletoes in puce suds, and flung open the door.

'It's your boss on the phone, dearest one,' said Herbert.

As she stepped forward a sudden draught blew all the suds backwards into history. She was like the Venus de Milo with weightlifter's arms. Herbert fainted at her feet.

'Chief? Chief? That you?'

The phone made a pathetic whimpering noise, like a cashiered police dog.

'Chief?'

A police dog with its claws pulled out and its tail tied in a reef-knot.

'Where are you, Chief?'

'Eurmmmmmm-errrrrrrrrrrrrrrr . . .'

Suddenly she couldn't hear anything if she tried. There was a strange whizzing sound coming from outside and something was banging on the living-room window. She stepped over Herbert's body and, still straining to hear the inaudible whimpering on the phone, dripped into the living-room.

Filling the long window, which usually had a vista of gasworks, more high-rises, a weeny football pitch, and endless traffic-jams leading to the M25, was a helicopter. Windscale was stuffed inside it. He was trying to attract her attention by banging a police dog against the window, swinging it on its leash, with occasional delays as it stopped for a shave in the rotor-blades. But the whimpering wasn't the dog's. It was Windscale's! She'd never seen him in such a state.

She stepped out onto the balcony, her five-feet long chestnut hair blown on end by the whaft, and deftly caught the dog.

'WHAT'S THE TROUBLE, CHIEF?????' she yelled above the noise of the helicopter.

'EUEUMMMMMMMMMMMMMMMMMMMMMMMM-MMMMMMM . . .' yelled Windscale. 'IT'S HIM! MMMMMMM! HIM! HE WANTS TO SEE ME!'

'WHO DOES'

'SIR CYRIL! SIR CYRIL HIMSELF! PERSONALLY!'

At this point the helicopter pilot, in noticing Petherwick's nakedness, forgot how to fly helicopters and the thing suddenly veered off, blowing washing from 300 balconies.

Windscale tried to resist the inevitable by holding tightly on to the dog's leash. Petherwick helped by gripping the dog by the tail, but it wisely slipped its collar and the helicopter lurched towards the gas works. It disappeared into a mini-Hiroshima, an explosion that rattled the spoon in Sir Cyril Passey-Wix's saucer ten miles away. Employees of the Gas Board, meanwhile, shot past Petherwick's eyes still reading their newspapers and chewing Toffee Crisps.

Several more explosions followed, prawn-red fireballs bursting through plumes of black smoke that were fast blotting out all daylight. Down distant streets could be seen fire engines, their sirens getting faster and more anxious. Then they too were covered by smoke.

It all looked oddly unreal to Petherwick as she dried her hair in the warm cindery blasts that came her way, lifting her off her ample policewoman's feet. Suddenly, a knock on the door. The dog answered it.

Windscale stood in the doorway, scorched, still holding the dog's leash. He'd acquired the Italianate complexion of a smoked kipper, and his clothes had gone brittle like old tracts.

'SIR CYRIL HIMSELF! PERSONALLY! I CAN'T DO IT! I CAN'T!'

Petherwick sat him down, wiped his tears, and tried to calm him by feeding him the contents of her fridge. Then she sat in his lap and with a motherly expression picked glass out of his chin.

'This evening at 4.32! I'm to be there!' blubbed Windscale. 'Me, myself, actually in his presence!!! I'll not be able to say a word! I'll stand there like an artichoke. You'll come with me, won't you sergeant?'

'Of course, Chief. Wouldn't miss it.'

Windscale's clothes suddenly turned to ashes. So, yet again, he was naked in Sergeant Petherwick's company. But this time her fiancé was also present. Herbert had just come back to consciousness with a bar of soap in his mouth, floating in Petherwick's bathwater. He thought he was drowning somewhere off the Dogger Bank. Then he remembered: April the Fourth!!! But when he came dripping into the living-room there was his fiancée nude on the sofa with an equally nude hippopotamus.

'Cheryl! Who is this naked person?'

'This is my chief, Herbert. He just popped in for a bite.'

Herbert could see the bite: Windscale had been absent-mindedly chewing Petherwick's shoulder in lieu of Toffee Crisps.

'BRAZEN HUZZY!!!!' he yelped like a prayer-sore Sanhedrin and raised his hand in a moral outrage to slap Petherwick across her jowls.

Ever the gentleman, Windscale caught the blow in mid sweep and flung Herbert out of the window.

Petherwick seemed to feel the unslapped slap anyway. She gazed at the empty window. 'You've . . . killed . . . Herbert,' she said softly.

'Naw, he'll be all right,' shrugged Windscale, and kicked the dog out after him to reassure her.

Sir Cyril Passey-Wix gazed out on a dull official London through blinking feminine eyes set in a dull official's face. Then, his spectacles cleaned with a handkerchief monogrammed *C P-W*, he replaced them on his nose, hiding the almost pretty eyes with the glint of the lenses. He could see everything better now, but it was just as dully official. News was coming in of a major disaster in south London, but his thoughts this afternoon were devoted to murdered comedians.

Loveridge came in silently and surprised him.

'Chief Superintendent Windscale, sir.'

'Ah! Send him right in, Loveridge.'

'I'm afraid you'll have to see him in the outer office, sir. He'll not fit through your door.'

It wasn't, in fact, Windscale who saw the dapper-dan approach with one of Marlborough's victories behind him. Or rather it was and it wasn't . . . At the last minute Windscale had chickened out of the encounter, pulled up his collar and stuck Petherwick down his shirt with his trilby on her head. The result was an impossible beast with a balloon for a body and an aspirin for a head. Worse, because Petherwick kept slipping down so that the head was forever disappearing and in kicking herself up again it looked like this impossible beast was having a heart-attack but didn't know it.

Sir Cyril offered the beast a limp handshake. Windscale responded with a single wet finger. He groaned a belching rapture when the finger was touched by his hero.

'Excuse me,' said Petherwick, and in watching Sir Cyril dry his hand on Loveridge's shirtfront, was kind enough to mew: 'What lovely nails you've got, sir. How do you keep them so nice?'

Sir Cyril blushed like a fourth former on her first date. Even the glint of his specs turned red. Then Petherwick's hair escaped from the trilby and momentarily wrapped around his face before whipping away leaving an aroma of crushed almonds in its place. Loveridge was floating away on the smell, remembering a past encounter. But Sir Cyril was suddenly vexed.

'How long since you had your hair cut, Chief Superintendent?'

'I had my split ends done . . . ooooo, when was it?'

'You will have your hair cut to regulation length as soon as you leave this office! Do I make myself clear?'

'Yes, sir.'

'And, just to be sure, you shall send me the hair from the barber's floor when he has finished with you.'

PLETHORA OF GITS

(Petherwick later sent him the tail of a police horse, which her local salon coloured and highlighted to match what had exposed itself that day in the Home Office.)

'This letter!' Sir Cyril brandished it. 'Do you have evidence to substantiate these most serious allegations against the Bulgarian Consul?'

'I do,' said the disappearing head. She read from one of Haddock's monologues, being held more-or-less near her face by the blind Windscale.

Sir Cyril paced while he listened. When Windscale peeped, the great man seemed to be stalking up and down the field of Oudenharde, oblivious of French darts and the curling flight of cannonballs.

'This is a most serious situation we have ourselves, Chief Superintendent. On the one hand the country is losing its best-loved comedians in the most distressing circumstances, but on the other hand we are faced with an international incident of cataclysmic proportions if it does indeed transpire the Bulgarian government and not just the Consul is behind the killings.'

'You said it, sir.'

Sir Cyril gazed out of the window, cleaning his spectacles again, seeing an innocent slice of English street where nothing untoward had happened since Mrs Pankhurst and which should have waited for drizzle in peace for all eternity, but suddenly all of Haddock's wildest fantasies seemed alive and throbbing in the air.

'Chief Superintendent!'

'Yes, sir!'

'I have formed the opinion that these murders are the responsibility of the Bulgarian Consul alone. I have met the man on three occasions and he is undoubtedly insane. Of course, I could have him accused of spying and deported, but then we'd never know, would we?'

'Would we what?'

'We would never know for absolutely certain that he is our man. I could never be happy unless we have incontrovertible proof of his guilt.'

Windscale squeaked an impersonation of Petherwick: 'Your happiness, O great one, is the desire of my every corpuscle!'

'Errr . . . thank you, Chief Superintendent. I want you to follow the Consul. Don't let him out of your sight for a minute, do you understand? Where he goes, you go!'

'Yes, sir.'

'If and when the swine attempts the life of another of our comedians you are to arrest him on the spot. Got it?'

'Aye-aye, sir.'

The Windscale/Petherwick beast was waddling blindly in the general direction of the door, dislodging several Disraelis from their plinths, when Sir Cyril called it back. 'Oh, Chief Super . . .' he stroked his sleek black quiff. 'Don't mind me asking, do you – what shampoo do you use?'

Loveridge hiccoughed.

Windscale wanted a good look at the Bulgarian Consul in order to know who he was following (he only had fuzzy photos from an MI5 file to go on) but when he turned up at the Embassy in Queen's Gate Gardens claiming to be a Bulgarian onion-man in distress, he was told that the Consul, Lazlo Rotweiler, was 'resting'. Further investigation established that Rotweiler never emerged from the Embassy during the hours of daylight. A lengthy surveillance seemed inevitable . . . and there was nothing, ever since his days pounding the beat in Reading, that Windscale hated more than surveillance.

He positioned himself across the road from the Embassy, ingeniously disguised as a road-mender. Sheltering from the miserable rain in a striped plastic hut, filling it like an elephant in a dog's kennel, he grew seriously bored within fourteen seconds. Shooting spuggies out of the trees with his pistol didn't prove particularly entertaining. Petherwick provided some alleviation. As her part in the surveillance she kept passing every few minutes in a different outfit, supplied from quick-change vans at either end of the street. Every time she passed, Windscale shouted out in character: 'Cor! Look at the bum on that!' Or: 'Here, let's have a butcher's of them dumplins, darlin!' Petherwick playfully obliged.

All morning . . . No Rotweiler! All afternoon . . . No Rotweiler! Windscale was bored to death. He looked about for something to read and found the instruction leaflet of his roadmender's drill. He took it all in in an eyeful's trice and thought . . . why not? So he punched it into rattattatatatatating life and bounced along drilling foot-high letters into the road outside the Embassy. His message stretched right down the street, then back the wrong way up:

PLETHORA OF GITS

LAZLO ROTWEILER IS A SLIMY BULGARIAN ARSEHOLE

He was quite exhausted by the time he finished drilling. He retired to his hut and was soon eating Toblerones in his sleep. The rain patted against the plastic. His snores, louder than the drill had been, did not frighten the cats who stealthed in the Embassy grounds, carrying away murdered spuggies. All over England people were eating their tea.

When Windscale woke up with a start at seven o'clock, yellow from the streetlights, there were less cakes in the world then there'd been when he slipped into his snooze . . . this thought made him miserable and extra hungry. But, at last . . .

The Embassy door was opened by a bull-necked flunky. A pale man, thin as a hunger striker, swept into the damp air. Lazlo Rotweiler wore an ankle-length fur coat over his bemedalled evening dress. His black brylcreamed hair was combed back, but a kiss-curl suddenly snapped forward like a whip. He brushed it back with a white, red-fingernailed hand. His eyes were bloodshot as if he'd spent all afternoon weeping over the death of Stalin.

Rainwater had pooled into the letters of Windscale's declaration. Flotillas of sweetpapers floated in them. In the moments before his Rolls pulled up, Rotweiler studied the letters, turning his leering head on its side. He even took out his glass eye for a quick polish, but he couldn't make out the message. SAVE THE WHALE was his best bet.

'SLIMY BULGARIAN ARSEHOLE!!!' prompted Windscale from his tent.

Rotweiler stepped into the Rolls with a flash of his sharp yellow and gold teeth.

As the car pulled silently away Windscale discreetly jumped on to the back bumper, hoping not to be noticed. Nor did he seem to be, even though the car drove with its front wheels six foot in the air all the way to Piccadilly Circus. The mumpish driver assumed he'd set off a security device and after pressing every button he could find, continually ejecting people from their seats in nearby buses, he eventually electrocuted the outside of the car. Windscale spat off with a squish and the car uprighted itself with a polite bounce.

Windscale trotted along behind like a prize pig who'd drunk a swimming pool. He was determined to snatch a sample of Rotweiler's fur coat. If its hairs could be matched with hairs found at the scene of any future murders, then he'd have the proof the splendiferous Home Secretary needed.

7.32. Lazlo Rotweiler, the Bulgarian Consul, enters a Bulgarian restaurant and striptease parlour in D'Arblay Street, Soho.

7.33. Chief Superintendent Windscale requisitions four members of the general public to act as his fellow diners.

7.34. Windscale enters the restaurant, insisting he has booked a table for the 21st Birthday Party of his nephew Fred (played by an elderly jockey).

7.45. After some argument, and the laying out of three waiters, Windscale and his party take the table next to Rotweiler's. Rotweiler is already eating raw goulash. His fur coat is nowhere to be seen.

7.47. Windscale asks Rotweiler if he could please borrow the HP sauce. Rotweiler says he hasn't got any. Windscale calls him a greedy Bulgarian bastard. Windscale eats a plate of goulash and licks the plate clean.

7.48. Mademoiselle Hanki Pankov moves among the tables divesting herself of her clothing while singing Bulgarian folk tunes.

7.50. Windscale has another plate of goulash. He slices off Mademoiselle Pankov's beauty spots with his butter knife and flicks them on to Rotweiler's plate.

7.51. Rotweiler asks for more goulash with the little purple things in it.

7.52. Sergeant Petherwick arrives with eleven requisitioned nuns, one being naked, Petherwick having taken her habit as a disguise. They occupy a table adjacent to Rotweiler's.

7.53. Sergeant Petherwick asks Rotweiler if she could please borrow the HP sauce. Rotweiler says he hasn't got any. She calls him a greedy Bulgarian bastard.

7.55. Rotweiler tells Petherwick it is a waste of a good woman for her to be a nun. Petherwick says she is not a nun, only dressed like one. Rotweiler complains there are no purple bits in his new helping of goulash.

7.57. Windscale goes to the kitchens to lick the goulash pans clean, also looking for the whereabouts of Rotweiler's fur coat.

7.59. Rotweiler tells Petherwick she is the most beautiful woman he has seen since he was last in Plovdiv. If only she had a beard she'd be irresistible. Petherwick pushes his face in his goulash.

8.03. Windscale returns from the kitchens. Sergeant Petherwick and her eleven sisters are slumped at their table in a faint, holding their necks, their habits spattered with brylcream and goulash. Rotweiler has vanished.

It was always the same! Every night they followed the slimy Bulgarian arsehole! Every night he disappeared. Meanwhile, several comedians were murdered, alternative ones, turning up in dustbins in an alley off Leicester Square. When the Home Secretary phoned Windscale's workman's hut, the great detective was forced to admit that somehow, every night, Rotweiler managed to shake his tail. All Windscale knew was that he somehow got back into the Bulgarian Embassy before dawn. Yes, indeed, he could have committed the murders. Windscale wept with shame. The hut heaved with his manly sobs.

One night Windscale and Petherwick followed the pest into KOLAROV'S, a dingy but fashionable Bulgarian-owned nightclub in Kensington. Rotweiler danced the night away with dusky beauties and slumming Sloanes. Windscale stuck close to him, pretending to dance – in fact, his sergeant was repeatedly kicking him in the stomach, the resulting rippling effect up his flesh giving the impression of a brilliant new dance style. Ever the fashion queen, Petherwick was dressed in three belts and a J-cloth. Rotweiler's wolfish eyes were forever rolling her way, and he kept giving her aren't-you-lovely-but-where's-your-beard smiles, licking the needle-ends of his teeth with his chow's tongue.

On previous occasions Rotweiler had made his escape while Windscale was visiting the toilet. This time the bladdersome detective was determined to hold it in. But no . . . it was impossible! Windscale was a man used to urinating every seven minutes. Having missed three whole urinations, he was rubbing his knees together in time to the funky beat. Soon his penis was squirting down his trouser leg.

'An emergency, sergeant! Fetch me a crate of milk-bottles! Quick!'

Petherwick followed the order, found a crate in an alleyway and handed it over. With her high-kicking in front of him, Windscale filled the crate. He'd filled three more before the flashing lights, which all evening had been going from red to blue to green to off-altogether, then red to blue to green to off-altogether again, suddenly stayed off-altogether . . . altogether.

The record they were playing, Sophia Ruschuk and the Impalers singing *I LOVE MY TRACTOR*, stuck at Windscale's favourite bit. He threw a half-full milk-bottle through the darkness in the record-player's general direction.

A crash, a dribble . . . then silence.

'Hello?'

Silence.

'HELLO?'

Another silence . . . just like the last one.

Suddenly, the house lights came on, white and eye-smarting. Windscale was the only one standing up. Everyone was lying on the floor in a swoon, Sergeant Petherwick looking especially pale, her belts all in the wrong place. Rotweiler was gone.

Windscale banged sickly yuppies together in his frustration.

The surveillance dragged on past Bonfire night, a month of it. During that time 143 comedians were murdered up and down the country. Livid & Woebegone were found floating in the Thames outside Parliament, swollen-tongued. Commissioner Claeverlock himself dived in to haul them out. Afterwards, going for a brief snorkel to wind down, he found 61 further comedians on the bottom of the river, tied to garden furniture, fridge freezers and men-at-work signs. They loomed up at him in the greeny-grey murk, hugely depressed in such a jokeless environment. The Commissioner was so depressed himself when he got out that he produced the sawn-off shotgun he always carried and attempted to blow his head off. Fortunately, the gun was wet from the river and merely squirted him painlessly, or Windscale might've found himself at an interview for the Commissioner's job.

POLICEMEN SHOULD BE PAID ACCORDING TO THEIR WEIGHT was the subject of his most recent memo to the top brass. No doubt that was the sort of thing he might've said in interview.

But not now! Now he would never presume to aim so high! Now Windscale was a jelly, a mountainous blubbering jelly, as if all the jellies from every children's party since 1958 had been plastered together to make one miserable heap of a man. All his confidence was gone. He hadn't even managed, in all this time, to get a sample of the Bulgarian Consul's fur coat.

'Do you remember,' he said to Sergeant Petherwick with a sniff, 'that first night you worked for me?'

'Yes, Chief.'

'We sat outside Scotland Yard till dawn watching the sign go around.'

'I remember, Chief.'

'I was happy then.'

He looked out of the striped plastic hut at the drizzle-bound Embassy and let out a long sigh: the World going down like a crab-nipped beachball.

Having run out of spuggies to shoot, the depressed Windscale started shooting at passers-by. Petherwick kept having to jump in the way in a bullet-proof vest.

'I would only have winged the bastard!' shouted the disappointed jelly.

Truth was, Windscale's mind was slipping away from reality as fast as his bullets from their chamber. In his usual detective's manner he had studied his villain, Rotweiler, till he knew him better than he knew himself. But such was his concentration and so great was the pressure on him, that his mind started playing tricks that he couldn't help falling for. Windscale now saw Rotweiler's face wherever he looked. He saw it in clouds floating above Queen's Gate Gardens, with one cloud suddenly hurrying ahead of others to form a brief mocking smile. Even when he poured cans of baked beans into a tureen for his elevenses, off-orange beans on the top somehow drew themselves into the winking profile of Lazlo Rotweiler. He immediately penned a letter of complaint to the manufacturers.

But worst of all was that Windscale glimpsed Rotweiler's face on everyone he saw, every man and woman in the street, and all wearing fur coats. This made tailing the real Rotweiler impossible, even though by now he had the entire Metropolitan force at his command and Commissioner Claeverlock was finding spare coppers in all his old jacket pockets and from everywhere else in the country, so that a man in Middlesbrough could shoot his mother-in-law, rob Barclay's, Lloyds and NatWest, rape a schoolyard and walk on the grass without anyone around to arrest him.

Windscale sent these coppers in pursuit of everyone he saw, so that for several nights in a row everyone in London's West End had a policeman after them, but most of the policemen (who were also Rotweiler as far as Windscale was concerned) also had policemen after them, and so did they.

He even saw the pestilential man on the covers of magazines. Chasing an impossible number of Rotweilers into King's Cross Station he passed a newsstand . . .

'Cor, that bugger doesn't arf get about!' he yelled, requisitioning copies of *Time, Newsweek, Vogue, Woman's Own* and *Penthouse*, all smacked with the same pale red-eyed face.

Petherwick didn't realize what was wrong until one day in a taxi Windscale pulled out his beloved photo of the Home Secretary and ripped it in four.

'What am I doing with a photo of that bastard in my pocket? I know what he looks like!'

He then attempted to strangle the taxi-driver.

Even Petherwick wasn't safe. Several times Windscale's eyes, from gazing at her with benevolent affection turned into the eyes of a wronged ostrich while his pudgy fingers twisted into claws.

'It's me, Chief! Me! Me!'

'Slimy Bulgarian goat-poking git!!!!'

She had to strip naked and do pirouettes singing what she could remember from *South Pacific* before Windscale came to his senses. She usually performed the entire musical twice before he was properly calmed down

Doctor Beckenbaur, Windscale's psychoanalyst, was sent for. He turned up at Petherwick's HQ in the quick-change van. He was dressed as a Waffen SS Field-Marshal, but when Petherwick politely asked him why, he demanded some of her pubic hair for his collection. When she told him she didn't have any he moaned quietly over a drain for half an hour, in which time Windscale winged a milkman and four passers-by.

Eventually, he was shown in to Windscale's tent and stood in the only available space, between the big man's thighs.

Windscale smiled at him like the man-in-the-moon.

'So, at last,' he said. 'You've come to give yourself up. Conscience got the better of you at last, eh, lad?'

'Pardon?'

'Pardon? No chance, squire. You've killed yourself 237 comedians. 237, average age 48, that makes eleven thousand . . . three hundred . . . and seventy six years for you, maximum security, solitary confinement. Don't worry, though, I'll visit you every Thursday and KICK YOUR BLEEDING GUTS OUT!!!!!!'

'No, you are mistaking me for someone else, Obersuperintendant-fuhrer. I am Doctor Beckenbaur, you remember me, don't you? You hate me because I remind you of your fazzer . . .'

'What you saying, mush?'

Windscale snapped his thighs together, and the bad Doctor was mush indeed.

'Your fazzer! You hated him because he was thin! Zat is why you are so fat!!'

'I'm nowhere near fat, you Bulgarian dung-bucket!!!'

'Bulgarian? BULGARIAN! I am a true Arian! Look at how tall and blond I am!' (He was short and dark.)

'Mebbees they'll let yerh have a telly in yerh cell, eh? Eh? I'll make sure they shows yerh old programmes full of all the poor buggers wot you done in. Wouldn't that be nice?'

Windscale ground his thighs together like whales canoodling in a trench. Tiny bones, including both ulnas, cracked in the psychoanalyst. Had this been done to Freud he'd have taken an even dimmer view of humankind.

Doctor Beckenbaur swang his watch back and forth in his teeth in a desperate effort to hypnotize Windscale.

'You must push from your mind this perfidious delusion, Obersuperintendantfuhrer! Zink of nice things: ze green fields, babblink brookys, unt ze tanks trundling peacefully over ze hills into Sudetenland.'

Windscale, indeed, went heavy-lidded and glassy-eyed. How strange he felt! His real self was walking around in his head in heavy traffic.

His father, as thin as an After Eight Mint, was directing traffic, and all his way!!! Buses, coal-waggons, Ford Populars, muddy Wolseys, E-type Jags, Panther tanks both dinky and war-sized . . . all heading for Windscale's open maw. Up a ramp that was his tongue they drove, then dropped down into his watery innards, like vehicles driven by lemmings off Brighton pier on a moonless night. Meanwhile, back in the real world, a robotic Windscale was handcuffing Doctor Beckenbaur's legs to his arms, growling: 'Let's see you try to get out of this, you spittle-gobbed snake-in-the-coccygealium!'

He was kicking his prisoner down the street when the prisoner squealed: 'Ask yourself, Obersuperintendantfuhrer, would an official of the Bulgarian delegation be wearing ze uniform of a Waffen SS Field-Marshal??????'

Windscale waved goodbye to his father as the lids of his eyes grew lighter. 'What did you say?'

The Doctor repeated himself.

'Got yerh!'

'Um?'

'You told me it were the cheese, you bloody liar.'

The Doctor was beaten. He left on the next flight for Paraguay.

But Windscale was completely cured! He shook the hands of total strangers, saying how delighted he was to see them again. He received numerous luncheon invitations, even a half-hearted proposal of marriage. Meanwhile, every day the country lost another comedian . . .

Maxwell Drear spun the big wheel on his game show BIG WHEELIES and it fell off its spoke, splattering him flat in mid-catchphrase. Someone had undone the nuts at the back. (And all this in front of 16 million viewers!)

Windscale was held entirely responsible by the Home Secretary, Commissioner Claeverlock, all the newspapers, the relatives of the succeeding victims, everyone. If he didn't get a result soon he'd have to resign from the force. And for Windscale not to be a policeman was like a life of roast beef and Yorkshire puddings without the beef, without the puddings . . . with just Yorkshire, in fact, on a wet night during a power cut.

Windscale was muttering . . . 'Slimy Bulgarian arsehole, slimy Bulgarian arsehole . . .' over and over like a hari-krishna dribbling his mantra.

PLETHORA OF GITS

Rotweiler was on foot in the Bayswater Road. Windscale, ten paces behind him, had draped himself in washing to be disguised as an arab. If anyone he saw looked in debt he flung a fistful of change at them. Exhausted from all that following he kept falling over. In the moment of impact his eyes couldn't help closing for an instant – in that instant Rotweiler always managed to walk an impossible distance up the road. Windscale had to put on a jogging wheeze to catch up. He stole a child's skateboard, but it snapped when he put his weight on the thing.

It was a grey moonless night, with occasional scarves of fog twining themselves around the lamp posts. As the traffic-noise quietened into a jam, Windscale could hear a newspaper seller way back at Marble Arch yelling: 'ANOTHERFOURTEENCOMEDIANS-MURDERED!'

Rotweiler turned off into Sussex Square heading towards Paddington, his fur coat flapping behind him. Windscale fell over again, rolling into the gutter like a felled ayotollah, underpants shedding from the washing that enwrapped him. When his eyes snapped open again Rotweiler was gone.

'You seen a Bulgarian about here a minute ago?'

'Wot's a Bulgarian when it's at home?'

'A Bulgarian!' gritted Windscale and threw the man halfway to the Serpentine.

Everyone was in restaurants, at the theatre, having a bath! The streets were empty! Then Windscale saw a ravished young woman leaning on a postbox in a faint. Her neck was bleeding from what looked like a recent tracheotomy. Perhaps she'd dismissed herself from a nearby clinic after a botched operation.

'Excuse me, miss, but yerh hassent seen no Bulgars about, has yerh, by any chance?'

She nodded dazily.

'Where'd the bugger go?'

She pointed up the street to a handsome Edwardian building whose fierce red lights turned a taxi scarlet as it pulled up outside. Two chortling young men paid the driver and hurried up the steps.

'Thank you, miss,' said Windscale and flung a fistful of change at her.

There was no plaque on the door, nothing. Windscale pushed the

83

bell. A woman in her eighties answered. She was stark naked except for a straw hat and a bootlace around each ankle.

'MacTavish sent me,' said Windscale.

It was what he always said. MacTavish had been sending him places for twenty-five years. It never failed.

'MacTavish?'

'He sent me.'

'Did he?'

'MacTavish.'

'MacTavish?'

'Big man. Red beard. A tatoo of the Battleship Potemkin under his vest.'

'Ah, yes, of course. Mr MacTavish is one of our regulars.'

Somehow, it never failed.

The old woman led him down a dark corridor. Her posterior was a haze of cracks. Sporty prints of frisky women wrestling minotaurs decorated the walls.

Then they were at the end of the corridor with nowhere left to go. Suddenly the floor beneath their feet span, together with the wall and half a sporting print. Suddenly Windscale was in the plushest, reddest room he'd ever been in his life. It was like being in Liberace's stomach. Red velvet everywhere. Deep pile carpet: he sank up to his swollen ankles in its fluff. Huge paintings of naked women escaped from behind the drapes in a bobberation of curving flesh. At the far end of the room, past enough marshmallowish sofas to stuff Harrods, was a rosepetal-strewn swimming pool where young Indonesian girls skinny-dipped daintily. It looked like they were swimming in pink champagne. One splashed another, yowling playfully. A mote of the splash landed on Windscale's lower lip. He licked it. They WERE swimming in pink champagne!

An effeminate negro brought Windscale a glass of the stuff (with an elastoplast floating in it), together with a plush folder. He sat down on a marshmallow, knocked back the champers, spat out the elastoplast, and perused the folder. It was full of photographs of naked women.

HI I'M DEBBIE, No. 28. She was upside-down, hanging from some gymnastic equipment. He couldn't make out where her head was. Unless that was it? No, that was something else.

FENELLA, No. 42. HOW'S ABOUT IT, BULLBREATH? She

was a woman with a face like a slaughtered sheep whose bosoms had never heard of Isaac Newton.

Windscale gripped his truncheon as he realized. 'This is a b . . . b . . . b . . . brothel!'

The two young men he'd seen get out of the taxi were ascending a Hollywood-style staircase, still giggling. One was arm-in-arm with Fenella, the other was being carried by the negro.

Windscale's arab dress was sodden with his panicky sweat. A brothel! Mice ran up his spine, dragging refrigerators. Swordfish fenced in his guts.

The old woman again: 'Have you chosen yet, sir?'

'Errrrrrrrrr . . .' He flicked the pages in dread.

'Perhaps you would like to SEE our girls?'

'Urgh, don't get them up . . . errr, let them out, on my account, please.'

The old woman clapped her hands officially. For an instant there was the remains of a wondrous beauty in her face. She clapped again and was like Marilyn Monroe in purgatory punishing flies.

Girls trotted up on their toes, from all directions. There were enough to make all England happy on a Whit Monday. They smiled like a litter of Cheshire cats, doing high kicks, twanging each others' brassieres.

'. . . Errrrrrrrrr . . .'

'Come, come, now. Sir must make up his mind. Or perhaps would sir like ALL our girls.'

'All?'

'If sir can afford it.'

He smiled back at the girls, helplessly, turning the pages of the folder to match them up with their names. A wicked voice had switched itself on in his head. He could afford it . . . He could!!! He had pocketsful of confiscated credit cards. What's more, he needed the sexual experience as badly as a spider needs legs. A night with a few of these and he'd be able to show Petherwick what a real man was made of! In a few hours he could catch up on the education he'd missed out on for forty years!

'Errrrrrrm . . .?'

He surveyed the skinny line. 'These bints – you haven't got any nearer my size, eh? More as Rubens would have daubed them.'

She didn't. She tied several together to make one big one, but it looked like something from the wet dream of an octopus.

The girls were getting bored, pouting, angry. They were drifting away to continue their flower arranging and what-have-you. Windscale had to make his mind up quick. He walked up their line and pulled them out by their noses, just as he pulled out volunteers for traffic duty.

'These'll do.'

His blush was as red as the carpet as the girls giggled him up the stairs. They pulled away swathes of washing till he was down to his policeman's boots and trousers. He was a Gulliver in a pornographic Lilliput.

But suddenly his policeman's mentality surfaced. He bellied some of the girls against the bannisters.

'Any of yous lot Bulgarians?'

They squealed not.

'Bet yerhs is!'

He inned and outed his belly, shaking them till their false eyelashes were floating down into the pit of the room, like feathers from a gunshot crow.

'CONFESS! CONFESS!' This was the most exciting part of policework.

The only Bulgarian who worked there, squealed the girls who were nearest to falling over the bannisters, was Magda. She was engaged with a client at present . . . but if sir would be patient.

Windscale rushed up the stairs and flung open every door on the landing. 'POLICE!' he shouted. 'POLICE!' But Rotweiler wasn't to be found. Then . . . AH HA!!!! Someone was hiding under a pillow made to look like a Chinese nipple. Windscale undid his police badge and stuck the bastard with the pin.

'Arrrrrrrggghhhhhhhhhhoch!!!!!!!'

It was Commissioner Claeverlock wearing a red beard.

'Commissioner!!!!!!'

'MacTavish.'

'Who?'

'Me. MacTavish. I'm undercover.'

'You never are, are you?'

'What are you doing here, anyway, you blimp? You're supposed to be trailing the Bulgarian Consul.'

'I am. He's here.'

PLETHORA OF GITS

'You bloody liar! You're here for the same reason as I am!!!'

Claeverlock chased him out of the room. Before he clicked the door shut he winked with pathetic Scots whiskylessness, saying: 'You won't tell Moira, will you?' (Moira was Mrs Claeverlock.)

The instant after the door clicked Windscale heard a distinctive laugh. He'd heard it ten thousand times in the previous weeks. It was the laugh that vanished up alleyways, that frightened greyhounds to a halt at the dog track, that was suddenly above your head in a pea-souper. It was Lazlo Rotweiler's laugh, coming from a room at the end of the landing's curl.

The door opened. It was Rotweiler, nude, skin like the skin on warm milk. Apart from his scarlet lips he was as white as a virginal cricketer who'd never left the house. His long wormish penis was snapping like a piranha out of water. His bible-black brylcreamed hair was on end, all messed up. It had hands in it. Magda's hands. She was behind him pulling him back to the bed. He shared an astonished gaze with Windscale before kicking the door shut, as her black nails scratched scratchless lines across his chest.

Windscale was dashing towards the door before it was half closed, his folds of fat applauding him forwards. The momentum was irresistible . . . he almost had his mit on the knob of the closing door . . . but physics was again confounded in this illegal place. Windscale was suddenly stilled. His beauties had nabbed him at the last moment. Their long experience taught them exactly how to control a man's sudden urges. They especially knew where a man was ticklish. Windscale was helpless, incapacitated by chuckles from the hands of this bevosity of Delilahs.

They scrummed from all sides, manoeuvering him like an out-of-petrol bus into a puce room on to a puce waterbed smeared with lipstick, sprinkled with mascara and plastered with . . . SIN! SIN! SIN!

Windscale shook like a blender full of broken glass. Three dozen naked women had been crawling all over him for several hours. There was a permanent tickle of approaching ecstasy at the roots of his genitalia which occasionally burst forth into the full-blown thing, like the Flying Scotsman crashing into the buffers and tasting summer fruits. Then: a brief relaxation, like Atlas in the moments before laying down the World, before the tickle filled his bloated body full of budgies mating on the wing, then macaws doing the same, and in occasional lewd peaks as his trembling fingers found girlie bits, there were pterodactyls filling him, squarking obscenities under a red dome of rippling passion. (This place certainly gave you your money's worth!)

By the early hours he was too sore and exhausted to feel any more. How long before the girls using his belly for a trampoline broke through his paunch to be melted by his gastric juices? Others had sucked his toes till the nails had gone soft and if felt like he'd made a barefoot pilgrimage to Rome on a gravel path. One girl had been plucking his nose hairs (a favourite eroticism of Plantagenet Kings), but when she started reaching too far up he drenched her with ecstatic sneezes. These extra-helpings of ecstasy brought him to his absolute limit!

But there was more. A pleasure he had never felt before! Feelings he did not know that human flesh could have. It began at his neck and flapped through his system till it hit his heart, turning it into a blood-spraying Catherine Wheel, till it hit his brain, turning it into an inexhaustible floating mine blowing up every ship that sailed the porpoise-leaping seas. On the closed lids of his eyes he saw dances of the seven veils done by every policewoman he had ever coveted, in a vast police station . . . hoi, wait a mo! The policewomen had bats where their pubes should be! And how come the desk sergeant was wearing a fur coat? IT WAS ROTWEILER!!!!!!

When Windscale woke up dawn was on the net curtains. He felt his neck. It seemed he'd cut himself shaving without actually shaving. He brushed sleeping girls off his chest like a man swearing off jelly babies. What was this? There was something in his hand. He looked at it till his eyes came back into focus. It was the sleeve of a fur coat.

The morning had other discoveries. Sidney Night, the Australian comedian and female impersonator, was found in his dressing room at the Prince of Wales Theatre. He'd been strangled with the flex of his hair dryer.

Windscale had to drop off the sleeve at the police lab, and have several large meals, and try out some of his new expertise on

PLETHORA OF GITS

Petherwick in his tent . . . so he didn't turn up at the scene till nearly noon.

'Any prints?' he asked, then howled like a wolf. (He'd been doing it all morning and couldn't think why!)

'Naw,' said Mr Sparbrooke, a baggy-eyed old wreck who attended to such things. 'Just a few hairs in the face powder.'

'Let's see them hairs, then.'

Windscale held the little bag containing the hairs up to the light. Black hairs, each about an inch long, browner at the root. He picked at his coat where some hairs from the sleeve had rubbed off. They looked the same.

He telephoned the lab from the manager's office.

'We've gone over that sleeve you gave us, boss.'

'And?'

'No doubt about it. Wombat hairs. From a wombat's armpit.'

'Black hairs, each about an inch long, browner at the root.'

'That's them.'

He rushed the plastic bag over. Indeed, they were also wombat hairs. Ordinarily, a slain Australian with wombat hairs in his vicinity would not be thought suspicious, he coming from a country that abounds in such creatures, there being a million ways in which hairs from a stray wombat could have found their way into his luggage and thence into the face powder. But this was different.

As a precaution Windscale had the wombat in London Zoo arrested. If it ever came to a trial the defence would obviously attempt to implicate it and get their boy off. But with a watertight alibi from the wombat there was no way that Lazlo Rotweiler was going to escape the clutches of justice. Windscale had the proof he needed! The day was saved!

Another phone call, to the boys down town.

'How you doing with that wombat?'

'It's being grilled, sir.'

'Save a double portion for me, sergeant.'

'Its keeper says it was locked in its cage all night, sir. I've taken his statement.'

'That's good enough for me.'

Windscale then telephoned the Home Secretary.

'Esteemed paragon!'

'Speaking.'

'Your humble adoring servant, Chief Superintendent Windscale here.'

'Yes.'

'WE'VE TUMBLED THE BASTARD!!!!! WE'VE GOT HIS SLIMY BULGARIAN ARSE!!!!! INCONTROVERTIBLE EVIDENCE THAT HE'S THE BUGGER WE WANT!!!!!!!!'

'Oh, good-O!' said Sir Cyril Passey-Wix, who'd been on the verge of resigning because of the crisis.

Petherwick was in Windscale's hut painting her toenails when the police cars arrived. Every police car in London! Then blue vans full of scuffers in riot gear. Within ten minutes the Bulgarian Embassy was more surrounded than 300 Jerichos.

Commissioner Claeverlock went inside with the arresting papers. He came out without Rotweiler, looking pale and howling like a wolf. He had to lie down in his car and eat raw liver.

Windscale took over, yelling through a megaphone: 'COME ON OUT YOU MURDERING BASTARD!!!!! YOU GOULASH SPOONING TURD-TONGUED VILLAINOUS GIT!!!!! YOU PIRAHNA-KNOBBED PALE-ARSED SNOTBAG!!!!!!'

As Windscale spat out each metallic insult, the assemblement of police repeated it into their own megaphones. The whole thing was heard as far away as ferries approaching Folkestone harbour.

'YOU SMARMY BRYLCREAMED PHLEGMPOT OF A BULGARIAN GOAT POKER!!!!!!! YOU LOUSE-RIDDEN BUGGERATION OF CONGEALED CONJUNCTIVITIS!!!!! YOU GANGRENOUS PUSTULANT HORSETROUGH OF GONORRHOEA SLIME!!!!! YOU UN-ENGLISH ABORTION OF PISSED-IN MILK!!!!! YOU SKINNY WOMBAT-SKINNING ILLEGITIMATE PINKO MUCUS UNDER THE BED!!!!! YOU CHISEL-TOOTHED SUPPURATING MEAL OF USED TOILET PAPER!!!! YOU SCROTUM-CHEEKED LEERING BOIL OF CANCEROUS VOMIT!!!! YOU POINTY-EARED ILLEGAL-PARKING FOWLPEST OF AN UNDERPANTS-STAINING BASTARD!!!!!! YOU GIT-BUMMED GITTYGIT-SPLURGE OF A GIT-BELCHING GITSTENCH!!!!! YOU SAGO-BALLED LUMBAGO-STAB OF A CATBIT DAGOPLOP OF CONSTIPATED CABBAGE SHITE!!!!!

PLETHORA OF GITS

YOU COWPAT-SANDWICH OF A SLAVERING SLAV-SUCKING PICKED-SCABBED GOBBET OF ADENOIDAL BASTARDING MAGGOTY-FACED BLOOD-PUKING JAYWALKING BULGARING BULGAR!!!!!'

This invective went on without pause for nine hours. Beyond the hot lights blazing against and around the Embassy was a cool crisp night full of stars and a crescent moon as slim as a corner of cheese caught between Windscale's teeth.

But even Windscale's encyclopaedia of invective was running out. By nine o'clock the pauses between insults were getting longer and longer, full of errrrrrrs, and by ten all he could think to say was:

'COR, BUT YOU'RE UGLY!!! COR, BUT YOU'RE UGLY!!! COR, BUT YOU'RE UGLY!!!'

His fellow police chanted this with him till their megaphones panted.

But still there was no sign of Rotweiler.

Windscale kept sending notes to the Home Secretary asking permission to storm the Embassy. But notes came back saying that the Embassy was, by international law, officially Bulgarian soil, so to storm it would be an act of war.

'SOD THEM BLOODY FOREIGNERS,' said one of Windscale's notes. 'WE'RE BRITISH AREN'T WE. WE CAN DO WHAT WE LIKE.'

The Foreign Secretary was consulted. He was listening to Windscale's invective on the radio at his club. He glared at the police delegation through a gold-rimmed monocle. 'Certainly not!' he said and put his ear back to the broadcast.

Rotweiler, meanwhile, was in his office, reeling from the nine hours of invective. The pinheads of pupils in his bloodshot eyes darted about like fleas desperately searching for each other in different bowls of tomato soup. Police spotlights penetrated his curtains and span around the room, astonishing his face at each of Windscale's convoluted jibes.

He pulled his wombat-fur coat over his head, seething with anger in its darkness as each insult struck home. He was reminded of his long-ago days in the military academy when the Principal had humiliated him on the parade ground in front of all the other cadets. He remembered how his classmates had chanted the Principal's insults while de-bagging him in the dorm. All had been well until that day on the parade ground, but afterwards he was never popular again. It was the same now! He was ruined!

'YOU... YOU... YOU... FUNGUS-FACED PIGEON-PLOP OF A DENTAL ASSISTANT!!!!'

No more! No more! He could take no more!

Windscale was going 'Errrrrrrrrrrrrrrrr...' forming another insult in a mouth pasted with salt 'n' vinegar crisps, when there was a crash from the Embassy. A window shattering! High up!

The spotlights lopped through the trees towards the stars. Something was up there! It was Rotweiler, flapping away in the night in a fur coat with one sleeve missing. He seemed dazzled by the lights like a moth flying into a convention of lighthouses. But then the beams span and span but couldn't find him. Only Windscale's trained ear heard a faint cackling laugh high up in the sky.

'CUT THE LIGHTS! CUT THE LIGHTS!'

Sudden darkness. Absolute silence. A police dog woofed. Everyone looked up into black, their eyes becoming slowly accustomed. The stars came out all over again for them.

Petherwick: 'There he is, Chief!'

Rotweiler's madly flapping figure could be made out as it interrupted stars.

'That's it, then,' sighed Claeverlock. 'The bastard's scarpered.'

Windscale stamped with the fury of a horse that had come second in the Grand National for the fourteenth year in succession.

'PACK UP AND GET HOME, LADS. BETTER LUCK NEXT TIME, EH?' megaphoned Claeverlock.

But as the police vehicles pulled away, Windscale saw the van of the Police Hang-Gliding Team. They'd been on their way to a competition in Milton Keynes but had stopped off to join in the action.

'Can you get me up in one of them things?' the 47-stone Windscale asked their top man.

'What, all of you?'

Next thing, Windscale was strapped into a hang-glider on the roof of the Bulgarian Embassy. A hundred of the Met's most strongarmish coppers were running around and around the roof with him, trying to give him the best possible launch.

Petherwick couldn't look. She was sure that when they flung him off he'd drop straight to the ground like a mortally wounded mallard.

PLETHORA OF GITS

He did. But at the same moment someone leaned on a switch and the spotlights all came on at once. The sudden heat from their lamps was like taking the lid off a saucepan of boiling soup. It created a whoosh of hot air that flung Windscale and his hang-glider high into the night sky. A minute later when the lights were switched off and their eyes were accustomed to darkness again, they saw the impossible aircraft scudding a brave flight above distant chimney-pots.

Windscale was over the Channel before he caught up with Rotweiler, who was lazily flapping towards Bulgaria, the occasional medal dropping from his jacket down into the dark sea to decorate fish destined to come up in the catches of chin-scratching Belgians.

'THIS IS THE POLICE, YOU SLIMY BULGARIAN ARSE-HOLE!!!' yelled Windscale. 'GIVE YOURSELF UP AT ONCE OR I'LL SHOOT YOUR BUM OFF.'

Rotweiler laughed as irritatingly as ever.

Windscale shot him, expecting his prey to drop down on to a snoozing Dunkirk. But he flapped on. Windscale shot again . . . and again. Blummy, but his aim was off tonight! He emptied every gun in his pockets into the beast. Nothing! Not even an ouch.

Sailing under the stars were small solitary clouds. Rotweiler kept nipping into these and coming out of them somehow miles ahead, flapping-on-the-spot, his slow sinister laugh like a spoon being repeatedly struck on a chicken's skull.

Windscale could do little to hurry himself up, except swallow great billows of air and flatulate them out his backend. This gave him little spurts, but didn't help him catch up.

Meanwhile, Rotweiler's arms were getting tired. He approached Vienna in a spin and clung to the great spire of the Stefansdom for a rest. Windscale soon came swooping along like a swearing angel and the Bulgar had to take off on the wing again.

Any Magyar sleepwalkers suddenly waking up with their feet in the shallows of Lake Balaton that night could have looked up and seen a most extraordinary chase while they crossed themselves. A British Police Superintendent ruling their skies in pursuit of a ruined Bulgarian diplomat . . .

But greater ruin was to come. Sofia, the Bulgarian capital, was almost in sight when dawn hurried above the mountains. Its first rays had Rotweiler in a panic, flapping-at-the-double back towards

Windscale and the night. Next instant the sun was red and round between two peaks and Rotweiler fell to earth like the ashy end of a tapped cigar.

Windscale crashed his hang-glider into a convenient medieval ruin. But by the time he reached Rotweiler he was sunk in his fur coat, in the final stages of decomposition . . . and without a confession to boot! The bastard!

Having puffed Rotweiler's ashes into an envelope, he stood about all perplexed, wondering how he could possibly describe any of this in his report.

A peasant came up and tried to sell him an aged sheep.

'Gerroutofit, you poverty-stricken bastard!' yelled Windscale, starting his long walk home by walking right over them.

BETTY AND GEORGE

BETTY AND GEORGE had been running for nineteen straight seasons. With new series or endless repeats it was never off the air. The early shows, with their frantic farcical energy and whirlwinds of denuded vicars, had attained classic status. Now the later, slower, increasingly tired shows were announced by the BBC linkman with: 'And now for a new series of classic comedy with those old favourites ... Betty and George.'

BETTY AND GEORGE was the Nation's Number One sit-com. Even if you hated it, and millions did, it was odds-on you had seen the most famous episodes at least twice, the damn thing being so hard to avoid. Hating it, in fact, wasn't easy ... Maybe you started by hating it, in the days when you were waiting for the Beatles' next LP to come out. But before you were too much older you found yourself enjoying your hatred of it and next thing you'd be watching the show for the comfort it afforded. Other shows had come and gone. Cast members had died till the survivors couldn't find each other among the replacements. But BETTY AND GEORGE went on and on ... It was a rare constant in times that had changed too much.

People didn't think to question their assumption that Betty and George actually lived together in their crises-ridden semi-detached suburban 143 Cherry Tree Drive.

It was the jumbled scene of many a dream: 'Guess what, pet? (Pet was what George called Betty and Betty called George) 'Last night I dreamed I was living in Betty and George's house.'

'Was I there?'

'You were Betty. I was George.'

Then they'd kiss each other, because in a way they wanted to be like Betty and George. No matter how many times Betty chased George with the frying pan, no matter how many chesty women George curled his lips and went 'Oooooooooooooooooorrrrrrrr!' at, they always remained loyal to each other, encased by a love-heart in the final credits. This unbreakable love, in a life that went on forever, was the show's secret weapon.

Nobody seemed bothered that the same jokes and situations returned again and again. Their regular outraged vicar (played by Ferdy Wells) was just as outraged every week, despite a history of similar outrages going back nineteen years which gave him a wider experience of outrages than any cleric since Pope Alexander Borgia. Similarly, Betty's WI cronies were forever amazed at finding George's underpants behind the cushion on the settee, even though they found them there on every visit. George, meanwhile, could always be relied upon to fall through the floorboards with a testicle-bruised grimace every time he attempted DIY, which was every week. On one famous occasion, when George's pompous boss had sent a tableful of important clients for Betty and George to entertain, the entire house blew up, leaving everyone, Betty included, with a testicle-bruised grimace as the familiar end music began to tinkle.

Even those folk who knew that Betty Kay and George Chowder didn't actually live at 143 Cherry Tree Drive would thoughtlessly bet their duodenums that Betty was really married to George, that George was really married to Betty. But George was married to Millicent and Betty wasn't married to anyone at all.

When Betty did chat-shows (George never did) she no longer bothered to point out that George wasn't her real husband. She used to. But the host never seemed to hear. Nobody did. Even her own mother, who'd recently died of a urinary complaint in a Hove rest home, had muttered over and over on her deathbed: 'Where's my son-in-law? George? Are you there, George? Take care of my little girl. Pity you never had children of your own.'

All this had taken its toll on Betty's psychology. When she and George went their separate ways from the set of their imaginary home, Betty returned home to Romford to a house which, over the years, had become more and more like the one she'd left behind at the BBC. Same gnome in the garden, same crazy-paving, same pebble-dashed walls. Stranger still, throughout the house the furniture was that of *BETTY AND GEORGE*. Even the double-bed, where she slept each night alone on the side Betty always slept, calling out in her sleep to hush the snoring of a George who wasn't there, was the same double-bed, identically blanketed, to the one where Betty and George listened pop-eyed for burglars. On the mantelpiece were pictures of Betty and George's wedding day, just like at 143 Cherry Tree Drive, and Betty and George on holiday in Majorca, and Betty and George feigning testicle-bruised expressions.

Her rare guests and the men who came to do jobs didn't think there was anything strange in all this. Nor that an actress who'd been at the top of her profession since as a child star she'd been hoisted on to Gracie Fields's shoulder in 'Sing As We Go' should be living in such lower-middle class surroundings. They reckoned they were in Betty and George's house, that George was away on a sales trip. The real Betty, meanwhile was a little posher and was a snappier dresser, called people 'darling' rather than 'pet', but she had the same over-the-fence laugh and if she was asked how George was she always had an anecdote which could be recognized as an incident from the show and she always looked over her shoulder to see if George was there before she hit the punchline.

The fantasy was an almost constant one. Betty bought food for George, cooked him meals, was always expecting him home-at-any-moment, got angry when he was inevitably late and she had to scrape the food into the bin. She put the frying-pan ready to chastise him with when he eventually arrived, just as the other Betty always did on the show.

Learning lines was a special joy because she could hear George's voice all around the house. She'd walk with the script from room to room giving a more muted, more genuine performance than ever made its way on to the small screen. But there were bleak silences with the fantasy put aside: Betty sitting up in bed weeping, Betty drunken in the garden swearing at the gnome, Betty staring at the mantelpiece with an expression of pain no sit-com could allow.

When the comedian murders were in full swing Betty became a wreck of worry. She loved George just as the TV Betty loved George, had loved him passionately for nineteen years of marriage. His chubby smile and flat Northern vowels were the only things that cheered her in a ridiculous World. If anything happened to him she'd be left alone with a bottle of pills and a locked bathroom door! Perhaps tonight, some hooded figure was creeping up on him with a garrotte. If only she could phone him, reassure herself he was okay, that tomorrow they'd be on the set again, husband and wife just as always. But like many double-acts they lived completely separate lives. Betty didn't know George's number, didn't even know where he lived.

* * *

George lived in Hummersly Hall near Sudbury in Suffolk. Built by Carstairs for the First Earl in 1650 on land given to him by Cromwell as a reward for being especially glum. The gardens were laid out by Ignance Wold. Constable made numerous watercolours of it. Tennyson had a heart attack there.

The third largest stately home in England, it was the only one untrampled by tourists. This because each succeeding Hummersly had made a brand new fortune of his own to add to his father's and his father's father's. They'd never had a wastrel or a flop or anyone who'd spent money just for the fun of it. 300 years of solid raking-it-in (and no bother with death duties because when an Earl died they kept it a secret) had made them the richest family in England. Rich enough to stand the occasional love-match, as when in 1954 the nineteen-year-old Millicent Hummersly married George Chowder. Churchill threw up at their reception.

But Millicent didn't marry a comedian, at least she didn't think she did. When George met Millicent at Henley Regatta in Coronation Year he lied to her, said he was in banking – after all, what chance would he have with such a starchy toff if she'd known he was Arthur Haynes's stooge staggering across a different stage every night with a broken cigarette in his mush! He'd maintained the lie for 37 years.

Fortunately, the third Earl had refused, since its invention, to have a television in the house. Continuing the glum religious traditions of his ancestors, he maintained it lowered moral standards and encouraged masturbation. So Millicent had only ever seen TV, and with a sneer, when passing shop windows in the Rolls. Meanwhile, she'd spent her life in the centre of a devout set of brow-knitted killjoys of identical upbringing whose evenings were spent reading Kierkegaard in the original while polishing horses unerotically. Little chance, therefore of her seeing the snippiest snippet of such vulgar nonsense as *BETTY AND GEORGE*.

Every morning George was driven to the rural dingyness of Sudbury station to catch the train to London and his job in Barclays Bank in the City. He was now, after 37 supposed years there, the head of the whole shebang.

Another bowler-hatted city-type on the platform: 'I say, you're not, are you? You know . . . HIM? That chap off the telly.'

George's toothbrush moustache bristled. 'Who might that be?'

PLETHORA OF GITS

'You know. Cripe me, but you're a dead ringer for . . . what's his name? George! That's it!'

'As it happens my name *is* George. Sir George Chowder. I'm in banking, you know.'

'So am I! Which bank?'

'Errrrrr . . .'

He sat with a *BETTY AND GEORGE* script hidden behind a copy of the *Financial Times*. By the time the train pulled in at Liverpool Street sometime after nine, George had that day's lines word perfect. He arrived on the set and kissed Betty on the cheek just as if he were arriving home from a day in the office. Gone was the plummy accent of the Hummerslys which he spoke at home better than they did, and up came the blunt Yorkshire of a Leeds greengrocer, which is what his father had been. It was a running joke of *BETTY AND GEORGE* that George was more common than Betty, but one famous time he dressed as a colonial bishop and confronted Betty's maiden aunts with a voice full of errant doubleyous such as were hunted in their time by the ghostly Hummerslys whose portraits worried the walls of Hummersly Hall.

For 37 years George lived this odd life, enjoying to the full his two great acting successes: one as half of the country's best-loved comedy team, the other as Sir George Chowder, banker, pillar of society. Life couldn't be more swish! No stiff-upper-lipped Hummersly loved the Hall more than he. He rode. He shot. Servants did his slightest bidding. He lived like a King.

George watched the tiny signs of the changing seasons with a special joy, supervising the vegetable garden with a zeal that was always in danger of showing (a Hummersly did everything as if he hated it). When he held up one of his prize Savoy cabbages, with the blue sky and the Hall's towers framing his view of it, he could hear his father's voice: 'By gum, son, thissin's a right snorter!' and a hiccoughing laughter drummed behind his lips, more delighted than any *BETTY AND GEORGE* had inspired down the years. His whole life had been a wonderful joke! He'd tricked them all and got away with it!

George was a happy man. Happy also with Millicent, even though she was the most miserable frosty-faced of women, thin, balding and sexless, eyes deeply ringed with a grief of being alive. Happy even with his grimacing children, sent away to a Scottish boarding-school noted for its cruelty. He even enjoyed the company of the third Earl, who locked himself away in a laboratory all day practising amateur taxidermy, not because he enjoyed it but because he didn't, because it was the last thing he wanted to do. The dour attitudes and tragic lifestyles of his family more than amused George, while the effort of pretending to be as dour himself stoked up the private joyousness that was natural to him.

But then Eddie Haddock had a kipper shoved down his gullet and everything changed for George. In succeeding weeks many old friends from his touring days left the bill forever in horrific circumstances. Maxwell Drear had been an especial friend. George was paralysed with fright. He was next! He was sure! Next! Help! Help!

He was so troubled that on several occasions he called Millicent 'Betty' by mistake and one day on the set his Yorkshire accent wouldn't come. He could only recite the sermons of Archbishop Tait with the occasional shriek such as the good Archbishop emitted only during his most hideous bed-wetting dreamings.

Millicent threw a devilled kidney to the corgis. As usual at breakfast she briefly perused the headlines in the *Telegraph*, looking for some further sign of moral decay and excessive masturbation about which she could rail all day long.

'It says here that the Bulgarian Consul is a Wampire.'

George wiped Oxford marmalade from his moustache, his nerves were a xylophone hammered by failed dentists.

'Sorry, pet . . . errrrr, dear?'

'The Bulgarian Consul. He's a wampire.'

'A what?'

'A wampire.'

'No!'

'Yes.'

'By gum . . .'

'Pardon!'

'Errrr . . . a colloquial expression, dear.'

'Don't be wulgar, George!'

She tossed another kidney to the corgis. The same corgi always got there first. It was very fat as a result, with legs that no longer reached the ground, and could only move with the aid of a roller-skate strapped under its belly, which ironically gave it the speed to beat the other corgis in a dash. The third Earl was eagerly awaiting its final heart-attack so that he could stuff it.

'It seems,' sniffed Millicent, 'that he's the one who's been kwilling all these dweadful comedians.'

'He what? Who? When?'

'Should give him a medal, I say. It's disgwusting how these frwivolous people tweat life as if we were put on this earth for our own amusement and not for the continuwal suffering the Good Lord intended. Are you quite well, George?'

George's lips were scaled with dry cornflakes. His eyes bulged like those of a camel forcing itself eye-first through the eye of a needle.

'The Bulgarian Consul, you say . . . he's been killing all those diabolical comedians, has he?'

'According to the *Telegwaff*, dear, though they're probabwly all Satanists even on the *Telegwaff* these days, I'm sure.'

'And they've collared the bas . . . they've apprehended the criminal, dear?'

She read disdainfully down the column. 'It seems he was last seen flying to Bulgarwia under his own steam pursued by a Chwief Superintendent in a hang-glwyder. What nonsense!'

George let out a long delighted giggle that sent the corgis scattering behind the furniture. It was the first peal of laughter in the house since the unhinging of the second Earl during the Relief of Ladysmith.

'Betty! Betty! I love you!' cried an ecstatic George.

Obviously, an evil spirit had entered him. The Bible was full of such happenings. Why not now, in these increasingly depraved times?

Millicent gathered the servants together. They stripped George naked, stripped naked themselves and beat both George and each other with branches of holly till the supper gong gonged. The evil spirit, who'd yelled for mercy all day in a broad Yorkshire accent, was pronounced cast out. Funny thing was, they didn't enjoy any of this one bit.

Betty was in her local Tesco's, sleepily lobbing tins of tuna fish into her trolley, when up the aisle came a smallish man completely wrapped in bandages, without even an eye-hole or a mouth-hole. He moved with the slow pained movement of a sodomized cellist. As he passed her, manoeuvering his own trolley (full of runny yoghurt, thin soup and plastic straws) there was a weensie movement in the bandaging around his face. Betty guessed he was smiling, so she smiled back. He nodded his head. She nodded hers.

Ten minutes later she was in the check-out queue and there he was behind her. She smiled again. He nodded his head. She nodded hers, then gave him a wink like the one in the opening titles of *BETTY AND GEORGE.*

The check-out girl: 'Cummon, dear. I hassent got awl day.'

'Sorry,' said Betty and started unloading her stuffs on to the belt.

But she couldn't help looking at the bandaged man. There was only a single wrap of bandage before his eyes. When he blinked his lashes brushed against the bandage . . . and they were wetting it! Staining it with tears! He was crying.

'You all right, darling?'

'Thank you. Yes.'

'You sure?'

'Quite.'

Outside, she was putting her shopping in the boot of her Fiesta when she saw him again, tripping over bollards and losing his yoghurt.

'Can I help you, darling?'

'My dog died.'

'Um?'

'I am totally blind,' he explained.

She picked up his dripping yoghurts for him and helped him to her car. She even mopped the pink dollops of yoghurt off his bandages with her own handkerchief.

'You sit down there, darling, and don't worry yourself. Tell Betty where you live and she'll drive you home.'

'Who's Betty.'

'Me. I'm Betty.'

'Are you a nun?'

She did her BETTY laugh. 'Just a friend.'

Sobs from inside the bandages: 'I don't think anyone has ever been so kind to me in all my life!'

They drove along the A118 towards West Ham. No conversation. The man sobbed occasionally, and once he blew his nose loudly inside his bandages, which couldn't be very hygienic.

PLETHORA OF GITS

Finally, at some particularly boring traffic-lights, he broke the silence.

'That's a very attractive dress you're wearing.'

'Thank you,' said Betty, but as they pulled off: 'I thought you said you were blind?'

'It comes and goes.'

More silence. Then at some Bromley traffic-lights, a sound like quadraplegics playing the Eton Wall Game in quicksand: he was sucking up yoghurt through a straw, weeping snufflingly at the same time.

'Accident, was it?' asked Betty.

'Sorry?'

'Your bandages.'

'Oh! Yes. I worked at the jam factory.'

This explanation seemed sufficient for him. Betty kept glancing sideways from her driving to see if he was gathering his courage to further explain his woeful condition. But he looked asleep, even dead.

'Fell in, did you?'

He came to life with a burp. 'Do excuse me.'

'You fell in, did you?'

'Into the jam. Yes. Blackcurrant. Strawberry would have been better. But I count myself lucky it wasn't apricot. I'd not be here today if it'd been apricot.'

The day had started bright, with warmth in the sun. Now the sun was lost. It was raining hard, stotting off the pavements in the Mile End Road. Betty pulled up at St Clements Hospital.

'They're taking my buttocks,' the man told her, 'and spreading them all over my body.'

Betty smiled sympathetically, ignoring the peeping horn of a bus stuck behind her.

'Of course, by the time they've finished I'll have no buttocks left, but Dr Mahmood says they'll grow back if I eat lots of yoghurt.'

'You sure you'll be all right, darling?'

'Thank you so much for your kindness.'

He got out of the car, gripping his shopping, and stood erect in the rain as others hurried past him bent almost double, showing pained expressions to the pavement. The rain wetted his bandages more than a plunge of tears. He raised a sickly hand and waved goodbye.

Betty wanted to see him safely through the hospital gates, but she was in trouble with the bus and had to drive off. Looking in her mirror she saw the bandaged man walking with a sprightliness of step down the street, not going into the hospital at all. And he had a handbag over one arm. Her handbag!!! The traffic pushed her forward into a handbagless life.

Betty was at home that night learning her lines, eating blackcurrant jam sandwiches with a vengeance, when the phone rang. A slow blank voice.
'Ms Kay?'
'Yes.'
'Ms Elizabeth Kay.'
'Yes.'
'This is Mr O'Crelli speaking.'
She thought her producer had been kidnapped by bookmakers again.
'No. It's Mick. Mick O'Crelli. We met this morning, don't you remember?'
It was him! The bandaged man!
'I stupidly walked off with your handbag. I hope you'll forgive me.'
It had all been a mistake. She forgave him.
'Perhaps I can make amends. I couldn't help noticing, in your appointments book, when I was looking for your phone number, you've nothing on tonight, no engagements, I mean. If you'd like . . . I know I'm a hideous monster of a man disgustingly scarred by jam and no right to ask this of an attractive woman such as yourself . . . but there's an excellent yoghurt restaurant in Walthamstow.'
Well . . . she had to get her handbag back, didn't she? She accepted the invitation.

Betty hadn't been on a date since the late Jerry Muckle took her to see a matinée of *The Sound of Music* in 1965. She put on the white satin dress she'd worn in the episode of BETTY AND GEORGE where Betty and George discover that they've never really been married because the priest who married them was a priest impersonator, who, it turned out, had also married their neighbours, the Braithwaites. In the double wedding which followed, with Betty looking twenty years younger in her white satin dress, George ended up married to Mrs Braithwaite and Betty to Mr Braithwaite who decided he liked things better that way.

Betty remembered the episode warmly as she searched Walthamstow for the restaurant. But when she went in and saw the bandaged man, Mick O'Crelli, at a candlelit table, a terrific pang of guilt hit her like a shoal of herring. She was two-timing George! No she wasn't. Yes she was. No she wasn't. Yes she was. No she wasn't!!! George wasn't her real husband. Yes he was. No he wasn't. Yes he was. No he wasn't. Yes he was. Her mind tortured, she turned to flee.

Just then, O'Crelli saw her. He waved. A loose strand of bandage passed through the candle flame. In an instant, he was doing a Jan Palach impression.

'Arrrrrrrrrrrhhhhhhhhhhhhhhhhhh!!!!!!'

A thoughtful waiter doused him with milky yoghurt and his screaming soon subsided. Betty couldn't help herself. There is nothing so attractive to a woman as a grievously wounded man. She advanced through the tables with a quiver of pangs stabbing her heart.

'Is that you?' asked O'Crelli as Betty sat beside him, dabbing him, all motherly instincts and fluttery eyes.

'It's all right, pet. I'm here.'

She'd called him 'pet', which was what Betty called George, not 'darling' which was what Betty called everyone else. This was significant.

O'Crelli thrust his smoking hand into a nearby ice bucket.

'It's brought it all back to me,' he moaned. 'The boiling jam. Sinking into it like the last wasp of summer.'

The last wasp of summer! What a beautiful thing to say. Betty was very nearly, not quite, in love. It all depended on what he said next.

His sight must've come back at that moment. He said, sobs cracking his voice: 'You shouldn't have worn such a beautiful dress, not for me.'

'Don't be silly.' She almost cooed.

Then he wambanged her with: 'But you can't possibly be the real Elizabeth Kay. The date of birth on the driving licence in your handbag is 1928, when you obviously aren't a day over thirty-two.'

All her wrinkles jumped under her hair. Her breasts hopped like spring lambs holding their breath. The rest of her mutton turned to cream. And her broad smile was suddenly the yellow of the inside of a banana rather than the usual out.

'Are you still there?' yelped O'Crelli.

'I'll not leave you, pet,' she said, and stroked the bandages that covered his hand. It aroused her to think that, although she was stroking his hand, she was also stroking his buttocks.

Betty felt that she'd been dead for years and had only just woken up. She was full of life and love like the brightest of all possible teenagers. She was no longer George's Betty! She was Mick's Betty!

On the set nobody could keep up with her. She had the pep she'd had in her Ealing comedy days, was full of suggestions for comic business, on how to improve her own lines and everybody else's. She moved faster, spoke faster. George, though inspired out of his usual cosy sleepiness, couldn't keep up. He chased after Betty in a tortoiseish dimension. But this contrast made everything somehow funnier. George found that his every slow gesture was a great pompous joke.

The two players rose above their material and viewers who previously had just smiled at *BETTY AND GEORGE* found their ribs splitting. Everyone agreed, the last two episodes shown that December, followed by the Christmas Special, were the funniest *BETTY AND GEORGEs* ever. They were also, it turned out, the last.

Meanwhile, Betty and O'Crelli spent their evenings together. They went to shows, casinos, dancing in West End nightclubs. The tabloids were soon asking: who is this bandaged man? It was rumoured Betty was having an affair with a member of the Royal Family!

And how was O'Crelli's treatment going?

'Dr Mahmood says I'll be able to take the bandages off soon,' said O'Crelli, a lasciviousness in his voice.

Betty looked at the bandaged lump at his groin and panted like a hot pekinese. She hadn't had sex since George accidentally penetrated her during a romping bedroom scene in the third series.

To keep away from the tabloids they started taking long rides in the country, Betty chatting energetically about nothing in particular while O'Crelli sucked yoghurt up a straw. She tried not to mention George or any of her other comedian friends, because every time she did O'Crelli went quiet and a sound of grinding teeth came from several places in his bandages. But this helped her personality

PLETHORA OF GITS

open out, she found a new Betty in her Georgeless nattering. And O'Crelli was all the more endearing for his tooth-grinding jealousy. Sometimes she let him drive and if his vision failed him, which was about every mile in three, he screamed for help and she steered with one hand till he could see again.

But one day George was reading a newspaper on the set.
'Who's this chap of yours, then?'
She went all blushificatious and couldn't speak.
'I always thought you were married.'
'No.'
'To a solicitor.'
'Not me.'
'I thought you were.'
'I never was married. Except to you, of course.'
They chuckled together. But minutes afterwards they were sitting glumly in separate corners, each upset for his/her own reason. When the next scene was called it was obvious that Betty had been crying. They had to hold things up till the red went out of her eyes. George, meanwhile, wandered slowly up and down, looking at his watch and barking: 'Bugger this nonsense! I should be at the bank!'

Betty knew it now. It was George she loved. She owed everything to O'Crelli. He had brought her to life, taken her from the strange fantasy life she'd been leading in her Romford semi. But it would be unfair to him to pretend he could ever mean as much to her as George did. Somehow, she had to have the real George. That, or nothing.

It was the week before Christmas. The same tree that stood in the blackened *BETTY AND GEORGE* set stood illuminated in Betty's living-room. The needles were already falling. O'Crelli's bandaged feet were hedgehogged with them. He sat grinding his teeth and hissing at the photos of George on the mantelpiece.

Betty had been standing in the hall for half an hour, trying to work out exactly how to tell O'Crelli that it was George she really loved. When she opened the living-room door O'Crelli was standing right behind it.

'I've some good news,' he said.
'Oh?'

'Dr Mahmood says I can take my bandages off.'
'When?'
'Now.'
'Now? Here? Tonight?'
'Let's go upstairs.'
Betty was suddenly, for the first time, frightened of him.

He took her by the hand with a firm almost painful grip and led her up the stairs. He'd never been upstairs before, not even to the toilet because he did everything in his bandages, but he knew his way about because he'd watched *BETTY AND GEORGE* like everyone else. He prodded her into the bedroom with a hand that was already unravelling.

Betty went without resistance. A) She was fascinated to see what he looked like under the swathe. B) If anything disgustingly sexual occurred why not pretend that she was doing it with George?

In the dim light of Betty's bedside reading-lamp O'Crelli wound and tore away his bandages, heavy-breathing all the while. He did his midriff first, exposing a deep dark navel. Then his left arm. Then his right leg. Betty couldn't see any scar tissue, no stain of blackcurrant jam. His flesh looked as clear and white as her own. Then his left leg. Then he turned his back and slowly the deeply shadowed crack of his fully-rounded buttocks showed above a tumble of falling bandage. Dr Mahmood was obviously a very good doctor.

When O'Crelli turned around he began exposing his face. But all the while Betty was staring at the swing and then the slow growth of his penis. His face had been bare and grinning at her for a full minute before she rose her eyes to it.

It was George! Or rather someone made up to look just like him. A false nose. Broken veins drawn on the cheeks in red biro. Betty was shocked and excited at the same time. She pulled back the bed covers, fetched her nightdress from under the pillow and began to undress. Tonight, at last, Betty would sleep beside George.

But when George climbed into bed beside her he was snapping a length of bandage between his fists. He wound it around her neck and strangled her with it. A grinning photo of *BETTY AND GEORGE* caught all the light under the bedside lamp. She reached out for it during her last gasp. All the while, she wondered why they hadn't mentioned this new scene in last week's script conference. It never occurred to her that what was happening was as real as anything gets.

The person who had called himself Mick O'Crelli wrapped Betty in her duvet and carried her into the garage. He stuffed her in the boot of her Fiesta and drove, dressed in Betty's nightie, howling with laughter, eighty miles to Hummersly Hall.

He buried her in a shallow grave in George's vegetable garden, between the Brussels sprouts and the leeks.

George was in a bad mood. He'd dismissed a footman that morning, which was always distressing, especially with Christmas coming. A good dig might cheer him up. He strode off across the wide lawns, swinging his spade at stray snowflakes.

He planted three lines of spring onions and, needing extra soil to sprinkle on the top, he thrust his spade into a lumpy bit between his Brussels sprouts and his leeks. The ground made a choking sound. He thrust the spade in again. The ground yiked.

The Day of Resurrection came early for Betty. She sat up coughing, her nudity brown from the soil, a leek on each shoulder.

George looked all around, terrified. What else could it be but a sickly beginning to a *This Is Your Life*? He helped Betty to her feet and flicked a worm off her left bosom. They smiled at each other as if reunited after a thousand years locked in separate cells.

'Good morning, George.'

'Morning, pet. Lovely day for it.'

(That was one of the catchphrases from their show.)

They walked up to the stables to give Betty a hosing down. Betty modestly held a cauliflower over her pudenda.

'If anybody asks,' whispered George, 'you're a balloonist on a nude ballooning pilgrimage to Canterbury to atone for a sinful life, and you fell out during morning prayers. Got it?'

'I think so.'

'They'll believe something like that around here.'

'Who will?'

George stuttered.

'This isn't your place, is it, George?'

George swallowed the way he did in *BETTY AND GEORGE* when he had something terrible to own up to.

'There are things I have never told you about myself,' he said.

Horses were hummering their heads over their doors as George sneaked Betty into the stable-yard. He'd never hosed anyone down before. It was rather fun. Betty squealed with delight as she lost her cauliflower.

'Shhhhhhh!' went George.

No, not cos of her squealing. He could hear blaring. Televisionish blaring. He turned off the hose and listened. Bloody hell! It was! Television!!! The theme tune of *BETTY AND GEORGE*!!! It was coming from the televisionless house!!!

George shot through the rose garden and across the croquet lawn towards the Hall's front steps with an expression of farcical horror bursting his face. In every one of the 200-odd windows glinting down at him in the sudden winter sunshine was a television set, all showing *BETTY AND GEORGE*.

He tripped up the steps three times before he got to the top. Inside, the blare was deafening. It came from every direction like God finally broadcasting his existence. Several sets sat on the little landings up the great staircase, their flexes dangling over the bannisters.

On all the screens George was having an embarrassing experience with the vicar. But the real George was in a huger panic. He snatched a golf-putter from the elephant's foot behind the door and smashed in his image in the TVs on the staircase. SMASH!!! SMASH!!! SMASH!!! Where was Millicent? He crashed into their bedroom. She wasn't there. Just the vicar with jelly in his lap. SMASH!!!

He swang into room after deserted room in floor after deserted floor. SMASH!!! SMASH!!! SMASH!!! TVs were in linen cupboards, shower cubicles, even in the third Earl's lab, watched by the blinkless eyes of ten thousand stuffed waterfowl. A pack of yapping corgis followed him excitedly from room to room, getting glass in their paws, yelping, savaging each other and tripping him up.

At last the only blare George could hear was the blare of his own wheezy panting. He covered his mouth, holding back a breathless terrified vomit full of heart-attacks. In the downstairs distance he could hear his own voice saying: 'NO VICAR, THOSE AREN'T MY UNDERPANTS! THEY MUST BE YOURS!'

He slid down the bannisters like the most reckless of schoolboys, collecting pocketsful of brass knobs on the way. The bannisters' retrouseé terminus launched him on to the antlers of a moosehead shot by Lord Byron from his deathbed in Missolonghi.

PLETHORA OF GITS

Perhaps Millicent was out shopping? Perhaps this was the day she caned those who'd asked awkward questions at the Sunday school during the previous term? He climbed down from the moosehead and limped into the Great Hall, a brass knob in each hand ready to chuck into his next victim.

Under the austere baubleless Christmas Tree in the Great Hall Mick O'Crelli had left a present of a King-sized TV. It had an excellent picture of Betty kissing a trouserless George. Millicent was watching this with the face of Saint Audrey during a pillage. The third Earl, proving his point that television encouraged masturbation, was masturbating under a cushion. George's hair-shirted children watched from behind their fingers, bottom lips pouting like those of mad emperors about to distribute hangings. A glut of domestics stood with O-shaped mouths, as outraged as crocodiles in a handbag factory.

George threw a brass knob at the set. It missed. The congregation turned its angry eyes upon him. At the same moment, Betty came in, nude and dripping, her feet slapping the tiles like a seal's half-hearted applause.

'Errrrrrrrr . . .' began George, who'd already concocted an explanation. But no one had time to hear it. Just then, the King-sized TV exploded. Red and white and in a blinding flash George saw bits of his family flying towards his already splinterful face.

'George!' yelled Betty.
'Betty!' yelled George.

The autopsy revealed that Betty was run through by a corgi. George was brained by the brass knob which the explosion had googlied back at him. Millicent, a red haze in the fireplace, was collected in butterfly nets. The children dripped from the chandelier for days. A policeman caught them in his helmet.

The only survivor was the third Earl. But he never masturbated again. He spent what time he had left crawling along the drains of his estate, bitter and confused, muttering obscenities in dog Latin.

The local constabulary arrested a footman for the murder. Apparently, George had dismissed him that morning and he'd sought an immediate revenge. In a rigorous interrogation he admitted to being an admirer of the Bulgarian Consul.

Mick O'Crelli cleared himself away like the washing up. But as sure as bellies rumble with unusual appetites there would be horribly slimed plates piled high tomorrow... from a party without comedians, without jokes, with only tears that remembered the laughter of *BETTY AND GEORGE*.

A PSYCHOLOGICAL NEED TO POLICE...

A huge grim grubby figure arrived back in London on Christmas Eve. It was Windscale. Such a long walk from Bulgaria! For countless miles he'd looked forward to eating whatever hadn't gone green in his fridge followed by a long snorey kip. But, limping down Oxford Street, surrounded by last-minute Christmas shoppers, he was suddenly lonely. He didn't want the oblivion of sleep. He wanted human company!

A thought spat nails at his heart: not one of these busy millions piled high with presents had come out tonight to buy one for him. So he grabbed one from under a man's arm.

'Thankyerh so much!' said Windscale, and unwrapped a train set which he played with in a shop doorway while resting his sore feet.

He snatched at a passing dowager.

'Oh, yer shouldn't have!' he said, unwrapping a cashmere sweater and a cruet set commemorating the drowning of Lord Kitchener. He tried to give her a kiss of gratitude but she was chasing a spillage of bouncing pearls, snapped from their string during his fight to retain her parcels.

Windscale was much happier as he bellied down the street, scribbling *TO CHIEF SUPERINTENDENT WINDSCALE* on the gift-tags of ten dozen Christmas presents. He'd never had so many! Then he saw a man returning to his illegally parked car. The sight of such illegalness made Windscale grim again. He collared the man and set about hanging him from the nearest lamp post with the noose he used as a trouser belt.

This caused him to remember! He searched in his pockets for his diary. Yes! There it was in almost microscopic writing: DECEMBER 24TH THE BRING BACK HANGING CAMPAIGN XMAS PARTY. Everyone he knew would be there! A warm, sentimental Dickensian Christmas spirit uplifted his flab. All his cells were Christmas puddings.

He immediately shoed it towards the venue: the Masonic Hall of his very own lodge, whose becoloured windows, though streets away, somehow already illuminated the expression of at-one-with-the-World smacking his growly face. He was as ecstatic as if the anus of his soul was being licked clean by a budgerigar. He tripped along like a cartwheeling carthorse moonwalking in its sleep.

Despite this, upon his arrival, he had his usual trouble with the narrow steps. The Victorian builders had gone everywhere on tiptoe, sneering into their hats. But in these more flat-footed days, Windscale's size 24s made him a Douglas Bader on blancmange legs. He made three attempts, but each time slipped back down again, a dropped blancmange, the steps rabbit-punching his chin as he slid down. But after the third slide he stood up in the path of a Number 43 bus whose driver was hurrying home to his new wife: Windscale was duffed at 60 MPH. Saying only 'Bug . . .!' without time for the '. . . ger!' he zeppellined over the steps through doors that even yet are swinging, leaving bits of his train-set embedded in the walls like a surrealist conceit, and making a wheels-up landing along a sumptuously laid table longer than a cricket-pitch whose layings he either swallowed, spat out or slapped into the cruel faces of the members of the BBHC. His sparks melting the police-blue and badge-silver trails of tinsel that jungled the room, he landed upside-down in the chair of Commissioner Claeverlock, who, fortunately, had just stepped up to urinate into the pot of a nearby ficus.

'I'd recognize that bum anywhere!' squealed the Commissioner, shaking his member like a strangled anaconda. 'Wilf, laddie! Best detective in the force, by thirty stones at least. Every stone an Elgin marble!' And he slapped Windscale's buttocks with a hand dripping with his own wee. (Slapping, it should be noted, was his usual method of expressing affection to men, women, and a succession of concussed police dogs.)

'Chief!' squealed Sergeant Petherwick, kissing Windscale a hello on the wrong end.

'That you, Stefanie?'

He'd called her Stefanie and with an f! Her orgasms were so

PLETHORA OF GITS

powerful they shot out of her spangled trouser-suit all the way down the table, causing a dozing bishop to rip up his collar and abuse the table-leg like an unpleasant corgi.

Windscale righted himself, slopping into his seat in a puff of Bulgarian dust. Speaking of dust:

'Here, sir, are the worldly remains of our comic killer!'

He handed over the packet amid the applause of the assemblage. Claeverlock accepted it with more slappings: of Windscale, Petherwick, that bishop, everybody. He put it in his inside pocket and slapped it energetically till he fell exhausted on to Windscale's knee (Petherwick was on the other one) and awaited his meal.

This was slow in coming. The waiters, falling in with the spirit of the occasion, had disguised themselves as Crippen and various other notables from the Black Museum. But every time one came in with a plate the guests, convinced by the disguise, set upon him and hanged him in the corridor. Thus, all the waiting ended up being done by a waiter who, wanting to be different, came as Carmen Miranda, who didn't, according to the records (someone checked), murder anyone in particular. He placed a tureen of spaghetti and meatballs before Windscale's salivating maw.

This meal was, Commissioner Claeverlock explained, symbolic of the occasion, the spaghetti representing rope and the meatballs the heads of the miscreants. The tureen was empty before he finished explaining.

'I've hardly had a bun since Zagreb,' said the policehog, snapping his fingers for a refill.

Just as it arrived, the lights went down. Tinny music started up and curtains parted to reveal a tedious little stage. It was to be a special entertainment devised by the country's surviving comedians, in honour of their saviour Commissioner Claeverlock (he having taken the credit for the apprehension of Rotweiler).

Dwight Hepple staggered on stage with a knife through his neck attempting to open the entertainment with a rendition of *McArthur Park*. Such black humour appealed to the room. Grins flashed white, like fridge lights shining in a darkened warehouse, showing up tongues wormed with half-chewed spaghetti.

Windscale, meanwhile, was slurping up a long rope of the aforementioned stuff when he suddenly felt something hard and hairy inside his mouth. It was Petherwick's head. She'd been sucking at the other end of his rope, but with an unequal suck. He spat her out as politely as he was able. Their lips met.

'Sergeant?'

'Yes, Chief.'

'I was thinking . . .'

'Yes, Chief.'

'While I was hoofing it over them Bulgarianish places and wherehaveyou . . .'

'Yes, Chief.'

'Bout you.'

'Bout me, Chief.'

'Yeah, you.'

'Me?'

'Bout asking yer somethink.'

'Like what?'

'I mean, we've heaps in common, hassent we, eh? You gets just as hotcollared when people says "pleece" instead of "Police".'

Every time he said a 'p' he inadvertently kissed her.

'I do,' she said. 'It's like putting a rabies victim in a sauna bath it gets me so hotcollared.'

'Me too.'

'So?'

'So what?'

'So what was you going to ask me, Chief?'

Something deep inside him clucked. 'Nothing.'

'Nothing?'

'No, nothing.'

'Nothing?'

'I forgot.'

'Forgot what?'

'It was nothing anyway, whatever it was.'

Their lips parted and Petherwick's eyes momentarily fell upon the blood-spurting figure of Dwight Hepple, who'd given up on *McArthur Park* and was staggering among the guests to their great amusement.

Windscale's liver stamped on the thing in his belly that had clucked. 'I've remembered.'

'What?'

PLETHORA OF GITS

'What I was going to ask you.'
'Go on then!'
'Will you marry me?'

Commissioner Claeverlock's laughing head was suddenly between them. He'd never seen anything so funny as Hepple's act. His head haw-hawed away and Petherwick's lips moved to begin an answer. Then the head came back vomiting cackles. Windscale pushed it down between his knees.

'WILL YOU MARRY ME!!!!!' he squealed.

She nodded and the glitter decorating her cheeks flew into Windscale's eyes where they formed into piles of inexhaustible fortunes. It was the happiest moment of his life. He took her hand.

'Shall we go and watch the sign going around to celebrate?'
'Ooooh, let's!' she said.

But just then Dwight Hepple dropped dead at their feet. The laughter stopped. The lights went up, a cold, unhappy glare. This was a dead comedian in an era supposedly bereft of such phenomena. Claeverlock's blinking face rose up from the folds of Windscale's crotch with the look of Jehovah finding Beelzebub eating the Virgin Mary in his sock-drawer.

'What all this, then?' he said.

'Something must've gone wrong with his trick knife,' said Windscale, pulling it out of the neck with two rubber-gloved fingers.

'Plainly an accident with his trick knife,' echoed Petherwick. 'Happens all the time.'

'Ooooh, all the time,' said Windscale, trying it out on a man sitting nearby.

'That tissent no trick knife,' said Claeverlock in his sinister policeman's whisper, his evidence being that the man Windscale had tried its trickiness out on was now lying beside Hepple going 'Uh!'

'Yes it is. There's just summink wrong with it.'

They adjourned backstage to ask the advice of the rest of the bill of performers, expecting showfolk to be expert in the matter of trick knives. In a tiny space, dominated by Masonic regalia, boxes of handshakes and aprons, the first they came upon was Sexton Ballard, hanging from a clothes peg with his tongue all blue and sticking out as far as a cuckoo ever shot from a clock.

'This?' Claeverlock indicated the problem with a sarcastic wiggle of his pinky.

'One of them extra strong mints, Commish. Must've been too strong for him,' was Windscale's explanation.

'They make 'em damned strong these days,' added Petherwick. 'A number of similar cases in West Hartlepools recently.'

'West Hartlepools?'

'So I believe, sir.'

Taking a swizzle-stick from behind an ear Claeverlock shyly lifted a length of fairy-godmother costume to reveal a tangle of legs, genitals and dickie-bow ties.

'And this?'

'Coo!' hiccupped Windscale. 'Isn't this new flu a bugger.'

Petherwick sneezed, fluishly.

'IT'S A BLOODY MASSACRE!!!!!' screamed the topmost cop, his loudness loosening the limp limbs of eighty-one further slaughtered comedians from stiffs stuffed into every possible stuffing point thereabouts. These limbs swang into view, their fingers all pointing at Windscale.

The furious Claeverlock pulled out the packet of Bulgarian ash and ripped it to pieces before Windscale's eyes. As each mote of ash touched the blood-spattered floor a tiny nude vampire picked up its clothes and ran for the nearest mousehole. Someone other than Rotweiler, it seemed, was their comedian assassinator.

'You useless stupid fat knobless git!'

'Fat?' Windscale was offended.

'This is your arse, not mine!' continued Claeverlock. His meaning was unclear to the non-policemen craning for a view of the carnage.

'My arse?' Windscale scratched it, affecting bewilderment.

'Your arse! See this!' Claeverlock dropped his trousers. Sergeant Petherwick held a fan before her eyes. 'This is my arse. Not your fat arse! My arse! And I'm keeping it, see! Nobody's getting this arse but me.'

'I should think not, sir.'

'Right, then. We understand each other.'

'We do.'

'I'll have it then.'

PLETHORA OF GITS

'My arse?'

'Your warrant card, toiletbreath!'

'Not his warrant card!' Petherwick's eyelashes twanged off, hitting Claeverlock in the face, giving him a Clement Attlee pretending to be Hitler sort-of-look. 'Please, sir, not that. He's policeman through and through, there's no life for him without coppering.'

But Claeverlock's hand was outstretched, awaiting the warrant card and Windscale was already searching for it in his pockets.

'He'll catch the bastard wot's been doing this, honest he will. You said yourself: he's the best detective on the force. Give him another chance! Give him 24 hours!'

But Claeverlock's heart was a stone goblin sunk in an icy bog halfway up the M6.

His hands shaking, Windscale found the warrant card in a froth of handcuffs and old wanted posters, deep in his inside pocket.

'There you are then. My arse.'

'Your arse,' smiled Claeverlock. 'Now sod off before I arrest you for wasting police time.'

Windscale plodded away slowly, arseless, into the empty glaring hall, his tongue as dry as a one-way ticket to Palookaville. Skins had formed on the scattered meals of spaghetti and meatballs. But Windscale was skinned and raw, broken into a million pieces not just in the mirroring glitterballs that orbited his dizzy waterfilled eyes. He'd had his policemanness amputated and there was nothing left but a hole where his arse had been, a hole through which his will-to-live was draining in a brown spewm.

Petherwick trotted out on to stage like a gallstoned Piaf, her bosoms heaving, one at a time, then both together.

'Chief! Don't go! Wait for me! You haven't said if you want a church wedding.'

Windscale didn't even turn around. 'It's all over,' he said. 'You shall never see me again.'

He dragged the BBHC's ceremonial gibbet with him as he went, to do away with himself in some quiet damp place, of which he had and knew many.

'Chief! Chief! Chief!' she screamed to the empty hall, but her only answer was the unsettling creak of hanged waiters gently swinging in their nooses.

Suddenly a glitterball snapped its wire and dropped heavy in a rush of colours. Petherwick stopped her ears and about-turned on her high heels. She would not hear or see it shatter!

It was a Christmas morning tradition in the Claeverlock household that the family should gather before the television and watch *The Blue Lamp* on video. When Jack Warner got shot, as he did every year, an emotional surge would cruise through the Commissioner's system and he would entwine his loved ones in his manly arms, stunning them with fatherly slaps. Looking like a family of shovel-bashed Jacobites on the day after Culloden, they all wept with smarting joy. Every year they wept like this. And the dogs howled, all 326 of them. (Mrs Claeverlock ran a home for retired police dogs in her spare time.)

But this Christmas the scene would be different. The presents sat truncheon and helmet-shaped under the tree . . . The cooking turkey smelled out the house . . . Steam from the boiling of vegetables dampened the crepe-paper decorations and settled on the lenses of Claeverlock's youngest, Dougall, whose secret was that he didn't want to be a policeman (he wanted to be a policewoman) . . . In *The Blue Lamp* Dirk Bogarde was backing away from Sergeant Dixon's oncoming body in cowardly evil . . . when Commissioner Claeverlock jumped to his feet and legged it for the hall telephone, scattering his bankrupt-stock furniture and leaving his in-laws impaled on the tree and his children feeling unloved.

'IT WAS HIM ALL ALONG!!!' he screamed down the phone to some sherry-nosed sergeant.

'Can you repeat that, madam. I'll take down the particulars.'

'What fools we've been! Windscale is the comic-killer! He thinks that whenever anyone laughs they're laughing at him for being fat. So he's gone on an orgy of killing to remove all laughter from the world.'

'I'm sure your cat will come home of its own accord, madam.'

In *The Blue Lamp* the crinkly-haired young constable is telling Mrs Dixon that she's a widow. Claeverlock is outside in the tartan-wallpapered dog kennel, 326 noses pointed his way, 652 paws over 612 ears (some had ears missing) thinking their visitor is about to commence a drunken carol service for them.

'Pay attention, laddies,' said the eminent Peeler. 'This is a picture of the most cunning mass-murderer since the brides-in-the-bath. The doggy who fetches him back here to me can have this biscuit.'

He held up a rather unimpressive chocolate digestive. He showed them both sides. They were impressed. Their claws scraped up splinters as they woofed out, each given a sniff of Windscale's warrant card as, with the eyes of an opium-smacked janissary, it sprang into the yard. They sprang! They sprang! They sprang!

Now came Claeverlock's surge of emotion. It filled his trousers as he watched the dogs leap the yard wall and scatter down the almost empty Christmas morning streets of Lewisham, knocking Pakistani boys off their new bicycles. Soon the barks were far away: barks heard by a deaf dog-catcher recovering his hearing while alone in the Gobi desert with a broken tape recorder. Then: silence. Just a faint weep over a bent wheel.

'Arf!'

Arf? A dog had stayed behind. Claeverlock absent-mindedly gave it the biscuit.

The quarry of their Holygrailish quest was, at that moment, floating senselessly down the Thames towards the sea.

The ruined Windscale had dragged the BBHC's ceremonial gibbet on to London Bridge and attempted suicide there with it. Drunken carloads swerved past, hooting at him, but he paid no heed. He climbed into the noose, his eyes tightly closed to create darkness, but so tightly that his optic nerves turned kaleidoscopes over his creased lids, showing him sunny days in childhood, brilliant sausages in fields of yellow mash, docksful of nabbed villains being clouted by the mute tinkerbells that flashed in these final moments. His optic nerves were keen to see more of the world. But they couldn't dissuade him. With the disgust of a Spanish waiter finding a gangrenous prawn in an otherwise perfect paella, he tweeked the lever. The trapdoor opened.

Real darkness. Wet, cold darkness. His eyes filling with ice. A last, tantalizing taste of spaghetti and meatballs. Then sleep and queer quick dreams as the cells of his brain were closed forever, a million doors disappearing as they were slammed shut, each on a lost moment. He dreamed he was sitting by the side of the road during the Trooping of the Colour, eating a police horse and the Queen came up to him, naked except for a neon sign flashing in her navel saying 'WE ARE NOT AMUSED'. He tossed her an intimate bit of police horse and when she caught it in her mouth she clapped her hands and honked.

Then he dreamed Big Ben was striking midnight making Christmas Eve into Christmas Day and he was in the Thames, floating past like a macintoshed iceberg. Skeletal comedians were chasing him in war canoes, all eager to tell him a particular joke. He didn't know what it was, but he was desperate not to hear it. He commenced swimming with all his might and suddenly he was a sea-monster leaping the Thames Flood Barrier with a mouthful of laughing skeletons.

Next, he was lying on what he recognized from a decade of childhood holidays as Frinton beach. At the same time he was high in the sky, falling down on to himself very fast. The Queen was falling with him, dressed in the QPR strip.

'Oh, Mr Pavarotti,' she cooed. 'I've got all your LPs.'

'Uh?'

'Would it be too much to ask – could you sing a snatch of Aida for me?'

'Erm, if you like, Marm. But I shall have to remove my clothes first.'

'By all means, maestro.'

He sang dreadfully, of course, and the Queen headed cabbages at him. At the same time she turned into Sergeant Petherwick. Windscale reached out to her, but the cabbages bounced him further and further away, hammering him down towards the ground. He fell into his beached self with a KO like all the KOs that ever floored a desperate boxer rolled into one. The cabbages kept coming but turned into kisses, big red reviving kisses that swallowed him up over and over again like a greedy boy being eaten by all the sweets in the sweetshop he's been pilfering for years.

Windscale really was on Frinton beach! Stark naked. Christmas morning. Bells communicating joy in the distance.

He stood up. Pebbles dropped one by one from his pebble-dashed buttocks till just their dents remained. Then a wave lassooed him with seaweed and he was on his back in the pebbles again.

An ancient, fleshless man came out of the sea, a whelk clinging to his left moustache.

'Every morning for eighty-three years. I've never missed my dip,' he said, pink with pride and blue with cold.

'You must be bloody mad,' said Windscale.

'Too much for you, was it?' He helped Windscale to his feet and helpfully kicked the pebbles out of his buttock-crack. 'Still, it's nice to see another chap having a go.'

Windscale shivered till his goosebumps quacked.

The ancient man suddenly frowned, stopped his running-on-the-spot and said: 'I say, this isn't a nude beach, you know.'

'Isn't it?'

'You'd better put your trunks on.'

Not having any, Windscale stripped the be-badged ones off the ancient man and strode tight-trunkedly up the beach with the air of ninety-one King Canutes sewn together.

His sister lived somewhere near Frinton. He hadn't seen her in years. There'd been a falling out, he couldn't quite remember what about, during the student riots of 1968. He'd seen her name on the all-in-wrestling posters from time to time, but he'd never been inclined to re-open contact. Winifred had married a man called either Pewter, Prendergast, Patel, or Pillbright. He couldn't remember which.

The defrocked detective borrowed a phone book from a lonely vandalized box and wandered about from address to address astonishing the Christmas mornings and eating the half-cooked Christmas dinners of numerous Pewters, Prendergasts, Patels and as many as eleven Pillbrights, till he stood before a tiny thatched cottage in the village of Great Bentley, so small that he knocked on the door with his great toe, a toe already sore from a day's barefoot tramping.

'It's me, Winnie,' he said to the mumpish pie-face that appeared at the door.

Winnie's jaw dropped. A half-chewed ball of turkey dropped out of her mouth.

'Look who it isn't?' she cried, and charged through the door like a bull at the beginning of a bullfight. She hit her brother with a forearm-smash and bodyslammed him into her vegetable patch before grabbing his head between her thunderthighs and slowly twisting it off. It was the reluctant lid of a pickle-jar from which the pickles would soon come bobbing. Oops! They came! She stamped them into the earth then went ricochetting off invisible ropes, back and forward, stepping on Windscale's paunch at each passing, shouting 'Eureeeeeeeeeeeeeeeeeeough!' all the while like a headless donkey with an unquenchable thirst.

They were wrestling just as they did when they were children. And, as usual, Winnie was winning. It was the baby brother's own fault for coming to the door in these purloined trunks. His sister had taken the apparel as an invitation for a re-match.

Finally Winnie ceased her rope-bouncing and fell upon Windscale so hard that his colon crammed into his head. With an enormous cry of 'Eureeeeeeeeeeeeeough!!!!' she flipped him over and did horrible things with his legs.

Sniffing out of a daze, Windscale saw what looked like one of his testicles orbiting the cottage on a skinny string. And that foot under his chin wasn't Winnie's: it was his left one, no his right, no right the first time, it was his left one, but the little toe was next to the great.

'Eureeeeeeeeeeeeough! Do you submit!' squealed Winnie.

'I do. Definitely. Certainly. I submit. Do not doubt that I submit. This is an official submitting.'

Winnie let him go and went all girlish. She was a foot taller than Windscale, and twenty stones heavier, that extra made up largely by bosoms that could suckle Australia, all topped by the face of a carthorse after disastrous cosmetic surgery.

Windscale got to his dislocated feet. An obliging muscle in his groin tugged his testicle home from orbit. He smiled at his long-lost sibling.

'You haven't changed a bit,' he said.

But she had. She'd become the image of their long-dead mother. Windscale sniffed back a snotty tear.

Pillbright, a pea-sized man in a ginger wig like a spot of tomato sauce atop the aforementioned pea, huffed hamsterishly in the doorway.

'Hoi, yous: the Queen's cummin on.'

They settled down with turkey legs to watch the Queen's speech. Windscale was a mite trepidatious: last time he'd seen his Sovereign she'd pelted him with cabbages.

'This is my brother Wilf,' Winnie explained to her Rumplestiltskinish husband.'

'Shut yer gob, woman. You got no respect!'

PLETHORA OF GITS

The Queen toffed through her speech watched in every living-room in the land. But no smaller living-room was there than this one. Two hippos in a lunar module would've had more room. Whist would've been impossible as they'd have been unavoidably nosing over each other's hands. Windscale's folds of fat folded in among Winnie's in a way that was almost incestuous. Her occasional playful forearm-smashes didn't help.

'To conclude,' said the Queen. 'We should like all our subjects to keep their eyes peeled for this ungodly man . . .'

A picture of Windscale flashed up. They'd found a particularly snarly one, an excellent likeness.

'. . . who is wanted by our police for the mass-murder of so many of our beloved comedians wot we have watched with amusement so many times at the Palladium.'

Winnie gave Windscale a 'you-little-bastard' look, such as he'd received when he'd put a toad in her sandwich box in days of yore.

'Wasn't me, Win,' he pleadingly peeped. 'Honest.'

An elderly police dog came barking up the cottage path.

Commissioner Claeverlock kicked in the door of Windscale's apartment, a one-room bachelor pad overlooking Willesden Jewish Cemetery. A reek of burnt mushrooms and unflushed lavatories caused him to push his moustache up his nostrils.

Sergeant Petherwick turned on the light. She blinked at the Commissioner and he blinked at her. They were up to their waists in sweetpapers. Their every movement was like the ultimate crackle of annoyance in a cinema. Their every step found a stale Malteser to crunch.

'Bloody rats' nest,' mumbled Claeverlock, who'd seen nothing like it since he visited his bedridden Uncle Angus on the Isle of Mull of 1962.

'The chief's a busy man,' defended Petherwick. 'He doesn't have time for housework.'

Claeverlock's ginger eyes fell upon the wallpaper. 'What's all this then?' he said.

It was made up of newspaper cuttings, pasted carefully in place, a mosaic of words and photographs of Sir Cyril Passey-Wix, the Home Secretary.

Claeverlock coughed Scottishly. He chewed his phlegm and kept giving Petherwick pop-eyed knowing looks.

'The chief is a great admirer of the Home Secretary,' she explained.

'Is he now?' His eyes rolled like those of a mad salmon in the wrong river.

'I've got pics of John Wayne and Sidney Greenstreet on my wall. So what!'

'I admire your loyalty, sergeant,' and Claeverlock struck the wall with a fist gummed with sweetpapers. 'But this isn't normal. I'll tell you what normal is: normal is a nice MacDougal tartan wallpaper or something puce with a Highland cattle motif. The man who'd plaster the Home Secretary all over his walls is an obsessive, a weirdo git, easily capable of mass murder. I ken these things, lassie.'

Petherwick daren't contradict her superior. She just tossed her perfume-drenched hair defiantly.

This tossing caused a slow stiffening of Claeverlock's libido. His eyes rolled towards Windscale's broken bed, then back towards Petherwick, who was glowering her understanding of his eye-rolling from behind a fringe visibly curling pubicly with anger.

'Ever played catchy-kissie?' he inquired.

'Is that where you chase me and I beat you senseless with this truncheon?'

'Yeah.'

And he took a Malteser-crunching step. But suddenly a forgotten omelette moved out of its blackened pan and jumped into the sweetpapers. Claeverlock and Petherwick ran from the room with cries of 'It's alive!!!'

They met a police dog on the stairs, dragging a huge man it had found in a chip shop in Bridlington.

'That's not him!' barked Claeverlock.

Winnie Pillbright didn't believe her brother when he said he hadn't killed all those comedians. But blood was thicker than water and her blood had been a warm honey of sisterly affection ever since she re-set eyes on the disgraced detective. She was determined to shield him and locked her husband, who was vehement for turning him in and fetching a reward, in the cupboard under the kitchen sink.

She set about easing the anger that had made Windscale do all those horrible murderings and was as nice to him as it was possible for anybody to be to anyone else. She gave him a room, the one her husband used to make his things in, and spread it among overfencenosing neighbours that her guest was a love child she'd had with Stanley Baldwin during the abdication crisis. They were suitably shocked and their noses were satisfied.

'Good morning, Mr Baldwin,' they'd say as Windscale came out for the milk.

'Uh?'

'I expect you'll be missing the ice-floes.'

'Uh?'

(Winnie had also said, to explain the love-child's long absence, that he'd been farmed out to Eskimos when still in swaddling and had spent a life slaying walruses and eating all their parts.)

But despite her ministrations, Windscale was desolate. He had, he explained, a psychological need to police. Without it, apart from food, life had no meaning.

Winnie cooked him impossibly huge pies, which he ate in bed in a room full of 'things' made from seashells, winkles mostly. (Pillbright had one of those hobbies that beset every spare room in England.)

Phoning people up and accusing them of things – a super idea of Winnie's – did alleviate Windscale's angst and rewarded him with brief smiling respites. He started with specific crimes, but his victim, dripping from its bathnight, usually assumed they were a wrong number. So he subtleified his approach.

'Hello, 37857674.'

'You did it, didn't you?'

'What?'

'You know.'

'No.'

'We've been watching you.'

'Who?'

He'd take a big bite of pie before answering. 'You know.'

'I've no idea, really.'

'We've seen you.'

'Seen me?'

'Oh, yes.'

'You couldn't have?'

'Have.'

'Haven't!'

'Have.'

A sob down the line. 'Look . . . I didn't mean to do it. I haven't been feeling well lately.'

A sinister chuckle from Windscale, before saying: 'We'll be around to get you later.'

Thus the ferries were full of haunted-looking people gripping all their possessions in one holdall. And all with names starting with A to F, as Windscale, with habitual systematicness, was working through the phonebook and had got as far as Frobisher E.J.

But Frobisher E.J. had, according to a hysterical answerphone, already been arrested for, of all things, rubbing out a zebra crossing. Windscale plunged into deepest despair. He'd never arrested anyone for that . . . and now he never would. He gave up the whole project and picked his nose till it bled.

'I've an idea,' said Winnie, helping him to his feet after a flying head-butt. 'Why don't you re-join the force, not as yourself, but as Stanley Baldwin Jr.'

'They'd recognize me.'

'Naw, not the local bobbies. Comb your hair back and speak with an Eskimo accent. You'll be just duckie.'

'Thanks a buffalo, Win.'

Twenty minutes later, this in what he imagined was an Eskimo accent: 'I want to join the police. Eep.'

'What was that?'

'I want to join the police. Eep.'

'I got the first part. What was that other part?'

'Eep.'

'Eep?'

'It's the lonely cry of the penguin wandering on the Steppe.'

The desk sergeant poured himself a coffee. His hands shook.

'I'm an Eskimo,' explained Windscale.

This, and the coffee, calmed the sergeant. He introduced him to a certain Inspector Hornbeam, the sort of copper whose shirt-collar is always too tight, now matter how loose.

'Well now,' he said, fingers down his shirt-collar. 'You're a nice big lad.'

'It's the blubber wot does it,' explained the desk sergeant. (He'd had a brief exchange about blubber with Windscale in the corridors.)

'Any experience?'

PLETHORA OF GITS

'I was in the Eskimo police for 15 years.'
'Hmmmmm. Many hard cases up there, are there?'
'Bears, mostly.'
'Bears?'
'They're bastards on a Saturday night.'
'I'm sure. Yes.'

Windscale beamed. He was almost a policeman again. The Inspector was loosening his shirt-collar while digging out the neccessary forms.

'Name?'
'Stanley Baldwin Jr. I'm the illegitimate son of the late Prime Minister.'

The Inspector was impressed.

'Age?'

This was a problem. Windscale was pushing forty or thereabouts, but Baldwin had been dead over fifty years. If he said 1939 he'd be too old to get in. If he said 1950-something he could be caught out.

'Nine comings of the great white seal,' he said.
'That's Eskimo counting is it?'
'I can't give you the other without my almanack.'

The Inspector guessed the great white seal came every four years, like the World Cup. That made Windscale thirty-six, which wasn't far out. This bloke wasn't an Inspector for nothing.

But for a guess at Windscale's weight only the most senior possible policeman would do. Which was lucky, because taking only the weight of his earlobes into consideration he was over regulation weight.

'This weighing machine's knackered. Eep,' said the recruit, having just sent its finger spinning at warp-speed.

'Humm, you don't happen to know your weight offhand, do you?'
'I'm ten stone four. Eep.'
'Eep?'
'It's the plaintive cry of the penguin at the door of a deserted igloo.'
'You don't say.'

It was a face of beatitudeidity that floated home amid the January snowflakes.

129

STEVE WALKER

'I start work tomorrow!' he yelled to Winnie as he bounced through the kitchen door.

She was gently strangling a police dog on the kitchen table. 'That's six this morning,' she complained.

The police-outfitters were defeated by Windscale. They sewed several jackets together to make one. This gave their new PC fourteen arms. It was the jacket of a bloated Hindu God, but you hardly noticed the empty sleeves flapping once he had it on.

'I'm putting you with Constable Fender, Constable Baldwin. He'll show you about our little manor. Eep.'

'Eep?'

'Yes, eep.'

'Oh, eep.'

'Eep.'

'Eep.'

Constable Fender didn't understand all these eeps. He sat at the wheel of the panda, too depressed to ask. His wife had left him for a launderette proprietor the previous night.

'Got any juicy murders for us?' enthused Windscale to his new partner.

'There's rumours of an axe murderer on the prowl, but he ain't axed no one yet.' His tongue flickered viperishly. 'Not yet he ain't.' Then, in an over-calm voice: 'In the meantime, we's after a gang.'

'Gang?' Windscale's lips bubbled with excited spit.

'Of kids wot's been graffiti-izing all over town for weeks. Glue sniffers, I reckons.'

'Glue sniffers,' humphed PC 665.

'It can lead to 'orrible crimes, glue can,' said PC Fender with the expression of a cod left alone in a bankrupt fishmongers.

Off they went in the panda in search of this dreadful gang. Windscale wouldn't fit inside. He sat on top with the flashing light between his legs. He rode shotgun with a blunt harpoon he'd found in an antique shop. He threatened contumelious-looking pedestrians with it, sometimes even had a practice chuck, but it never stuck in far.

They stopped on the Clacton Road under a graffiti-ized railway bridge.

PC Fender wound his window down. 'Look at that buggeration!' he yelled.

PLETHORA OF GITS

'Buggerationnnnnnnn!' yelled his echo.

The railway bridge was fully decorated with highly artistic penises, with, ingeniously incorporated into the overall design, a variety of weasels, unicorns and moose-like objects, all floating in a cerise fog, upon billows of which here-and-there lay draped a naked woman with swollen pudenda and a Rubensesque blush holding a half-peeled banana. Her name, depicted inside a heart-shaped tattoo upon a left buttock when she was faced that way, was *EVA*. Several of the penises also had *EVA THIS WAY* written upon them.

Windscale was disgusted. He gave a salty 'Harrrrrrrrr!', chucking his harpoon high towards a smutty brick. It made purple and yellow sparks as it chipped out the face of this Eva woman. Windscale made a W.G. Grace of a catch.

'Find this tart and we've found our gang,' said the Eskimo.

Just then a police dog came barking around the corner. Windscale stirupped the panda into a gallop. He gripped the flashing light over-anxiously till they'd turned three corners.

PC Fender stopped in front of a launderette.

'I'll just pop in and pick up some clean shirts,' he said, and off he went with a hatchet badly concealed under his helmet.

Windscale ate a few Toblerones, reading a graffiti-ized bus-stop while he waited.

Fender was no time. He returned with the expression of a shepherd who'd caught something off his favourite sheep. He fingered a pile of blood-spattered shirts.

'You oughta take them shirts back. They hassent got the blood out proper.'

Fender laughed like a pantomime villain.

Windscale wondered if he was overdoing the Eskimo accent.

They were down by the docks. An alley liberally festooned with swearing blue and orange graffiti up to a height of 5'3". The alley ground was littered with discarded pots of glue and crisp packets all but one of which was a cheese-'n'-onion, meaning, to Windscale's trained mind, that some glue-sniffer had stolen a box of cheese-'n'-onion crisps and brought them here to devour during a glue session. The thought of crisps made Etnas rumble in his deep.

A meek red light shone behind blackened windows, high up in a skid-rowish building, the one-time office of some tedious clerk employed by a banana importer. The company's tin banana sign had gone as black as the blackest banana. It hung in the middle of the pile of sooty brick like the insignia of a failed superhero. Fire escapes hoped for fires.

While the constables stood conspicuously among dustbins, the daylight ebbed and the meek red light in the blackened window coloured the alley with the red light of a pornographer's darkroom. The orange letters of the graffiti faded in this light, leaving a puzzle of blue letters, spelling out, Windscale was sure, odd Satanic messages.

'Did you hear that?'
'What?'
'That.'
'You mean . . . that?'
'No . . . THAT! There it is again.'

Their respective skins goosified. In a deep ghostly voice someone was singing either *Yes, We Have No Bananas* or *I'm Gonna Wash That Man Right Out of My Hair*. They couldn't agree which. Windscale bet fifty pence on the banana song.

Whatever it was, it was likely that the husky singer was Eva herself. As no glue-sniffing aggro boys had come into the alley for a glue-and-crisps party, they decided to mosey on in and investigate.

With a stealth learned from an observation of housecats hunting on waste ground, meowing under his breath, Windscale footsied slowly up the banana delivery ramp, stopping every third step to say 'Shhhhhhh!' to PC Fender, who was sniffing casually behind him.

Getting Windscale through the low jambed door marked KEEP OUT was like getting twelve sopranos through the eye of a needle. But they managed and stood wheezing softly in a sweet-smelling darkness.

Their usherettish torchbeams showed up circles of a peculiar place. A bankrupt banana warehouse. Boxes of gone-black bananas in white-wood boxes with wide gaps between the slats where the occasional banana boasted a rare circle of fading yellow, these piled here as high as the tops of a rugby goalpost, here only as high as the crossbar. Rusty iron girders caught their beams high up, where the ropes that the Banana Co's directors had hanged themselves with were still knotted like reminders on the finger of a forgetful widow who habitually forgot to buy bananas. Higher still the occasional bat hung in a doze, like a blackened banana bored in its afterlife.

Windscale pussyfooted between the high aisles. Sugary mush dripped out of the boxes.

'Look!' shhhed Windscale.

In the dusty floor were the clear prints of a woman's high-arched naked feet. They followed them along several aisles. Here and there she'd skipped an escaped hand of bananas, which had expired in a crawl towards the faint squares of light hitting the floor under night-blue skylights. Then she'd been inspired into the dance of a bee-stung Salome. Her footprints – and toeprints, heelprints and her bum-print when she'd failed like any drunken skater in a quadruple double-twist – filled a crossways between the aisles and seemed to set off again in three directions.

'We'd better split up,' whispered Windscale. 'You go that way.'

'Wait . . . Listen!'

Quite plainly, from high above, the singing of *I'm Gonna Wash that Man Right Outta My Hair*.

'Bugger,' said Windscale, and handed over a fifty pence.

PC Fender went to the left. Windscale strode straight on with occasional cat-like zooms until his torchbeam began climbing a rickety length of wooden stairs. He climbed after it, each step a creak.

'Meowwww!' went Windscale, pretending to be an unusually heavy cat.

At the top was a cracked wooden door with a 1973 calendar pinned to it: semi-clad damsels in queer hairdos all being affectionate with bananas. Miss September, Windscale noticed with reference to the face on the brick in his mit, was the younger self of this Eva person whom he sought.

He was just working out what Miss December was doing with her bananas when the door opened. Red light drenched him in the face. He dropped his truncheon. It dropped sixty feet into an open box of decomposed bananas, its splashlanding emitting an embarrassingly extra-disgusting 'plurp' sound.

'Hi there, snookums.' It was Eva, tickling one of his chins. 'Come on in, then. Don't be shy, honeybun. What can the little girlie do for the big strong man?'

She twirled in her see-through negligée through an air pink like a froth of daphnia. She twirled and twirled, at each twirl a reddened tattoo flashed EVA, EVA, EVA, on her red-cracked posterior, EVA,

EVA, EVA, till she fell with a dizzy *kawhump* in the middle of the room.

Windscale noticed that beyond her dirty feet were pudenda not nearly so large as the ones in the graffiti. But she had a fetching spare tyre bigger than the bag under Windscale's right eye, sticking out immediately under a lickable bellybutton as big and red as the gunshot that blooded Nurse Edith Cavell.

Windscale helped her to her feet.

'A genuine gentleman,' she oozed. 'Aren't we the lucky girl tonight!'

The old clerk's office was as silkily draped and plushly cushioned as any whore's palace anywhere. A plastic Rodin's *Kiss* was kissing redly in one corner. The only eccentricity was the hands of vermillionized bananas who cockroached the floor.

Eva arranged herself on a redly cushioned red divan, her hair falling into her redshot eyes like a squirt of ketchup into ketchup.

'Hand, mouth or all the way?' she asked.

'Errrrrrm . . .' panicked Windscale.

'Would you like some glue while you're making up you're mind?'

'Glue, yes. How nice.'

He sat on the divan red faced, red macintoshed, red booted, while she fetched the glue.

'Hand's a pound, mouth is five pounds and All the Way's a tenna.'

'Very reasonable,' blushed Windscale, adding 0.00001% to the red of the room.

He didn't know what to do with his gluepot, so he smashed a porcelain elephant and commenced sticking it back together. Eva, meanwhile, had taken a snort of her glue, and was attempting to bite the buttons off his macintosh in an erotic manner.

It must have worked. Windscale pressed a shy pound into her very hand.

She pulled off his now buttonless macintosh. Luckily, the blue bobby's uniform underneath was painted red by the room, allowing Windscale to claim to be the Commissionaire at the Odeon.

'But the Odeon's closed down.'

'I know.' He affected a made-redundant chagrin which, surprisingly, touched Eva's heart. She turned away with a sob.

'I didn't always do this sort of thing,' she said softly. 'My father was Sir Edward Straight, the owner of this banana business. When he went bankrupt and hanged himself there was no other way I could earn enough to pay off his debts and open the business again.

Windscale didn't like sob-stories. He punched her schoolbullyishly in the small of the back. That, and the gluey stench, lightened her mood. She squeaked coquettishly and pulled off his trousers.

'Perhaps I could ask your professional opinion,' queried Windscale stiffly. He was on his back with his spread legs in the air. 'Do you think it's big enough?'

Eva was still looking for it.

'Go on. You can tell me. I won't be upset.'

She found it.

'Well?'

'Hard to tell,' she said. 'Maybe it's not so small as it looks. Its just small compared with the rest of you.' Finally, she was discreet. 'I reckon it's bigger than some.'

This satisfied Windscale and he laughed with derision at all those small-penised men over whom he had an advantage. Meanwhile, Eva was setting about further satisfying him.

It didn't take long. His penis spat like a bronchial flamingo into one of those sickly-pink sunsets they get over Mombassa. But it was a short-lived ecstasy, for, as its beginnings tickled at the root of his truncheonette, the vision of Sergeant Petherwick came plodding a beat in his mind's eye.

'Stephanie!' he cried, just as Romeo would have shrieked 'Juliet!' could similar circumstances have been arranged.

Eva helped him on with his trousers and fourteen-armed jacket. 'Who's this Stephanie, then?'

'We were going to get married,' he sniffed.

Eva patted his arm understandingly. She shoved a frothing gluepot into his nose. 'This'll make you feel better.'

It didn't. Next thing he was vomiting into a sink in her red-lit dressing-room. She was practising dance steps while saliva stringed from his exhausted lips. A banana with a single bloodshot eye was looking at him from inside the mirror. But when he turned around it wasn't there.

'I'll be all right in a minute,' he said and then shrieked for a little while because he'd somehow eaten the banana in the mirror.

She left him alone to recover. But, ever the policeman, he instantly started going through her dressing-table drawers, vomiting lightly into some of them. All prozzies kept address-books with the names of their clients inside. If he found it he'd surely find the names of the ringleaders of the Graffiti Gang.

'Ah ha!' He held it in his hand, flicking through it in triumph. But a tick-tock later his eyes had focused on something beyond it. A screen of the sort showgirls undress behind. It was festooned with sellotaped-down publicity photographs of comedians.

Windscale shone his torch on it. Its white light showed that most of the faces had been angrily crossed out with red lipstick, faces belonging to recently-murdered drolls: Frankie Moss, Eddie Haddock, Jerry Muckle, Betty and George, etcetera, etcetera.

'Eep!' went Windscale.

The comic-killer was a client of Eva's! The monster's name was probably in the little red book he held in his hand! It was the greatest moment of his policeman's life!

Just then PC Fender came through the door with the calendar on it and saw red. It has to be admitted, that very morning, in a jealous rage, this same policeman had fallen so far as to cut up his wife and her lover with the hatchet which he was already aiming at Eva's unfortunate head.

'Another Commissionaire, eh?' was the last thing she said. Her see-through negligée, sadly, was exactly like the one his wife had been wearing when he'd found her snogadoodling with the launderette proprietor atop the laundry basket arear the launderette. PC Fender went into his second red fit of the day. Eva's blood increased the red in the room by 13.09%

Windscale dragged the screen into the room.

'Which bugger's is this?' he demanded. Then his eyes took in the scene of yet another bloody crime.

'He's been, has he?'

PC Fender just cackled.

'Can you give me a description?'

PC Fender sang *I'm Gonna Wash That Man Right Outta My Hair*! kicking the corpse to make a beat.

Windscale ran out on to the stairs. He shone his torch. Its white beam cut through the red cloud that surrounded him. It slid along the warehouse floor. Dark figures flitted there. He swang the torch to and fro but could only catch a last flitting footstep . . . and another . . . and another. 'I arrest the lot of yerhs in the name of the law!'

Childish glue-high giggles from behind boxes. It was the Graffiti Gang.

'If I come down there I'll be beside you!' threatened this constable bigger than *The Haywain*.

But smoke reached Windscale's nose-holes. They'd set a fire of banana-box wood under the stairs. Great! He could nab them for arson as well! But the stairs were already well alight. Windscale couldn't get down without making a Joan of Arc of himself. He tried to urinate a path but he ran out of urine after the third step and had to run to the top shaking his fists at the figures who'd ceased to flit and had come to warm their giggling faces before the fire.

'I'll see yous all hang!' yelled the desperate Windscale, his eyebrows singeing, his buttonless mac flapping in the heat rising from the flames.

They laughed all the harder, glue dropping out of their noses like ectoplasm from an antipope.

Windscale dashed back into the red room.

'Pull yourself together, man,' he screamed into PC Fender's ear.

Fender had now dressed in a spare negligée and was about to hatchet his own head.

'This whole place is alight! Bananas and all!'

But his partner was unreachable.

Windscale opened his buttocks wide and placed Eva's address book there for safe keeping. He then skipped across the smoking floor as far from the door as he could get and commenced an Olympic run up. He pelted for the door with the desperation of an athlete who hadn't bothered to train. He ran into flames. The top step cracked as he dived from it. Far below the Graffiti Gang were screaming: glue from their noses had glued their feet to the floor and flames were all about them now. Windscale caught a satisfied glimpse of them as he dropped earthwards like a devil thrown from Heaven for eating God's God-sized helping of manna. He crash-landed on a pile of banana boxes. The boxes splintered. Bananas squished. Windscale disappeared in it all, drowning in mashed banana, thrashing with his spare truncheon, wading and swimming in an ever-sinking plurping pudding, down, down, deeply down towards more pudding and the strokes of a thousand banana-skins to trip his descent to where the pudding bubbled and cooked thicker and harder, a running lava that ran him around and around the warehouse floor, his narna-stuck hands grabbing all the while for an outside of puddingness that was Atlanta in flames.

This is it, thought Windscale, his lungs filling with a warm, sweet flambéed banana that was his hero's death.

Dawn came to a dockside that reeked of burnt sugar. Where the warehouse had been was a long, low banana surprise: a dense overdone cake leavened by bricks. Amused firemen roped the thing off. It was still bubbling tunefully in places, through weaknesses in its scabby crust. An audience of small boys, stray dogs and the unemployed stood at the rope and were mildly entertained.

But when Windscale's charred face broke through the scab like a black beanstalk from a plurped-over Pompeii greenhouse, they all ran away. A pained Windscale climbed on to the crust of the cake, scratched his scalds, and made a brief moonwalk before crashing back through and surfaced with every swear word he knew unable to break through a clog of banana.

'Hoi, Larry,' said a fireman. 'There's a bloke in there.'

'Never is.'

'Straight up. Huge black fella.'

Windscale made another brief appearance.

'Wait there, mister. We'll get the ladder.'

They cranked the ladder over where Windscale was treading banana and although he over-balanced their machine and lost them three of their colleagues, they did get him out.

'Good work,' he said, congratulating the fireman in charge, giving him a manly banana handshake. Then with a whump of glee he remembered the address-book between his buttocks.

'This time I've got the bugger good and proper!' he screamed and thrust his hand right up.

But all he came away with were ashy flakes of paper that immediately took to the breeze. He was so put out that he threw everybody nearby into the banana-cake. Once calmed down, it took him all morning to get them out again. He also retrieved the corpses of poor

PLETHORA OF GITS

Eva, PC Fender, the Graffiti Gang, and a number of burnt-out police dogs.

Sighing heavily from this latest thwarting, Windscale wandered off in search of lunch. If anyone offered him another banana he'd ... he'd ... he'd ... he'd eat it probably.

ZULUS ON A RIDGE

Inspector Hornbeam was pulling at his restricting shirt-collar while giving a pep-talk to his squad. That night Bingo Sarkie was giving a special charity performance at Clacton's West Cliff Theatre, just around the corner from the station. (It was a sign of the times that the charity in question was for the families of slain comics.) The entire local constabulary would be in attendance, on stage with riot shields, to protect the comic.

Windscale strolled in during the pep-talk's third quarter.

Hornbeam was furious: 'There's a banana in your ear, constable.'

'Ooops, sorry,' said Windscale and shoved it down his superior's shirt-collar.

'Coo, that's much better, thank you.'

Sirens made their noise. Sarkie was screeched into the station in a police van, disguised as a WPC, surrounded by police marksmen in bullet-proof vests. He was, after all, one of only four comedians left alive in an increasingly jokeless realm. When they got him in, he was wrapped in a carpet and taken down to the cells where he changed into the parrot costume in which he was to begin his act. He then sat down and smoked cigars, writing jokes on toilet paper between puffs.

Windscale popped in for a visit.

'What are you?' asked Sarkie. He was too astonished for a better crack.

'I'm yerh bodyguard. I'm to stand in front of yer during yerh performance.'

Sarkie's creased tortoise's head breathed smoke out of the parrot's beak till, with perfect timing: 'What about the audience?'

'There isn't going to be an audience.'

'No audience!'

'Too dangerous. Any one of them might be the Comic Killer armed with an ingenious plot.'

Sarkie went crazy. He wouldn't perform under such outrageous conditions! He pulled on the bars like a lovesick gibbon, yelling through teeth clenched on his cigar: 'I'll not do it! I'll never do it! You can't make me do it! I'm a professional! Goddamit, this ain't no police state! Lemme outta here, you bluebellied bastards!'

Inspector Hornbeam came down and a compromise was reached. 1) There would be an audience, but trussed and gagged. Sarkie was satisfied he could make a joke of that. 2) Windscale would stand in front of the comic, but with his legs wide enough to have material shouted through. 3) Rather than give the box office takings to charity Sarkie and Inspector Hornbeam would split it between themselves.

But how to get Sarkie into the theatre! Those few steps from the police van to the stage-door were the most vulnerable, during which most presidents and their wives get popped at. Windscale saved yet another day! With the aid of a chair-leg and a hidden talent he did himself up as a larger-than-fiction Long John Silver and, with a cigar-smoking parrot that was Bingo Sarkie perched nervously on his shoulder, he limped bravely round the corner and straight into the theatre without any assassin's bullet being fired.

'Arrrrrrrh, Jim!' he went, attacking the confectionery counter and helping himself to the sort of confectionery you get in theatres.

He couldn't have been more satisfied with his revival of the role. But behind stage, in Sarkie's dressing-room, he was gripped with the most terrible stage fright.

'But you don't have to do owt but stand there!' screamed Sarkie.

'I know. I know. But in front of all them people. All them eyes, staring . . . all them eyebrows meeting horribly in the middle . . . all them fingers forcing toffees through their gags . . . all them spines iced with the fear of imminent murder . . . all them bladders whose only entertainment is to go wee-weeee . . . all them hats loaded with wax fruit covering minds contemplating the most dreadful crimes!!!!!!'

This succeeded in giving Sarkie stage fright for the first time in his career. He hid under the sink squawking 'I'm a professional.' When five minutes was called Windscale had to prize him out with his Long John Silver leg.

They trembled on to stage like children towards their first day at school. And why no applause!?! (In their tizz they'd forgotten the terms of the recently-reached agreement.) Not a patter or a

PLETHORA OF GITS

slap! Not a sausage! A silenter silence they had never heard . . . They walked up to the mike to the sound of sloshing water in Windscale's water-on-the-knee.

The policeman parted his legs and Sarkie commenced his act with a funny dance. From the back of the stalls what perhaps were chicken's feet could be seen skipping about. From elsewhere: nothing. A squawking could be heard, but no one in the gagged, trussed audience connected it with anything in particular.

Sarkie ribtickled his way through a five-minute opening patter, increasingly desperate. No laughter! Not a titter! He was dying! In forty years he'd never died like this. Not even on the night he went on blind drunk at the Lyceum, Crewe and fell asleep during his Al Jolson impression.

He elbowed Windscale: 'They're not laughing!'

'Hum?'

'This is sure-fire stuff and they're not laughing!'

'They should be, should they?'

'They always have before.' His parrot costume was moulting despondently. Then, with new confidence: 'I'll go into my Hitler-and-the-tortoise routine, shall I?'

'Yeah, can't hurt.'

So while Windscale scoured the dress circle for the glint of an enemy rifle, Sarkie went into his bestest ever routine with all the gusto his experience could muster.

'There'll never be another! There'll never be another,' he began, goose-stepping behind Windscale.

But his bodyguard had problems of his own. His eyes had picked out Commissioner Claeverlock in the third row of the stalls, struggling in his bonds because he'd recognized this so-called PC Baldwin as Public Enemy Number One. Windscale screwed his eyes tightly shut and pretended to be somewhere else.

In Claeverlock's gagged squeal Sarkie thought he detected an uncontrollable fit of laughter. But when the gag worked a little loose it was easy to hear that it was someone mumbling 'Bastard' over and over again. The desperate Sarkie reached the part in his Hitler-and-the-tortoise routine where the tortoise says 'I've never slept there myself'. This was his biggest belter. It couldn't fail. Any second, he'd have them in the palm of his hand!

'. . . I've never slept there myself.'

Nothing! Not a hiccup.

Sarkie ran out from behind Windscale with his hair in his fists. His eyes missed the rest of the trussed-up audience and fell upon one member of it: Claeverlock, furiously kicking the seat in front of him, his ginger eyes rounded with hate.

No comedian had ever received such a rebuff from his public. It gave him a brain haemorrhage. He dropped dead on to Windscale's boots.

When Windscale opened his eyes there was a dead comedian underneath them. The wings, meanwhile, were crowded with snarling police dogs, pawing slowly forward into the lights.

His teeth full of knots, Commissioner Claeverlock broke Samson-like from his bonds and pointed at Windscale with the scream: 'ARREST THAT FAT GIT!'

Police marksmen arose across the curl of the dress circle like Zulus on a ridge. Windscale put his hands up and emptied his bowels all over the stage.

'I am innocent!' howled the huge man squeezed into the dock, Court Number One of the Old Bailey.

'OH NO YOU'RE NOT!!!' yelled the court.

'Oh yes I am!' he insisted.

'Oh no you're not!!!' scathed a particularly plummy voice. It was his own barrister.

The BBHC couldn't have been more energetic in its campaigning. But the special hanging vote in the Commons was 324 in favour and 324 against. The Speaker thus had the deciding vote and, having recently shot a friend's butler and buried him on a moonless night somewhere in Gloucestershire, he played safe by voting against, thus saving Windscale's bacon. Sir Cyril Passey-Wix squealed like Fay Wray.

Windscale was sentenced to life imprisonment for each of the 1,340 comedians he was supposed to have assassinated. He did a sum on his cuff. Say thirty years for each life sentence: that made 40,200 years . . . meaning he wasn't due for release till the year 42191 AD, an impossible year to visualize, full of aluminium hats worn by people called Zog. Even with a third off for good behaviour, taking him to circa 26800 AD, he'd be long dead anyway. Worse

PLETHORA OF GITS

still, history would remember him not as one of its great police but as a slaughterer of clowns.

Sentence having been given, the humourless judge added some words about the value of comedy in a free society while Windscale was yelping in the dock. He wasn't in fact complaining about the severity of his sentence: he was being shot in the bottom by a delighted man from London Zoo.

Windscale woke to a drowsy consciousness with a tooth missing, his limbs hanging limply through the holes of a rope bag containing the rest of him, all this suspended from a helicopter buzzing across a huge slow landscape of sharp little churches poking from lightly snowed-upon brown fields: like a box of drawing-pins flung on a chocolate cake the shape of England. In the years of incarceration ahead of him, when he often fantasised himself as a bird on the wing, he always remembered his heavy-lidded vision of his country: but the churches became sweetshops, and in swooping low the signposts did not say DURHAM 123, but in weensie writing contained details of the countless pleasures an Englishman could enjoy on any day of the year.

The helicopter was due at Durham Jail during one of those aforementioned pleasures: tea time on a dull snowdroppy day in early March. The rear rotor-blades shaved Windscale's legs for him as the copter turned a tight corner around the cathedral and dropped towards the twisting grey river like a thirsty dragonfly. Rowers approaching Prebends Bridge snagged their blades in the grey plash as an angry noise shook their water. Windscale swang past in his bag, briefly begging for chocolate by pointing a finger at his small hurt mouth: a burning crater pouting from a stubbly moon. It hung in the air on the eyes of those who had seen it long enough for them to toss a few Smarties at it, none of which it caught.

Windscale, meanwhile, was high over the picturesque city being winched down into the prison. A new wing was being built especially to house him. The foundations were already done and its grim workmen were standing tools-in-hand ready to commence building Windscale's cell around him. They were hard, cruel men. So hard and so cruel that they did not take pity on their caps which the downdraft had flung from their pates into storm-tossed puddles. Any man soft enough to pick up his cap would've been shunned by his whippet when he rolled home that evening.

'Ugly bastard!' Windscale growled at one from the comfort of his bag.

'I'm ugly me, ugly, bloody ugly me,' said the man and hit himself in the face with his trowel to show how hard he was.

But Windscale knew such types, he'd arrested thousands. Tell them their mammy has choked on a cornflake and, even though they know its not true, the very idea makes them blub like kiddies who've over-scratched their chickenpox.

The copter let him go and whizzed away. The rope dropped from his shoulder like a nightie from a statue of Lenin seen in a fairground mirror. Slowly the breeze-blocks arose in a close square around him.

TIME

Five years later the bored Windscale was gently masturbating in his cell, day-dreaming about the day on which he'd finally nab the real comic killer. Outside, it was a very different England that had forgotten all about him.

Meanwhile, no further comedians had been killed, so Windscale's guilt, had anyone bothered to ask, was obvious.

Commissioner Claeverlock had retired from the force and done a Gauguin. Abandoning his family, he'd gone to Benbecula in the Outer Hebrides . . . to paint. His tumbledown croft eschewed all comfort, just a straw mattress, a rusty tap over a bucket, and his busy easels. Within days of his arrival the walls were covered in ginger self-portraits and dark sunsets daubing over Loch Uskavagh. His only concession to civilization was three policewomen he'd kidnapped and kept chained up in his byre in case he felt an urge.

Sergeant Petherwick had likewise lain down her truncheon, some months before Claeverlock or she might herself have been one of those kidnapped three. In a pepful Chelsea wedding Petherwick married her boyfriend Herbert's best friend, Lord Rupert St Mawes-Godolphin, who immediately transported her to his family home on the Goonhilly Downs in Cornwall. Thus she sat before a stately fire, wolfhounds at her feet, dreaming of her endomorphic lost love like any Arthurian heroine. The fire was like a branch office of Hell, so hot that it dried her tears before they even left her eyes. Her husband, meanwhile, often dressed in a favourite suit of armour, kept trying to make a time machine in the kitchens, electrocuting a string of butlers along the way. He was a melancholy sort, but endearingly desperate to be cheerful, who blamed all his problems on the fact that his mother was also his aunt, his father both his uncle and his brother, and his grandmama his third cousin twice removed.

Bad news, alas, about Windscale's only living relative . . . his beloved sister Winnie went on an all-in-wrestling binge to raise money for the FREE WILF WINDSCALE CAMPAIGN, of which she was the only active activist. As a publicity stunt in Leeds she wrestled a mountain gorilla who happened to be in the audience. It was an effective stunt, but to keep public interest she had to think of something even more outrageous . . . but could only come up with wrestling two gorillas, which she did . . . then three gorillas . . . then four gorillas and so on until it was standing-room only in the ring. At London's Albert Hall one steamy July night Winnie climbed in with 213 gorillas (16 were, truth be told, Scotsmen in gorilla suits, this due to the regretful international shortage of gorillas for any purpose). But this time it was to be no pushover. An unusually sentient gorilla (or Scotsman) came prepared with a deadly fight plan. Winnie began, as usual, dashing from rope to rope, excusing herself through the crush, issuing slow forearm-smashes like tickets from a vague bus conductor in the rush hour. But then she found she couldn't move. The gorillas had linked arms in a fierce black scrum and begun a push in their opponent's direction. Winnie's chubby hands were seen sticking from the shove of hair in silent submission. Suddenly the gorillas (and the Scotsmen) took fright and ran off screaming into the audience, which simultaneously scattered through the exits. When the ref put his broken spectacles onto his sorely tweaked nose he saw at the centre of the empty monkey-smashed hall the last sigh of Winnie with her brother's name on it wisping between the cracks in his vision. Winnie had burst all over the stage like a stomped-on brown-paper bag of bruised tomatoes.

A screw shouted the news to Windscale under his cell door just before lights out. In the seconds-later darkness he had never been more alone. He wrestled Winnie in his mind's eye until it was more bloodshot than his other eyes, all three at the centre of a sleeplessness alerted by sudden clanks, far away and near.

Meanwhile, during Windscale's five years out of 40,200, the world of comedy underwent a regeneration. Within months of Windscale's incarceration new blood had arisen over the spilt blood to hog the limelight and divert the nation from its cares. It was a new kind of comedy, more modern, more literate, more politically aware, more caring of the afflicted, which looked back with a sneer at the antics of its pratfalling forebears. No catchphrases. No mother-in-laws coming on surprise visits. No Pakistanis. No Pats. No Mikes. Hardly any jokes at all, in fact.

Writing in *The Guardian* Epping Chowder described these new comics as 'transplanting a private comedy onto a public stage'. He also praised their 'essentially schoolyard interface with contemporary reality, creating for the viewer a second-hand camaraderie redolent of the microcosmic empathy between the Lower Fifth and the lonelier freneticism of an increasingly insecure advance into middle-age . . .'

The schoolyard reference was peculiarly incisive because by a strange chance all these new comedians – there were forty-one of them – had gone to the same school, and at the same time . . . in the same class, in fact. In the schoolyard of Burton Agnes, an obscure but progressive mixed public school in Oxfordshire they had stood in twos or threes doing impersonations of Mr Nafferton, the headmaster, and showing their bottoms to each other, items never to be excised from their comedy acts in future years.

The schoolyard pairings-off, also, were maintained into the real world. Of all the comics only Snog Duffie did a single. The others cross-pattered in double acts, triple acts and quadruple acts which were constantly scattering and, like a splurge under a dirty microscope, forever making new beasts. But it was like God getting his needle stuck and making an aardvark over and over again, because these double/triple acts weren't made up of one biggun and one skinnyun, or one hairyun, one baldun and one with a Methuselah beard. Though each had his or her own special personality, all forty-one comics looked exactly alike, as if laid by the same frog . . . a frog which, it must be admitted, had only known one joke, now shared out among its tadpoles together with a compulsion to endlessly retell it.

Of the girls, Hecate Smedley was regarded as the 'pretty' one by her clan, but they all had the same plump smile, irony-seeking eyes, child-bearing hips, and three more were called Hecate.

In the group's swashbuckleizations on stage and TV it was always Hank Dean who ran the others through but he was as slight a mummy's boy as the rest of them. Had he been a cavalier he'd have gone around dressed as a tree-trunk till the Restoration was well ensconced. Had he gone to the Spanish Civil War he'd have spent it playing flip-football in a Benidorm arcade.

Also like denizens of the schoolyard: though they rarely stopped honking with laughter every night on TV they always seemed on the verge of tears – one slap, one name-call would do it. Davey Buttermere, in fact, did a crying act and like in Haddock's old monologues you could never be sure if it was only an act. He was probably the most gifted of them but being the least popular among his classmates (they'd bullied him mercilessly since his milkteeth days) he was never allowed to do very much. He did a sometime double-act with Peggy Lewes, who usually appeared naked in a long clinging wig and who knocked him over if he said anything, giving him the latest in a long line of hilarious nosebleeds.

The BBC were desperate when they gave them their first show, anyone else who might've dared describe themselves as comedians being on Boot Hill, but were now smugly delighted, dryly inventing new shows for them, all of which proved popular, spawning more, then spin-offing more still, till there was nothing else left on the box but the news and the old films which the group spent so much time pastiching, interspersed by commercials in which the same forty-one comedians came with their mops, breakfasts and bankbooks selling their souls with a smile.

Their irrepressible animalistic wildness, their natural drollness, their disrespect of everything they were supposed to scrape at, and their never-standing-still-for-a-moment youthful oompahpahpah energy gave their public plenty to look at, a new pantheon of jesters to wheeze at in the long debt-ridden armchairs of life. It was perhaps as Epping Chowder suggested: they made a schoolyard of the whole country, nothing seemed so deadly serious, anything might happen: the man rushing by dressed as a half-sheep/half-prominent dentist might bequeath you all his money which you'd spend on trumpet lessons and a fleet of submarines.

But this delicious wildness was short-lived, made to seem longer because of the incurable hic-hic-hiccupping repeats. It lasted the length of their first series, no more. After that their private world was redefined for them by accountants and producers uncomfortable among jokes. The old private world had constantly added to itself with new in-jokes, new extravagances and over-the-topnesses. It was suddenly frozen under an older skin impermeable to new invention. They became, every one, more like other people and less like the strange brood that had grown in an obscure place. If any had understood the source of Haddock's greatness, that of a man who

PLETHORA OF GITS

never left his own head, he may have led the others down a new road to Funnyville. Alas, the childish bitterness that had fizzed on their hungry plate became a picked-at cabbage-supper of adult tedium. Their padded-cell wildness dissolved to reveal a tax inspector back at work after a nervous breakdown.

Marriage was the sharpest whip that tamed these lions. Within a year of their emergence all forty-one paired off with someone else from the forty-one. Hecate Smedley, being a particularly modern woman, married several of her fellow comedians and a number of other people as well. Marriage was fun, adding hilarity on-stage and off. Sex became real at last, and dirtier than they'd ever dreamed. But soon the girls were duff-bellied . . . and so ever after! Between them these jollyfolk sprogged enough children to support a whooping cough epidemic in Pyongyang. Peggy Lewes, being prone to multiple births, had eleven offspring in two years: two sets of three and a five.

A numbing domesticity flopped over their comedy like round pages of milky pastry. Their hugely popular award-winning ensemble pieces, whose first series had been gaily plotless reinterpretations of the classics of English Literature, suddenly turned into a mad housing estate of hatchback-in-the-drive family comedies with the ghosts of Betty and George flitting between the vol-au-vents and the sherry trifle. Even Snog Duffie's stand up, once full of jaggaling genitals and furious send-ups of Sir Cyril Passey-Wix . . . five years on was dominated by amusing anecdotes about the potty-training of his youngest and other observations of problematical married life, even daring to mention the surprise visits of mothers-in-law.

An odd regression infected the rest of the group, which was soon rich in spiv acts, 'Englishman, Irishman, Scotsman' jokes and finished by nosediving into a jam-flicked semolina of pie-throwing, slow falling overs and comic Cockney songs, with all the pace of Medea played in a school for eyeless hydrocephalus sufferers at the bi-annual Delft treacle festival.

But the less funny they got the more their audiences liked them . . . and the TV companies patted them on the back . . . and they got famouser and famouser . . . richer and richer . . . happier and happier.

Windscale, meanwhile, had lost weight: from 703 lbs to 194 lbs. The thin man inside his fat man had gotten out. Five years of a chocolateless diet of thin chilli-con-carne and Ready Brek had made him into an apple-core of his former self. When they'd built the cell around him he couldn't take a step. A little while later he could take one in any direction. Now he could take lengthy circular walks.

The prison Governor was sure that Windscale was escaping from the prison a pound at a time and had the screws gadding about in search of butterballs of fat which he supposed were rolling through the guttering, slowly joining up on the outside where the golem of a Windscale was filling out in someone's attic. Windscale's sleep was constantly being disturbed so that they could check to see if his belly-button was still there.

It was: in the tight flat belly of a Sicilian youth. Windscale had slimmed into a beauty. Never had there been such a before and after! His long body, that of a prison-pale Apollo, lay on his bunk in a jungle of stripes that was his fatboy's gone-baggy outfit. His single chin rested on a chest whose spread-out hairs had come back together in a curly black mat. His head was one sculpted by Praxiteles at his most inspired. A large handsome nose, nostrils flaring at each sighing breath. Lips made for the kissing of fruit curling between leonine cheeks all the more manly for the lengthy stubble of his latest beard (he shaved with a torn fingernail every second Tuesday). Sorrowful clear eyes, azure even after lights out, making the smallest movements as if judging a woman's changeable heart, but in fact re-reading yet again the copy of the *Daily Express* he'd had with him since the day he came in. It was his only reading matter, full of news of his own trial and on the TV pages an interview with an up-and-coming comedian named Snog Duffie. Most beautiful of all was Windscale's skin: it glowed, wrinkleless and pure, blued by the occasional vein, pinked by the occasional memory of Sergeant Petherwick riding a police horse nude on Hampstead Heath. The grey at his sunken temples was that of a middle-aged man. The smooth eye-sockets swept by his stiff lashes were those of a boy. An other-worldly contrast in a room without contrasts locked away from the world.

But suddenly the door opened.

The prison Governor wrote a 300-page letter to Sir Cyril Passey-Wix about Windscale's escaping butterballs. He was immediately retired. The new Governor saw no reason why Windscale should

PLETHORA OF GITS

remain in solitary confinement, especially as he was now slim enough to walk around the prison without bending the ironwork.

'Fancy some exercise, fatso?' yapped the screw.

Windscale gathered his baggy outfit around him and stepped into a new space for the first time in five years. Taking deep mote-filled breaths he followed the screw on a clanking walk to the exercise yard where he was left alone: alone with a daisy growing from a crack in the concrete! Alone with the vast blue spring sky! Alone with the sweet fresh air and the sun's warm touch!

A sudden campanology practice from the cathedral! He'd strained to hear this from his cell for the past 260 Sunday mornings. Now it was clear and bright, the perfect soundtrack to one of the most perfect moments the ruined detective had ever known. He hadn't felt so ecstatic since the day he arrested the Melditsi brothers at the 1975 Grand National.

Yikes! The door in the dark prison wall opened and his fellow prisoners sauntered into the yard. It was a mugshot book come to life. Windscale backed away into a mossy shadow. He recognized most of them: they were his own nabs!

'Here, you, this is my place. I always loiters here.' It was none other than Dan Melditsi speaking.

'So, sorry.'

'Don't fret yerhself, kid. Yerh just in, tissent yerh. Yerh wassent ter know.'

'I didn't, no.'

'Here, doesent I know yous from somewheres?'

'Um?'

'Yeah . . . yeah . . . It's cummin . . . YEAH: yous never is! Yous is! Yous Fingers Norton's boy Harry!'

'Errrrmmmmm . . .'

Due to a boyhood accident Melditsi's nose was on the side of his head. He wiped it with a sleeve and then examined the little line of wet his dew-drop had made.

'I was there at eees end, yer nar. When that fat git plod stuffed the jockey down eees throat. Horrible, it was. I still gets nightmares.'

'How distressing.'

'Yeah.'

Melditsi sat in the shadows against the wall. He inadvertently stretched out his legs into the light but when he saw them there

153

he kneed up. Windscale politely sat next to him, pulling his feet into the shadows after a prompting from his new friend.

'He's here, yer nar.'

'Whom?'

'Him. The plod wot did for your dad.'

'No!'

'Bloody is, mate. They got im bricked in somewheres with nart but eees knob for company.'

Melditsi took out a small dirty comb and set about his moustache's toilet. His nose being on the side of his head, the moustache was in the middle of his face. It was round, like a hairy bullseye, six inches in diameter, surrounded by a skid of moles. He kept smiling coyly at Windscale, who smiled back.

'They did im for doing in all them comedians a few years back. You must have eard.'

'I've been abroad . . . Bulgaria.'

Windscale then described, to the entranced gangster, the scenic beauties of the Rhodope Mountains, adding that safes were particularly easy to crack there but that they sometimes had goats inside rather than money.

'Goats?'

'Popular things, goats is, thereabouts.'

Melditsi put his comb away and took out something wrapped in shiny purple paper.

Far away in the Home Office a 300-page letter suddenly metamorphosized and splurged a filing cabinet with scrawled fat.

Windscale's brow swote. 'That's not . . . chocolate, is it?'

'I's forgetting my manners.'

Melditsi snapped off a square and tossed it into Windscale's hand. It balanced on the end of his middle finger like a stray sexual part. He watched it for a full minute, mantra-mumbling the magical word *Cadbury's* over and over again, before putting it between his teeth with the smile of a Mexican bandit who's accumulated every peso in Mexico. The pleasure that followed was the ultimate advertisement for that particular confectionery. But twas over too soon! Too soon! He wanted more! MORE!

'Like chocbars, does yerh?'

Windscale's lips were a tremble. 'Uh-huh.'

'Gis yerh the rest of this for a snog.'

'Errrrrr . . .' But it was too late: the snog had begun. He was selling his body for seven squares of chocolate!!!!!!!

But all in all the snog was no worse an experience than having the President of Egypt eat a meal of snot and shoelaces with one's tongue as the plate.

The Melditsi brothers had been famous rally drivers in their youth before their natural criminal bent disclosed itself with their robbing every bank on the route of the Paris-Dakar rally. (They came third.) The cell they had shared for sixteen years in Durham Jail was a junk shop of car parts and motoring magazines. Two steering-wheels were fixed to the walls, one afore an Alpine scene, the other afore a desert. The brothers spent the long shut-in evenings racing each other into these pinned-up landscapes with a brrr-brrrrrrrrrring of the lips that infuriated the imaginary grannies in the Lancashire Granny Killer's cell next door.

Windscale spent many repulsive hours there, on the burst backseat of a Hillman Minx, swapping his snogs for chocolate. When Dan Melditsi had had his snogful, Windscale would tuck away his chocolate prize, because now it was Sandro's turn for a snog.

Sandro was the older by two weeks (a painful birth, apparently) and in the same childhood accident which left Dan's nose on the side of his head Sandro's was shifted to the top, where it stuck out of his thinning hair like the fin of a joke shark dropped among unhealthy kelp.

'Oh, Harry boy,' he fluttered to Windscale, with the voice of a cement-mixer full of plaster saints, 'You's my dreamcar of a fella. Come, lerrus motor ter Lover's Lane and park under the stars.'

If he opened his eyes during Sandro's snogging he could see Fanzio winning the Monte in 1930-something, tattooed where the creature's nose should've been. (Dan had a snap for this under his own tache.) But the brothers didn't match in the tongue dept. Sandro's was half as long again . . . It flicked down Windscale's throat with the power of a catfish flung out for the night in Gomorrah.

Windscale tried to ease the pain by imagining that the Melditsis were Sergeant Petherwick. (Their jowls were not dissimilar.) This allowed him to put some effort into his end of the snogging, which sometimes encouraged the brothers to bung him an extra chocohunk, and sometimes he got carried away enough to moan: '. . . Oh, Stephanie!'

'I loves it when he calls me Stephanie,' said Dan when he was alone with his brother.

'He calls ME Stephanie, not you!'

And they threw the engine of a Triumph Vitesse at each other far into the night.

Windscale, meanwhile, sat in the tombdark carpentry room, occupying one of a wild-west-saloonful of crooked chairs, enjoying a meal of hard-won chocolate. His hands kept nervously brushing across his face to remove a phantom snog that wouldn't stop coming at him, like Fanzio eternally around that noseless bend.

Suddenly, from the darkness, a mellow voice: 'Can I have a bit?'

'Bit of what?'

'That's chocolate you're eating. I can hear the paper tearing.'

'I aint got none. Bugger off!'

But, despite himself, Windscale couldn't help handing over the chocolate, every bit of it, to a small cold bogeymanish hand.

A wandering screw turned a light on in the corridor! Glass panes at the top of the room shone like TV-sets showing camouflaged skiers fizzing on the Beadmore Glacier. Woodshavings brushed into heaped piles on the floor shone as white as yetis put through a pencil-sharpener. But sucking in most of the light was a snow-capped little man like a whitewashed gnome perched several deranged chairs away. He was finishing off Windscale's chocolate.

'Here!' snarled the bereft one. 'I gave you my dairy milk!'

'Thank you. It was most appetizing.'

Windscale's fists rose to batter this cocky little sod, but they disobeyed him and set about making rabbits on the wall.

The gnome was mildly entertained. He looked like a priest impersonator or a dipper, but he was a much rarer birdbrain than that. This was Maxwell Einstein (no relation) who had lived an easy life hypnotizing bank clerks all over the globe into handing him drawersful of money before being wrongly convicted for the bombing of an army barracks in Aldershot (causing the deaths of three buglers and a regimental mascot), from which all his hypnotizing skills were not enough to extricate him, this due to the unfortunate presence of eleven Welshmen on his jury. (Welshmen, of course, cannot be hypnotized.)

'Why'd I do it?' wailed Windscale, as his rabbits teased him with a picnic of chocolate cake that nearly dislocated his thumbs. 'Why? Why?'

Just then the wandering screw sniffed in yapping: 'Here, what's yous doing in here. It's way after lockup.'

'You are the proprietor of a sweetshop,' said Einstein in a slow, low voice.

'Yes, master,' said the screw and immediately dropped his mask of cruelty and assumed the mean of the sort of pleasant old gentleman who ran sweetshops during an endless school holiday of long ago.

'Shall we go in . . .' said the mesmer, inviting Windscale and his rabbits with a sweep of the hand.

'Go in where?'

'The sweetshop, silly.'

'Sure, yeah, the sweetshop.'

Windscale decided to humour him. But on his way across he tripped on a woodshavingheap and found himself in the middle of a sweetie-filled sweetshop. His rabbits, before they mixamatosised themselves down the rabbit-hole of his sleeves to hop out as Malteser-snatching hands, gambolled across shelves lined with jars of translucent candies.

'Help yourself to a pick-and-mix, sonny. Everything's free today,' said the screw-turned-shopkeeper.

'Can I? . . . Can I really?'

'Some mint creams, perhaps,' suggested Einstein.

Windscale commenced a gleeful scoff, grabbing something of everything and forcing it into a brown hole spangled with lemon drops in the middle of his face. Chocolate-covered Brazils zonked from side to side in his mouthful like their countrymen doing the tango in a mud hole, before slipping out denuded of chocolate on to a wrapper strewn floor.

'There's too much! I'll never eat it all!' celebrated the chocaholic.

But Einstein further illustrated his power. Toothy chocolate-hungry mouths opened all over Windscale's arms and legs, he having stepped unashamedly out of his prison-striped swathe in his eagerness to scoff. These new orifices snapped lap-doggishly as the shopkeeper tossed walnut whips their way.

This couldn't be happening! . . . was the unsummoned thought that megaphoned in the deep place where Windscale's mind did its speaking to him. Suddenly he was wised to a treasureless reality . . . the mouths healed up, the sweetshop flickered, letting through the carpentry room at each flicker.

'It's a bloody con!' he whinged, his tongue white as sawdust . . . but had he been a bank clerk he'd had given away a drawerful of monkeys by then.

Alerted by these previous minutes of whooping, the Governor peeped in.

'Can I interest yerh in a sugar mouse?' asked the still-hexed screw.

The Governor looked straight at Einstein. 'Been up to your old tricks again, Maxie?' he said with a voice whose burr rather than its vowels betrayed a Welsh origin.

Einstein smiled a smile sickly enough to suggest he'd eaten all the chocolate that Windscale thought he'd put away himself.

Maxwell Einstein was the only villain Windscale had ever liked. The small white man did a wonderful thing for the choc-starved beanpole: he made him a gift of an imaginary Mars Bar. This incredible object could be unwrapped and eaten an infinite number of times. Exactly how many times, in a meal of 40,200 years, was a cheerful prospect for the unfortunate, whose cell walls were covered with crossed-out sums attempting an exact calculation of how many Mars Bars he could eat in that time, allowing for 15,000 years of munchless sleep.

The Melditsis, meanwhile, had seen the collapse of their snog-for-chocolate racket and had turned as nasty as a cheekful of yellow-and-green gumboils, defiantly slamming cell doors on their genitals – an equally terrifying sight from either side of the door – before Einstein mesmered them a muscle beach in a corner of their cell. They tore about on beach-buggies, buried tanned youths in the sand, snogged and swam and stole credit-cards from the back pockets of jeans. Bliss. It was more than they deserved.

Windscale had long, lazy snogless chocolate-filled days. The Mars Bar was his perfect cellmate. It lulled him, a mother's teat, into forgetting all his nightmares, into forgetting everything but itself. Windscale was like a great cavalry charge, without horses, without cavalry . . . he had at last completely forgotten who he was. This

PLETHORA OF GITS

terrible process had begun the day he'd handed over his warrant card to Commissioner Claeverlock . . . and continued as the waves of time had beaten on this dune of a man, making of him a slip of a thing who'd permit nose-skew convicts to snog him without him once growling 'Villain!' down their little red lanes. When talking to prison visitors he nodded warmly at their liberal musings, rather than filling his slop-out bucket and drowning them in it, the automatic action of his better self. The policeman had died in him leaving nothing but a seven-foot sop as dull as a prawn pressed between the pages of a history of Belgium.

But after a week or two the Mars Bar proved itself a true friend. Windscale was putting on weight. Flexing his cheeks in his parrot's-cage mirror he saw a real man returning, mightily comfortable sags under all his creases. True, it was a phantom weight – if he had an itch on his side he had to plunge his arm up to the elbow in imaginary fat before he could locate it. But its presence peppered his gravy and something of his copper's manner returned: he arrested people in the corridors, kept saying 'Mind how you go!' and in the exercise yard he chased everybody whistling like a horse (it was excellent exercise for one and all).

He was in a just-broken-a-big-case mood, having solved the disappearance of the communal bar of soap from its string in the showers (someone from the Melditsis' muscle beach confessed) . . . with the Mars Bar going down for the 7,249th time, when he found himself paying greater attention to the animated notebook of memories that floated thoughtlessly across the surface of his policeman's mind like helmeted porpoises skimming briefly from thick soup. He remembered a detail of an old case from the early '60s when his then boss, Chief Inspector Hartburn, had fetched in a hypnotist to hypnotize a woman into remembering the movements of her husband's finger while it dialed their hall phone. This had led to the phone number and thence to the arrest of her husband's elder brother who'd been living a double life in a Cinque Port . . . Windscale forgot which Cinque Port . . . under the name of . . . he sought the name during thirteen Mars Bars . . . no, no, it wouldn't come.

But Maxwell Einstein's eyes widened a bit and Windscale saw Piccadilly Circus circa 1963 with the name Ludovic Crutty flashing in neon where the Coca-Cola sign normally excited the night.

'Ludovic Crutty,' grinned Windscale. 'The alias of Sebastian

Arthur Towser, arrested in Hythe-on-Sea for convoluted bigamy at 7.35 PM 19 August 1963.'

Einstein's lips curled like money drying before a fire. He was making notes for future crimes in a weensie address book.

Windscale snatched it off him. 'Here, if I was to flick through this, just flick through it mind, without actually reading it as such, could yerh make me remember what I'd seen?'

More money dried in Einstein's smile.

'Could yerh? Could yerh?'

The white hairs up his nose waggled like the legs of albino spiders as his conceited little snort said he could, of course, do anything, anything at all.

Windscale had remembered the little red address book, scorched to ashes between his buttocks, which he'd had briefly in his hands in Eva's dressing room.

'You are feeling sleepy . . . sleepeeeeeee . . . sleeeepeeeeee . . .'

'I am feeling sleepy,' yawned Windscale.

The prison library went the colour of Eva's nest. Its walls melted, books slipped down to become one big book with ten thousand beginnings, middles and a jumble of softening endings, with shoals of footnotes running away into a spineless sunset of alphabet fountains . . . he was at Eva's again, standing in the dressing room, vomiting glue into a pink sink. A banana with a single bloodshot eye was looking at him from inside the mirror. But when he turned around it wasn't there.

'I'll be all right in a minute,' he said and then shrieked for a little while because he'd somehow eaten the banana in the mirror.

He was alone, searching a drawer filled with erotic underwear. Over his shoulder he was aware of the screen covered with publicity photos of comedians.

'I have it in my hand . . .' said Windscale, gripping *The Cruel Sea* upside-down, but seeing Eva's secret file of clients.

'Turn to the first page,' said Einstein softly. 'What do you see?'

'I see a villain's name. Attwood, Jeremy, 24 Bildeston Road, Wattisham.'

Einstein turned to the As in his own address book and noted down this name and address, just as he noted down the seventy-four names which Windscale afterwards chanted to him.

PLETHORA OF GITS

Windscale was finger-snapped out of the prozzie's dressing room into a policeman's joy as great as if he'd saved Lincoln from being shot by throwing Hitler in the way. Einstein handed him the address book and he turned its pages with religious awe. Excluding the names beside which Windscale wrote *'Graffiti Gang'* in his miniscule writing, the following names remained:

Arbuthnot, George – 54 Juniper Rd, Frinton, 756642
Banyard, Igor – The Crossways, Wivenhoe, 310555
Bardsley, Carl Gustave – 20 Walnut Way, Chelmsford, 507853
Cruttendon, Rev Samuel – The Vicarage, Bilsington, 666556
Cumber, Broderick – Poacher's Lane, Lower Melford, Bury St Edmunds, 709822
Dickenson, Philip – Dickenson, Fooch and Son, High St, Notley, 85319
Fairweather, Wendel – 396 Queen St, Haverhill, 878540
Fooch, Rex – Dickenson, Fooch and Son, High St, Notley, 85319
Foxnash, Digby – 3 Conifer Close, Clacton-on-Sea, 224099
Gimbal, James – Gimbals Farm, Duck Lane, Tiptree, 429527
Goudie, Albrecht – 19 Hawkwood Road, Witham, 73893
Harris, Christopher – 42 Feldstead Drive, Oaklands Estate, Clacton-on-Sea, 547431
Haygreen, Osbert – The Poplars, Colchester Road, Brightlingsea, 9387511
Hornby, Binkie – Cromwell Rest Home, Dukes Meadow, St Osyth, 22255567
Ince, Steven – 15 Woodpeckers Way, Hundunmunden, 865331
Jennings, Peter – 34 Winnock Avenue, Bury St Edmunds, 756841
Jubb, Bardolph – 8 Boars Tyre Road, Ipswich, 339883
Keefe, Eamon – 98 Brownings Ct, Southend, 981726
Lawther, Angus – 16 Falkland Avenue, Colchester, 372471
Leggett, Clive – Mill Bridge Antiques, High St, Nigly, 937861
Ling, U – 4 Tye Green, East Bergholt, 238667
McMarney, David – Dog & Monkey Pub, Armoury Road, Southend, 349008
Mabbott, Jerome – 21 George VI Crescent, Walton-on-the-Naze, 245981
Moore-Crosby, Lionel – 7A Buckweed Court, Sudbury, 590281
Openshaw, Oliver – 61 Shinnington St, Felixstowe, 8900436
Parker, Michael – 105 Hoomdownway Park Road, Yeams-on-Sea, 432436
Pordage, Dwight – 55 Juniper Road, Frinton, 768123
Quarkell, Yitzhak – 'Glencoe', 541 Mirabel Buildings, Finkle St, Tel Aviv, 918195642
Redpath, Alexander – 3 Tower St, Colchester 262678
Thirlwell, Nicholas – 88 Coppins Close, Uplands Road, Coggeshall, 874631

Tillinghast, Boris – 'The Merry Lady', Snoods Wharf, Jaywick, 746321
Upchurch, Dwain – 11 Myrrh Bend, Chaucer Park, Solburtonberry-on-Colne, 278213
Vickers, Brigadier-General Theodoric – Officer's Mess, Colchester Barracks, 438921
Weeks, Enoch – 17 Sycamore View, Broom Knoll, Stoke-by-Nayland, 356742
Wilmoteson, Henry – Bunnywunny Cottage, Bures Road, Colchester 676743
Younghusband, Findlay – 79 Malthouse Road, Sudbury, Suffolk 298561
Zorba, Clifford – Bovington Hall, Bovington, 4

Windscale held the book to his convictly-striped bosom. Although with just Einstein for whirly-eyed company, this was his drawing-room scene where he could say: 'The person who liquidized the butler is in this room.' Because the comic killer, he was dead certain, was one of the names on this list.

'The person who killed a generation of British comedians,' he said in his best detective's voice, 'has his name somewhere on this list.'

'I thought you did them larks yerhself,' said Einstein.

Windscale threw him over the railings into the pit of the prison. He kept slapping him back into the net every time he bounced up.

Petherwick, or Lady St Mawes-Godolphin as she now was, lay perspiring on the fireside rug of her vast new home. Her face had the loose-ended languid look of a mastiff in a world without cats who cannot find anything else to hate quite so much.

She had so severely sexually abused the servants that they had barricaded themselves in their attics, leaving her frustratedly shooting the eyes out of numerous lengthy Gainsboroughs, now all starelessly miffed on their staircases. Her husband, meanwhile, was so happy with his scientific experiments that she thought it best to leave him to it. So nowt to do with her life but lie there, listening to the fire crackle and her wolfhounds bleeping in their sleep. Her police-blue nightie stuck sweatily to her long curves, her sweat-pooled navel being a chiffon-covered swimming-hole for the fleas travelling from wolfhound to wolfhound.

'The post, marm . . .'

It was a masochistic butler hoping for a drubbing down.

Petherwick saw the Durham postmark and her sweat instantly

PLETHORA OF GITS

dried. It was a letter from her old boss and love: WINDSCALE!!!

While her eyes held the tiny writing up to the firelight, the butler removed his clothes, assumed an attitude of crucifixion and awaited punishment from the ceremonial mace he'd placed at his feet.

> **Dearest Stephanie,** went the letter, **I hope yous hassent forgot your old Chief Super and the great days wot we had together way back when. Yous got proper big instincts as good as any copper I ever knew – you knows the truth, doesn't yerh, eh? Everybody thinks I'm the bastard, but I'm not the bastard is I? I've got this fab new lead on who the bastard really is, but can't gerrout of here for another 40,195 years to catch the bastard's neck so could yerh please drop everything and come and do a bit of nosing about to crack this bugger and put things back like wot they were before.**
> **Fondly yours, Ex-Chief Super W.E. Windscale.**

Petherwick ignored the butler completely. He was overwhelmed. Such exquisite humiliation! And so much of it . . . she'd rushed out of the house, leaving the door banging in the wind, perhaps never to return, leaving him in a lifelong expectation of pain! His perversions panted like cut flowers in an airless florist's.

'STEPHANIE!!!'

Windscale grasped her hands over the table in the visiting room under the eyes of a dozen hard-hearted screws.

'I've missed you terribly, darling!' she said.

'Terribly?'

'Ooooooh, terribly. Have you?'

'Have I what?'

'Have you missed me terribly as well?'

'Terribly. I think about you all the time.'

'All the time?'

'Every minute.'

'Every minute?'

'Of every day.'

'As much as that?'

'I think about you riding a police horse nude on Hampstead Heath.'

'How sweet of you.'

'You don't mind, then?'

'Not a bit. I'll have some photos taken as soon as poss – police horse, Hampstead Heath, nude. I'll make a note.'

'Yerh'd do that for me?'

'I'd do anything for you, you big hunk.'

'So you still . . . care, does yerh?'

'Care, of course I care.'

'Oh STEPHANIE!'

'Oh, CHIEF!'

'So you have too then, have yerh?'

'Me?'

'Have yerh?'

'Have I what?'

'Have yerh thought of me at all?'

'Uh-huh.'

'Every minute of every day?'

'Every second of every minute of every day!'

'Oh STEPHANIE!'

'Oh CHIEF!'

Windscale's copper's-shirt-blue eyes were pinked with the reflection of the rapturous Petherwick, whose own Windscale-full eyes sizzled like turquoise-yolked eggs frying under the laser of his big sentimental face.

All the screws overlooking them were sobbing into their handkerchiefs, knowing no one would ever feel for them what this woman felt for this lag. Windscale took the opportunity to slip Einstein's address-book into Petherwick's hands.

'?'

'It's in there,' whispered Windscale. 'A list of thirty-seven names. One of them is the name of the bastard wot we want. It's up to yous, sergeant, to find him out.'

She hadn't been called sergeant for a while. It stiffened her vertebrae and set her teeth grinding with pride. She slipped the address-book down the front of her velour catsuit.

'You can rely on me, Chief,' she said, leaving the room in the style of a prehistoric Ines De La Fressange.

A little while later Windscale was back in his cell playing whist with Einstein, who'd won every hand he'd ever played with anybody,

PLETHORA OF GITS

when Petherwick, who wasn't there, said: '*Big Mama to Lovebird. Over. Big Mama to Lovebird. Over.*'

It was coming from a Madeira cake she'd left him. There was a US Army-approved walkie-talkie inside, recently famous in a scandal involving senior officers of the Belgian Navy who'd been caught using it to communicate with their bookmakers back ashore. Windscale freed it from the cake's crumby grip and replied: 'Lovebird to Big Mama. Am receiving you loud and clear. Over.'

'*Am proceeding on the southbound carriageway of the A1M. Will report in one hour. Over.*'

'Oh, STEPHANIE!'

'*Oh! Oh! Oh! Oh! Oh!*' went Petherwick, who wasn't in ecstasies: she was running over a line of bollards.

Petherwick commenced her enquiries with a call to the residence of Digby Foxnash who was innocently taking tea with his wife and children. Mrs Foxnash led the visitor into a puce-carpeted lounge.

'*I'm entering the premises now. Over.*' she told the faraway Windscale, who listened while she questioned Foxnash . . .

'Digby Foxnash?'

A small man stood in his socks. 'Mmm-hum.'

'I understand you were in the habit of visiting a prostitute know as Eva Straight of . . .'

'Erghhhh . . .!' He led Petherwick aside.

His wife was selecting a kitchen knife from the rack.

'I'm sure we can come to an understanding,' he smarmed and wrote Petherwick a cheque for £500 pounds.

Further questioning established that Foxnash hadn't been out of Frinton in nine years, except for one brief visit to Eva's red room which had been a male-menopausal lapse which he had ever afterwards regretted.

Clive Leggett ran an antique shop in nearby Nigly. He was polishing spoons when Petherwick burst into his shop and stood on his chest in her high heels.

'*Thissun's a real villain, Chief. Over.*' she told the walkie-talkie.

Leggett admitted to being a client of Eva's, his excuse being that he could only maintain an erection if there were a good number of bananas in the room. In saying this his eyes strayed towards a fruitbowl half-full of bananas. Movements in his corduroy slacks, meanwhile, suggested a hamster trying on hats in a collapsed tent. Petherwick hated every penis in the world but one. She didn't like hamsters either. A casually dropped vase dispatched another penis/hamster to wherever they go when they die.

Checking through old receipts she established that Leggett was busy selling junk in his shop on the days of enough of the murders to convince her of his innocence. Two down, thirty-five to go.

Brigadier-General Theodoric Vickers was so frightened by Petherwick's interrogation that all his war wounds opened. Bardolph Jubb gave himself up and showed Petherwick where he printed the money. James Gimbal had been in a coma on his kitchen table since before the last edition of THE EDDIE HADDOCK SHOW. His elderly sisters saw to his needs. George Arbuthnot had been walking in the Pyrenees long enough to provide an alibi. Wendel Fairweather was at an athletics meet at Troon the day Sidney Night was throttled with his hair-dryer. Albrecht Goudie was a definite possible: he maintained he'd been at the pictures every night for the past twenty-nine years, enough to get him off everything since Profumo. But it turned out he was a projectionist in Southend. Rex Fooch and Philip Dickenson had been closetted with the auditors of their animal foodstuff business during a crucial slice of the time in question. Rev. Samuel Cruttendon initially mistook Petherwick for somebody else and answered his door wearing nothing but a layer of custard and a well-placed cherry. It was later established that too much of his life was spent namecalling over fonts for him to have had time to murder anything except babies called Trevor, a name for which he had a particular loathing. Igor Banyard had recently died, but he too was ruled out, having been in prison for compulsive shoplifting during all but a few days of the 1980s, days spent visiting Eva's banana warehouse.

By now Petherwick had completely lost faith in Windscale's list. She was just going through the motions, walking up the pathway of one Broderick Cumber, in the sleepy English village of Lower Melford near Bury St Edmonds.

She picked up a dandelion clock growing among purple-and-white pansies.

'*Big Mama to Loverboy. Over.*'

Windscale awoke from a snoozy dream of sailing a Swiss roll in a chocolate ocean.

'Loverboy, here. Over.'

PLETHORA OF GITS

'*He loves me, he loves me not, he loves me, he loves me not . . .*' She puffed away at the clock, finally announcing the result: '*He loves me!*'

'Who does?'

'*You, silly.*'

Windscale blew kisses into his walkie-talkie. Petherwick blew bigger ones back, tearful because she despaired of ever clearing her hero's name.

Suddenly Broderick Cumber was beside her, dandelion seeds floating across his pale pixieish face.

'Mr Broderick Cumber?'

'Yes.'

'I should like to ask you a few questions. It shouldn't take very long.'

Cumber looked at a silent plane crossing the sky. 'What sort of questions?'

'Just to eliminate you from some enquiries.'

In his buff cardigan, tea-stained shirt and red slippers he was the epitome of English reasonableness. 'Come along in,' he said.

'*Am entering the premises of Broderick Cumber*,' reported Petherwick.

She stooped under the overhanging thatch and entered a cosy little timber-beamed room. Every shelf and alcove was filled with a collection of glass figurines. Sunlight cut the room in two. Cumber sat in the bright half, pouring tea. His hands entered the normal light, offering a cup-and-saucer to Petherwick. She sat down with it.

'What lovely knees,' complimented Cumber, boyishly.

'Thank you,' said a businesslike Petherwick between sips of tea. Her policewoman's instinct told her that a man who compliments a girl on the quality of her knees is incapable of murdering 1,340 comedians.

'Where were you on the night of October 21st, 1989?'

'Manchester.'

'Manchester?'

'Manchester.'

The light was so bright she could barely make out the expression on his smooth, newly-promoted prefect's face. The glass figurines caught the light and sent shards of rainbow all over the room.

Petherwick made a note next to Cumber's name in the address-book. He was in Manchester the night Eddie Haddock died.

'Do you remember where you were on November 3rd, that same year?'

'As it happens, I do. In Smethwick.'

'Smethwick?'

'Smethwick.'

On that night in a working-man's club in Smethwick Barney Fawkes told his last joke. Petherwick made more notes.

'And could you tell me what was the purpose of your visit to Smethwick?'

'Business.'

'What manner of business?'

'Personal business.'

The sun went in, darkening the room. She could see the comic killer properly now. He looked back at her with the dangerous calm of a sheep made of bees. The figurines, she noticed, were mostly men in battered hats, some were of men prodding other men in the chest, one was a man with a goose under his arm . . . doubtlessly Frankie Moss and Herman.

'These ornaments, do you make them yourself?'

'A harmless hobby of mine.'

'How many have you made exactly?'

'Exactly? One thousand, three hundred and forty.'

Petherwick reached for the walkie-talkie, but her arm was heavy and wouldn't move. She struggled with her eyelashes but they kept banging shut, snowing mascara on to her suddenly sore lips. The pencil fell from her fingers making the lightest of marks in the address-book.

Cumber was very close. He was sitting on her knee. He was shouting obscenities into the walkie-talkie. His face kept spinning up to her eyes: a planet of stone about to collide with a planet of flesh. But no pain. No feeling at all. Perhaps he was kissing her. Perhaps he was pouring more tea down her throat. The New Scotland Yard sign kept going around and around and around. The especially-favourite doll of her girlhood came walking stiffly from a night whose blackness was falling over clifftops into a waveless sea.

CUMBER

On 14 July 1958 a certain Sylvia Pitt was seated in an ice-cream parlour in Great Yarmouth, hunting a submerged cherry in her Mr Softy, when Pringle Dicks and his enormous stooge Sy breezed in in camel-hair coats which still reeked of camel.

These were the last days of Variety and Pringle Dicks was in his own last days of touring England telling the same forty-two jokes he'd told for as many years. Baggy-eyed and boozed up he sustained himself with the belief that a man is as old as the woman he feels. He looked up from his banana milkshake and felt his youth stiffening under the table as he caught the eyes of Sylvia Pitt, sitting some tables away in the otherwise empty establishment.

Sylvia was a virginal sixteen-going-on-seventeen who'd lived a secluded life in the demure seafront hotel run by her mam. She'd never seen a look as evil as the one on Pringle Dick's long mush. He bit his straw in the middle of a smile lascivious enough to snap the strings on the harp of any angel cloud-floating directly above.

The lost cherry was on her spoon awaiting a) her lips, b) her mastication, c) the juices of her belly. Dicks winked, shocking her into a sudden intake of breath which sucked up the cherry . . . straight down her gullet in one! Her admirer, meanwhile, sucked the last of his milkshake, continuing the suck to make a disgusting noise as long as Aida.

Sylvia wanted to bolt for the door. But the end-of-the-milkshake noise somehow kept her pinned down, as if under gunfire. He had to draw breath sometime . . . he had to . . . had to. He did. She ran for it . . . her freckles spinning around her nose, past Dick's imploring eyes, his shy snatch, the acromegalous guffaw of his stooge. She ran into the calm salty air and hung over a rail on the promenade.

A boy from the ice-cream parlour found her there. 'Here, you hassent paid for your ice-cream.'

She'd been sick and was pawing through the sick in panic, saying: 'It's not here! It's not here!'

'What ain't?'

'The cherry . . . it's gone. GONE!!!'

The boy retreated a step.

Her fingers were down her throat. She retched. Nothing. She tried again. Nothing.

'One and threhpunce,' asked the boy.

Pringle Dicks and Sy were walking along the promenade towards them, Sy the proud owner of a red balloon with a face on it.

'HIM!!!' screamed Sylvia, pointing at the approaching Dicks and grabbing the boy by the lapels of his white coat. 'HE'S JUST GOTTEN ME PREGNANT, THAT'S ALL!!!!'

Dicks lifted his pork-pie hat to say good afternoon, but Sylvia pushed the boy into him. Sy let go of his balloon with a horrified mute gasp, more tragic than any he'd ever done on stage, he watched it rise ever smaller into the stratosphere.

Sylvia tripped down some steps, over a sewerage-pipe redoubt and dashed between sandcastles to put as great a distance between her and Dicks as between Sy and his balloon. Losing both shoes in the sinking sand where the waves were crawling Bermudaishly but cold. Every time she looked back he was still there, waving and smiling. But at least she couldn't see the yellow of his smile, then she couldn't tell him apart from the figures gathering around him. She was alone with her bellyache and the tiny stickleback of a Pringle Dicks suddenly alive in her womb.

Sy, meanwhile, couldn't be persuaded to move from the spot, or take his eyes off the sky. It was dusk before his head dropped. A Salvation Army band passed by and it broke the spell of his misery. But his small sorrow had made a broken man of Sy. He died in Whitby that winter in a bed much too small for him. Another giant took his place in the act and no one was the wiser.

Sylvia, meanwhile, had panted into the tea-time at her mam's hotel. She removed the scarlet ribbon from her hair and shook her curls free.

'I'm pregnant,' she announced.

Crumbs whirled around the cake-tray.

PLETHORA OF GITS

Her mam instantly blamed a recuperating acrobat, Humbert Cumber. At that moment he was limping in from the garden with a balloon he'd found.

'I shall marry the girl, of course,' he said.

Nine months later, on April Fool's Day, 1959, at 4.22 in the afternoon, Broderick Cumber was born, in room thirteen of this same hotel, the Battenburger Arms, Yarmouth. At that precise moment PC W.E. Windscale, a mere sylph in those days at 28 stones, pounding his beat in Reading, a small blue helmet on a head big with a youthful bloatedness, was fishing a drowned dog out of the Kennet Canal and slopping it at the plimsolled feet of its grief-paled owner.

Cumber was a strange baby who became a strange infant who became a strange little boy. The death of his father in an acrobatic slip-up and the conversion of his gran and mam to Evangelical Christianity had the effect of making him even stranger.

Always a little unwell, he only had to hiccup and his mam would say: 'Better not go to school today, precious.'

So he wandered the hotel, playing long, lonely games which always ended with him hiding in a wardrobe of one of the rooms. One day Eddie Haddock stayed in the hotel. Cumber sat in the cupboard and watched him through a knothole. He was running through one of his monologues or just talking to himself, it was impossible to guess which.

'... So he catches all these prawns hisself, see, and trains them up wiv a whip, singing them Bulgarian songs, wot they sings to themselves later on when they've been put in the wellingtons. My rabbit, he knows why he does it but he won't never say. Sez who?' Silence for a moment, a gap for applause, maybe, but then, looking sadly at the looming wardrobe, 'You's there, isn't yer? Cummon, I knows you's there. You's one of them Bulgarian spies or I'm a kipper.'

Cumber slowly came out, a six-year-old boy in his pyjamas.

Haddock was on the bed, shaking with fear. The bedsprings creaked.

'That's a better disguise than yer lastun.'

'I was hiding from me mam.'

'I've got a mam 'n all. Yer won't kill her, will yer?'

'What wiff?'

'Prawns,' said Haddock, as if it were obvious.

But Cumber wasn't always lucky enough to be mistaken for a Bulgarian. One time he fell asleep in the wardrobe of Room 9 and woke up to see through the crack a stout woman doing her exercises, wearing only socks and a faded tattoo. The crack kept revealing different lengths of her, like a pornographic bacon-slicer with a furball stuck in its works.

In search of a mirror on the back of the wardrobe door, better to observe her knee-bending and stomach pulling-in, this health-conscious guest screamed at the sight of two beastly eyes spinning in tune to the wobble of her purple breast-ends.

Mrs Cumber had him by the ears.

'Are . . . you . . . a . . . Christian?'

'Is!!! Is!!!'

'What . . . does . . . Jesus . . . do . . . to . . . naughty . . . little . . . boys?'

'I doesn't know!!'

'YES . . .' A slap. '. . . YOU . . .' Another slap. '. . . DO!!!'

'He . . . he . . . heshrivelsuptheirwee-weething!!'

'That's right. He . . . shrivels . . . up . . . their . . . wee-wee . . . thing.'

'He wouldn't, would he? HE'D NOT NEVER!'

A melting. 'Course not, mammy's little treasure. Jesus loves you. He loves us all.'

But if Jesus loved us all, why did he allow Gran to fall over the bannisters, down the stairwell, killing herself and bonging the gong with its last and gonggggggggggmost gong? Jesus was after his wee-wee thing . . . he was sure.

It was his first major anxiety . . . Cumber was in constant fear that his wee-wee thing would shrivel up. He kept feeling it, twanging out his shorts for a quick look, and under the bedclothes he watched it for hours with a torch. Sometimes it did indeed look shrivelled up and his heart beat fast and he sobbed all night, saving each sob for a clank in the clankity plumbing: if anyone heard him sobbing, he'd be taken away and made to dig graves for the soldiers.

He also developed a small anxiety which was to grow huge with the years. It was an idea seeded by Haddock when he suggested the boy was in disguise. Cumber thought that he wasn't really himself, but a complete stranger disguised as a child and that any minute he'd be exposed and disappear, popping up to lead an entirely different life somewhere else. In a way it was excellent news, this idea . . . after all, if he popped up somewhere else it would take Jesus ages to find him again and his wee-wee thing would be safe.

'That's me,' he once boasted in the TV room to a red-nosed guest. 'There look, in the black hat.'

Bonanza was on the screen.

'Ah, you're a cowboy, are you?'

'Bang!'

'I'm an injun.'

'Why you here then, in that disguise?'

'Hum?'

'You escaped from the reservation, has yerh?'

'Uhk?'

He worried about this little exchange for years. Meanwhile, long hours were spent in the bathrooms of the hotel, alone with the tunes of dripping taps, examining his face in extendable shaving-mirrors, searching for a sign of who he might be, yanking his cheeks, hunting up his nose. And always trousers-down, his wee-wee thing in one hand. He was terribly worried about it. If he was an adult in disguise, why was his wee-wee thing so weenie . . . why wasn't it long and hairy and fat like the ones he'd seen swinging from the groins of salesmen on their way to the third floor bathroom.

It must be in disguise too. His real wee-wee thing was inside him, huge, sleeping on a bed of its own hair, like a serpent in a storybook cave. In his nightmares Saint George – there was a painting of him dragoning in reception – kept galloping up his poosy bottom into a long darkness that was like an endless corridor of the hotel. He kept opening doors looking for Cumber's real wee-wee thing, only to find naked women of all kinds, surprised before their mirrors, every one with his mother's limp face in their make-up-mucky hands.

He'd wake up screaming. Deep down, it was the thing that terrified him most. If he was someone else, and he certainly was, and if he disappeared, he'd lose his mam forever. He loved his mam passionately. He wanted to be at her skirts always. But if he was someone else, and this was undoubtedly true, then he wasn't his mam's son, which meant he could marry her when he was a bit older. This idea kept him warm for a whole termtime. Then a penny dropped into the sinister pool that was flooding his young mind, a penny that fell through his slot towards other pennies after his cowboy-injun exchange with the salesman . . . if he himself was in disguise, why wouldn't everyone else be in disguise too . . . and why not his mam also? Perhaps his real mam was long dead? Or was that drooping aspidistra which had replaced the gong in the stairwell his real mam in disguise? Once when Sylvia Cumber slapped his legs for wetting his bed he blurted out: 'You're not my mam! Take that disguise off!' And he snatched at the crease under her chin, expecting to get her face off and find a witch underneath.

The child was not yet wholly insane, but well on the way. Lots of things started him off, but what really launched him, there can be little doubt, was that suggestion of Haddock's. It was the cue for Cumber's lifelong mad screech. After that idea filled his mind he was lost for always. An idea suddenly popped up like a log in the stream of consciousness, can block the stream and generate chirruping beavers who madly make new landscapes full of frights and distortions. Such an idea can come to anyone, anytime and can ruin a life . . . once had, it can never be rubbed out, it creates a new world, seen through its own perceptions. True, in this life of snakes and ladders, some are prone to snakes, others to ladders. Cumber was one of those who always have a hissing at their feet, are always about to drop. Haddock passed him the dice with which he threw his first snake's eyes, thereafter many queer ideas were his slides in a park loomed by sinister red skies and trees gone unreal. Cumber was ruined by a train of thought that got above its station in a musty hotel room long ago and that would end by clipping hellbound tickets for every comic who ever punched jokes down the line. And Haddock, having made his suggestion, though it came from the prison of his own weirdness, was an accomplice in his own dispatch, a slow throttle, coming twenty-four years later in Cumber's head of steam.

At age eight Cumber hid in wardrobes all the time, desperate to see someone removing their disguise. He saw many disgusting things, but never quite that. One ancient lady covered her face in white goo, and when she wiped it off there was an even older lady underneath, but this wasn't the spectacular proof he wanted.

Then one day he was in room 13, deep in the wardrobe behind a suitcase and some smelly shoes, when his mam giggled into the room with a mustachioed sales representative whose boily neck had fascinated him at supper last night. The rep next appeared before the knothole trouserless, his shirt flapping over boily thighs. He suddenly swan-dived onto the bed pulling his shirt off at the same time, showing a boily bottom and a boily back which flipped over to present a wee-wee thing redder and sorer than an explosion at a stop-sign.

Next thing, his mam was in the picture, nudified holding the rep's wee-wee thing, him going: 'Sylvia! Sylvia!' Her going: 'Dennis! Dennis!' Then her throwing a white leg over him and sitting on the wee-wee thing, bouncing up and down on it, not going 'Dennis!' now but: 'JESUS! JESUS! JESUS! JESUS!'

Cumber wet himself, weeing over and warming his entire crouching position. He was sure Jesus would appear. He'd been told he did, at suppers and on hikes, to worry people. He'd appear now, for certain. He'd shrivel that horrible wee-wee thing the rep was so proud of, for sure! But his mam! His poor mam! She'd have something horrible done to her too!

He crept bravely out of the wardrobe . . . his mam and the rep were too busy to notice . . . and tiptoed out into the corridor. He immediately ran as fast as he could screaming: 'HERE, JESUS! JESUS! JESUS! JESUS! JESUS!'

If he could get Jesus to catch him, perhaps he'd miss what his mam was up to. He slid down the bannisters, something he knew Jesus was particularly against, and rolled on to the doggy smelling carpet to come up against a man's dusty shoes.

Looking up he saw an unshaven man with a porkpie hat shoved over long hair and the most unusual eyes he'd ever seen.

'JESUS!' Yelled the boy.

The man pulled him to his feet, all gruff. 'You belong here, kiddo?'

An affirmative nod.

'I've been owt'n'in twice. Where is everyone? I got a room booked.'

They boy stood on a chair to consult the hotel register. 'Errr, what name might it be?'

'You know who I am. Everyone knows.'

'Course I knows yerh, course . . . but you'll not be using yer proper name, will yerh?'

'Pringle Dicks! PRINGLE DICKS!'

It was indeed, none other than . . . who he said.

Cumber gave him the key to room 34. Before he went up Dicks said something very strange to the lip-wobbling boy: 'Know any giants, does yer? Nother one just died on me.'

The boy hid in the leaves of the aspidistra, gripping his wee-wee thing with both hands, watching up the stairwell as the hand of the new guest slid higher and higher up the bannisters. When it at last let go Cumber looked at his wee-wee thing in amazement. Miraculous! It was standing on end! His first ever!

He found his mam in the pantry. She was wearing her dirty yellow dressing-gown, her black-soled feet slipping in and out of her furry slippers as she chastised herself with fingernails whose polish was three-quarters off. She muttered apologetic prayers.

'Mam.'

'I've been a bad girl. Jesus will hate me!' she whimpered to her beloved boy.

'He's here.'

'Who is?'

'Jesus. In Room 34.'

Windscale was desperate to find out what had happened to Sergeant Petherwick.

'Stephanie! Stephanie!' he kept moaning. 'Where art thou, Stephanie?'

Everyone who overheard him suddenly bent over with a tingle, kissed their own hands and went: 'Ooooooooourgh!' The prison governor sat squirming at his desk for half an hour while the great criminologist told him about Stephanie and this Broderick Cumber creature.

'I am innocent.'

'They all say that.'

'But I am!'

'They all say that as well.'

'It was him!'

'That's usually what they say next.'

'Oh, Stephanie!'

'Ourgh!'

'Stephanie!'

'No, stop it, please, no more.'

'STEPHANIE!'

PLETHORA OF GITS

'Oooooooooooooooooooooooooooooooourgh!!!!!!'

He had enough multiple orgasms to beat Sodom in the semi-final of an orgasm contest, meeting Gomorrah in the final.

Windscale's heart ached with worry. Cats clawed the fatty deposits from each ventricle, letting more blood through to his beset brain, awakening all his memories of Petherwick, who at that moment, sad to say, was being sawn into pieces by Cumber on his kitchen table.

Swallowing all pride, Windscale wrote to Claeverlock explaining the situation to him. But Claeverlock was engrossed in studying the way the evening sun over Loch Uskavagh affected his armpits . . . he was then painting his *SELF PORTRAIT WITH ARMPITS*, now on display at the National Gallery of Scotland, and which, with its ginger spots and lines, looking like bacteria in the bottom of a marmalade jar, is regarded as a potent symbol of Scottish manhood in a Jacobiteless age. Claeverlock sketched an armpit on the back of the envelope but didn't bother to peruse the desperate plea within.

Einstein suggested a rooftop protest and got the hippopotomic Windscale up there by deftly hypnotising him into believing he was a housefly. So, having flailed against a succession of windows for days, pursued by screws wielding rolled newspapers, Windscale succeeded in breaking through a skylight onto the prison roof, immediately unfurling a bedsheet on which this demand was broadcast: ARREST BRODERICK CUMBER.

No one took the slightest notice. The Governor sniffed Welshly saying: 'He'll come down when he's hungry.'

Indeed, if it wasn't for his magic Mars Bar and buns catapulted up by a passing anarchist, Windscale would have been quickly defeated by hunger pains. He held his fizzing walkie-talkie constantly to his ear, hoping for Petherwick's ookums voice to break the emptiness, but there was nothing to hear except faint fading-outs-and ins of faraway torch-songs which just as easily could have been wailing from his own lovesick subconscious.

Einstein improvised a megaphone from two toilet rolls, a toilet and a vacuum cleaner. When shouting into it, no actual noise came out, but by some method connected to the little man's psychic abilities, Windscale's explanation of the comic killings and the peril of his beloved Sergeant Petherwick came out of people's toilets over a fifteen-mile radius.

The Bishop of Durham spent a busy weekend unsuccessfully exorcising toilets and suffered a nervous breakdown when Windscale interrupted his usual subject to sing extracts from *The Desert Song* like a headless Pavarotti. He knew none of the words and had never heard the music, so the noise he made was like that of a self-destructive shepherd eating a sheepdog pie. Many swore they'd never go to the toilet again.

The rooftop protest was a flop. The local TV covered it only to say that the protestor had concussed the skulls of fifteen scullers by skimming rooftiles on the river.

'It was sixteen!' roared Windscale.

After three weeks of increasingly damp weather, sneezing through his megaphone, causing toilet seats to leap up as far away as Crawcrook, Windscale abandoned the protest.

A nervous Governor was waiting at the bottom of the ladder.

'The Home Secretary wants to see you at once,' he said.

'Ugth?'

'There have been certain developments in your case.'

'Developments?'

He showed him that morning's *Sun*. It had started again! Of the forty-one members of the *nouvelle vague* comedians, thirteen were already dead. Cumber was on the rampage.

Hank Dean, while doing a Zorro send-up, had been Saint Sebastianized by a hedgehog's worth of épées. Hecate Smedley, while doing one of her nude bubble-bath routines, where she lay with a toe up each tap talking of girlish concerns simultaneously soaping her bosoms, suddenly sank like a fleshy Lusitania. The investigating officer discovered two poison darts, one in each big toe, ingeniously shot along the plumbing system. Davey Buttermere entered a doctor's sketch weeping, a frequent feature of his act, and when he pointed out the writhe of red-and-white tubing spinning out of his belly the audience split its sides. But this was his large intestine unravelling itself between there and the taxi outside where Cumber had said his helloes. Peggy Lewes went upstairs to spank her children goodnight and found them tied-and-gagged on their rocking-horses. Cumber stepped out of the shadows and slit her throat with a Swiss Army knife. The children later wept in the arms of policewomen, telling of how Cumber had lingered for hours reminiscing about his own childhood. Snog Duffie had a lucky escape when, while on a visit to his stockbroker, a grand piano fell from the top of the Lloyds Building. It missed by inches, spattering his spangled suit with black-and-white keys like the spelling out of a tune from the spirit world.

Loveridge placed a plate of marmite sandwiches under Sir Cyril Passey-Wix's nose.

His eyelashes fluttered him out of his thoughts till he blinked over the sandwiches.

'I'm not hungry, thank you, Loveridge.'

'Go on, sir, just a nibble.'

With a long fingernail the great statesman lifted a corner where Loveridge's knife had missed a bobble of crust. He sniffed marmite and coughed delicately.

His rabbitish front-teeth were about to tear a morsel from a sandwich when there was a screech outside. Windscale tumbled out of a Black Maria like a single huge bean from a can.

Sir Cyril leaped from his desk, flew past Loveridge, leaving his tie embarrassingly erect in the air, and flung open the outer office door. Windscale was about to knock with a grubby convict's hand. Sir Cyril grabbed the hand in a sudden passionate tizzy.

'Oh, Chief Superintendent, you are here at last! You are my only hope!'

Windscale covered his eyes. He daren't gaze upon his hero, the man he most admired in all of human history.

Sir Cyril led him to the conference table, pushed two chairs together, sat him down and fed him a brief snack of marmite sandwiches.

'What can we do? What can we do?' mewed the Home Secretary, his hands pummelling the highly polished table with fists that squeaked.

Windscale gingerly opened two fingers over his eyes. He flinched! He saw Marshall Overkirk sweeping across the French flank in an angry depiction of Oudenharde that filled the wall opposite.

'Painted by Gainsborough after a row with his wife,' explained Sir Cyril.

A change of mood from Windscale, fingers out of his eyes, staring with the miffedness of a bear at the back of a fishshop queue who knows the fish will run out with the man in front. Sir Cyril's urine froze in his pipes.

'I've been up the river for over five years,' said the detective slowly.

'Have you? That long. Oh, I am sorry. Terribly sorry. So, so, sorry. Tell him how sorry I am Loveridge.'

'Very,' said Loveridge.

'See. I couldn't be more sorry.'

'Really?'

'Oooooh, yes,' and he stroked the back of Windscale's hand with an elegant white hand of his own.

Windscale went all bashful.

Loveridge, meanwhile, whose eyes had been crawling up and down Windscale's heft since he staggered in, was stroking his right knee to further placate him. Had someone said Stephanie just then Loveridge would have moaned like a platypus at the end of *Gone With The Wind*.

'By the way, I know who the comic killer is,' said he of the marmite breath.

'You do!'

'He does?'

'That's what he said. Who? Pray, who?'

'He's called Broderick Cumber.'

'No!'

'Bloody is.'

Windscale pulled out a roll of printout. It was everything on Cumber in police files. Sir Cyril was all smiles, even his quiff looked pleased. But there wasn't much info on the printout. His smiles descended.

'That's all we've got on im. He's a clever bastard and I'm going to have his arse.'

'His arse?' twitched Loveridge.

'In this hand!' yelled Windscale, holding a Zeus-like hand over its mahogany reflection in the scratchless tabletop, which otherwise reflected the host of pink cherubs that jammed the ceiling.

Suddenly a letter arrived, skating across the table from cherub to cherub. From Loveridge's vantage it looked as if it came from the hand of Prince Eugene of Savoy, who was making a letter-tossing gesture in the middle of Oudenharde. The letter skooted past Windscale's reaching fingers to be pinned by Sir Cyril's littlefingernail.

'For you, I think.'

It was addressed to FAT GIT COPPER.

'Must be,' said Windscale and opened it with the letter-opener Loveridge drew from behind his ear.

There was nothing inside the envelope but six Victoria Station left-luggage tickets. Windscale gulped.

'Opera?' asked Loveridge.

'Hm?'

'Tickets for tonight's opera?'

'Only if its one of them operas where they all gets marmalized at the end.'

'Let's all go, shall we!' Loveridge was in a skittish mood.

But Windscale's instinct was studded with policetunicbuttons: there was something deadly about these tickets. As they arrived at Victoria Station – Sir Cyril and Loveridge in the taxi, Windscale being pulled along behind on a sparking rollerskate – butterflies were using morse code to beat out their last wills and testaments on his stomach wall.

Loveridge handed over the first two tickets to a tired West Indian in need of a sunny day.

'Fetch these tout suite, my good man.'

He looked at Loveridge as if confronted by a zarnth, but was too tired to swap insults. On legs full of joints he soft-shoe shuffled into the racks of backpacks, haversacks and suitcases. He came back with two large trunks, dragging them effortlessly, his lips moving in a song of his own making which he would never sing again. Having pushed the trunks up to Loveridge's toes he rubbed his tired eyes with his black-and-brown fingers. Then a sudden massive smile which struck Loveridge's ego hard. It had the loss of Empire in it and worse: cricket balls caught in two fingers during an England collapse.

Windscale put a trunk under each arm and hurried down damp steps into the gents. Sir Cyril and Loveridge followed him into a cubicle, Loveridge being delayed in meeting several acquaintances standing dryly at the pissoir. Windscale cracked the first trunk open on his knee. The bodies of four throttled comedians bobbed out like jackinaboxes on a weak spring. Loveridge shrieked at length. (His loitering friends assumed he'd passed another kidney stone.)

'Comics, I suppose,' said Windscale, whose in-the-jug years left him ignorant of recent famousnesses.

But Sir Cyril, though faint, was surprisingly knowledgeable: 'Timmy Floot, Eric Munchie, Sarah Higgins and Brian Jakers. Poor darlings.'

As Windscale lifted the second trunk on to his knee Sir Cyril bit right through a handful of his pretty nails. He was unnaturally trepidacious, as if one of these comedians meant something to him: twas so . . . the politician's secretest secret was that Snog Duffie was his illegitimate son! After another shrieking kidney stone from Loveridge, he sighed with relief at the second set of stiffos. No Snog Duffie!

'Silas Gint, Perry Lonsdale, Ettie Sharps and isn't that Pelham Groome?'

'I wouldn't know.'

'I'm fairly sure it is.'

They climbed over into the next cubicle, Windscale accidentally flushing Loveridge back into the first one in the effort, and hot-footed it upstairs to the left-luggage again.

Sir Cyril handed over two more tickets.

'Make it snappy, will you,' he ordered.

The sleep fell out of the corners of the left-luggage man's bloodflood eyes. He snapped his fingers languidly as he walked off like someone walking a tightrope through a snowdrift. He came back with a tuck box and a battered suitcase with *Llandudno* and *Magaluf* on it in stickers.

The trio took these to the second cubicle.

'Hurry up, hurry, let's see . . .!' panicked Sir Cyril.

Loveridge stayed outside, telling a friend: 'I've had such a horrid day, dear, and now I've got this splitting headache.'

Windscale did some splitting of his own. A karate-chop on the tuck box let forth a packed-up picnic of bloody paper plates and jelly dishes with slops of raw liver in them. At the bottom of all this, so Sir Cyril pronounced with another sigh of relief, was Erwin Irwin, the cheeky chappie, whose cheeks were now ripped asunder, whose sorry eyes pled for just one more joke, just one, please, one more . . . but then another and another, all lost in darkness now.

The suitcase wasn't locked. Windscale's thumbs made clicks and hesitantly lifted the lid all by themselves. Sir Cyril sucked a Nuttall's minto with relief. Four hacked-at bodies were bent in a whirl of arms and feet, something left behind by a cruel ventriloquist who'd dropped showbusiness on hearing the Gestapo was recruiting again.

Sir Cyril identified: 'Rowland Meese, Queenie Tremayne, Gussy Todd and . . .' Windscale shook the contents for him. 'Errm . . . Blanco White, that's his nose, I'm sure.'

And so up at the left-luggage again . . .

Windscale handed over the last two tickets. He didn't say anything. He just looked, with all the menace of all the sharks on earth, grown legs and walking up the beach at Montego Bay.

The left-luggage man zoomed like a pinball collaborating with the player and dropped two holdalls afore Windscale with a single pant.

Sir Cyril couldn't wait. He unzipped one there and then and poured three heads on to the counter. He sighed with relief. But Windscale was staring tearfully into the other one. He didn't have to look any deeper. He recognized the knees.

Sir Cyril pawed in for the head like a duchess desperate for her lipstick. 'Don't know this one,' he said pulling out a pouting face by a chestnut pigtail.

'I do,' said Windscale, quietly.

'Oh?'

'STEPHANIE!!!'

A train crashed into the buffers. Windscale thought it was his heart breaking.

'This,' said Sylvia Cumber, her hand on the boy's head, 'is your real father.'

Pringle Dicks was alone in the dining-room, reading the obituaries column of *The Stage* while eating cold beef bourguignonne with a spoon.

'Bloody Nora!' he said.

'Daddy!' yelled young Cumber and ran through a haze of pepper that had been on its way to the bourguignonne before the shock of his mam's announcement had left Dicks overshaking in mid-air.

Dicks sneezed manfully. Mam sneezed orgiastically. Cumber came out of his childish sneezes to hug a man who'd never been child-hugged before.

Dicks treated him like something worrysome that canoodles you in a zoo car-park . . . he patted him on the head and said: 'There's a good boy.'

He didn't remember poking Sylvia Cumber. That leering day in the ice-cream parlour had faded from his memory. But he got drunk a lot, so maybe on a binge once . . . A father! Him! He laughed like Savanrola at the death of a Pope. Cumber handed him a napkin to wipe his snots away.

'Thanks, son,' he said.

Mrs Cumber idly ate melba toast while she sang *Ave Maria* and wept.

Pringle Dicks took over their lives, the hotel, everything. He moved into room 6 – it had the best view, including a bit of the theatre. When he wasn't on tour he sat in there in his vest and shorts smoking cigars, sometimes flinging open the window to swear at seagulls.

Every time he came back from tour he had a new giant.

'They're always bloody dying on me, the bastards.'

Cumber, to please the man, conceived a plan of growing into a giant himself.

'How come you's so big, then?' he asked the latest, a rake with a voice like soft thunder.

But he made no answer, having just died on the sofa in the TV lounge.

Dicks's giants got smaller and smaller, till they weren't much above his own height. It had ruined the act. There were places where his audience had always laughed before, lines that never failed. Now, it was like reciting the sermons of Archbishop Tait: the smaller and smaller giants were like his PRINGLE DICKS shrinking on the billboards, his belters wrong-end-of-the-telescoping into squeaks. He drank more. He took his troubles out on his new family.

'Stop singing that, you nasty little runt!'

Cumber had taken to following him about the corridors singing *Oobladee-ooblada*, a popular song of the time. He also had a habit

PLETHORA OF GITS

of saying: 'Jesus wouldn't like that.' and 'I think I'd better tell mam.' Especially when Dicks took the pass key and went kleping beer money off the sleeping guests.

'Jesus wouldn't like that.'

'This is for Jesus. I puts it in the box in church.'

'I think I'd better tell mam.'

'Naw, she'll only want to give more herself, ter outdo me like, then there'd be no dosh for sweeties, would there, son?'

'Here, what yous doing in my room? And my wallet!' A guest had returned from the bathroom.

'Collecting the money for your bill. You've been flung, mate.'

'But why? What have I done?'

'You know, you dirty bastard!'

'I think I'd better write to President Nixon,' said Cumber.

This, perhaps because he saw visions of President Nixon after a serious binge, worried Dicks considerably. 'Please don't! Please!'

Sylvia Cumber, now a buxom twenty-six, had become a mite over-religious. Taking her hint from a night of Dicks's drunken screaming, she conceived the conviction that President Nixon was the second coming. Cumber was informed of this and encouraged to write to him daily. Somewhat churlishly perhaps, he never replied. Mrs Cumber, who was fortunate in not living to see the Watergate episode, festooned the hotel with bunting left over from the 1969 Republican convention. It delighted the occasional American guest who added his horse to their one-horse town.

Dicks, meanwhile, was sure, with his brewer's droop, that every erection he had would be his last. He sat at his desk, chewing a cigar, and flipping through piles of erotic magazines. Occasionally the mysterious agency in his brain which allowed his excitement penile expression allowed his member to go slightly stiff. At these times he would rush about the hotel, holding the erotic photograph which had inspired stiffness in his mind's eye . . . and find Sylvia. He'd grab her and poke her, there and then, whatever she was doing, most embarrassing if she was pouring tea for a bevy of her religious friends.

'Jesus wouldn't like that!' Cumber would say, walking into a shocked room and seeing them at it on a table.

'Bugger off!'

'I think I'd better write to President Nixon.'

President Nixon ruined all Dick's erections. He hated President Nixon, hated Cumber, hated himself, hated everything. Dicks was a troubled man.

Then an evening of spoiled triumph which finished Dicks's career. He was second on the bill to *The Tremeloes* at the Wolsey Theatre, Ipswich, a charity do, and his act was going a bomb, even though his giant was 5'6", making all the giant jokes obscure.

'What's the weather like up there?'

The audience screamed.

'I'll fetch a ladder and punch yer narse for yer!'

When the audience finished rolling they were all in different seats.

Driving back to Yarmouth he said to his giant. 'Bugger me, if that wasn't the best audience I've ever had.'

'Yeah, must be nice for them to get out.'

'Huh?'

Apparently, the audience had been made up exclusively of loonies, mongols and similarly afflicted persons on an outing from local bins. Dicks kicked his giant out at the next lay-by. He vowed never to appear on stage again.

Back at the hotel he climbed into a bottle and took his bitterness out on Sylvia and the now pubescent Cumber. He only climbed out of the bottle he was in to hit his family with it.

He wandered the corridors, catching people fumbling with their keys. He flung one arm around them and slurred a weeping and indecipherable monologue, suddenly breaking off to perform his act with a lampstand in the giant's part. If his victims didn't laugh properly he left them unconscious in their doorways.

Cumber's mam was always black and blue. She'd developed a permanent wink and one of her bosoms had gone down. Dicks attacked her several times a day and was especially adept at pushing her over the bannisters. He also found amusement kicking her into the dumb-waiter and hauling her up and down. His drunken laughter never seemed to stop.

'Jesus sent him here as a punishment,' she explained to Cumber, her head flung back to disencourage a nosebleed.

The boy flung his arms around her. 'I'll protect you, mam,' he said.

'The Lord will soon see that I have suffered enough.'

PLETHORA OF GITS

President Nixon seemed to be running around her as she swooned. It was his various pictures spinning into her eyes from a wallful of cuttings.

Cumber prayed hard but his mam's beating continued. He had two black eyes himself and was always picking broken bottle out of his head. He phoned a bishop on a radio phone-in show and put the problem to him.

The bishop didn't hear the question right. He thought it was about pollution. 'It must be stopped immediately,' he said.

'Should I stop it?'

'We are all God's instruments,' he said.

'Would it be okay if I killed him?'

'Yes, certainly, an excellent idea,' said the bishop and kindly played *Oobladee-ooblada* for him at the wrong speed.

Dubbed God's instrument by the bishop, Broderick Cumber set about planning his first murder.

Pringle Dicks's favourite food was jam roly-poly and custard. If he wasn't inebriatedly unconscious or hiding from stalking spiders he ate several helpings every Saturday and ordered cook to lace it with so much rum that it was to no one else's taste.

The next Saturday Cumber swapped cook's pudding for one he'd made himself in the cellar. It was bluish with rat poison. Cumber sat in reception reading his Bible. Like a playwright waiting for the audience to come chatting out of a first night, he waited for the other diners to rush out yelling that Dicks had collapsed dead at table.

Half an hour passed. No one came out. He turned down the Radio 4 play . . . silence from the dining room: no sounds of cutlery clinking on plates, no low humm of inane chatter. He peeped in through the swing doors. Everyone was face down in their place: Dicks, his mam, red-nosed reps, everyone. The bluish pudding had looked so unusual that everyone fancied a mouthful. A mouthful had been enough.

Cumber would have joined them in oblivion, but they'd scoffed the lot. He wound himself around his mam's ever colder black-and-white legs and chuckled like a small waterfall in the Trossachs.

Cook fainted when she came in to clear away and again when she returned later with the police. Their flat feet walked into a room full of stale bunting and dead eyes staring into thick-skinned custard.

Cumber was suddenly loud: 'None of this is real, you know. Oh, no. The world was destroyed years ago. Nobody told me at the time. I've only just realized. I'm not me, anyway. I'm much older. Everyone loves me. President Nixon will vouch for me. But he's not there, is he? And neither are you. There's only me. Only meeeeeeeeeeeeeeeeeeeeeeeee! And, guess what: I'm someone else who isn't there.'

He was in a mental asylum before the next cock crew.

Dr Helmut Scrapie had quarrelled with Freud over a card game in 1926 and shortly afterwards had left Vienna for good. He had fought on both sides in the war and lost all his limbs at Arnhem. In 1948 he founded *Scrapie's*, an exclusive bin in the Leicestershire countryside. It sounded so much like a health farm that numerous stout women arrived at the door wanting their fat scraped off. They were used in the Doctor's experiments and returned to society, sylphlike indeed, but with fixed grins.

It was to *Scrapie's* that Broderick Cumber was sent in the autumn of 1971.

'Night,' said the Doctor.
'Black,' said Cumber.
'Sun,' said the Doctor.
'Burn,' answered Cumber.
'Grass,' said the Doctor
'Cuttings,' said Cumber.
'Horse,' said the Doctor.
'Penis,' said Cumber.
'Penis?'
'Wee-wee,' said Cumber.
'Penis?'
'Death,' said Cumber.
'Penis?
A pause . . .
'Mother,' said Cumber.
'Penis?'
'Hm?'
'I sayed horse unt you sayed penis?'
'Horses have penises, don't they?'
'Not all horses, Broderick. Not all.'

PLETHORA OF GITS

'Wot, some gets them chopped, does they?'

This brought on the Doctor's castration complex, an understandable weakness in a limbless man whose penis accomplished for him an unusual range of duties. He'd trained it to write, and with a selection of attachments it could manage anything a hand could manage except to masturbate itself.

'How'd I do?' asked Cumber, peeping at the notes the Doctor's member had made.

'You are completely . . . INSANE!!!' he pronounced. This was his shock treatment.

'Oh,' sighed Cumber, and made a sound with his teeth like a pair of scissors beheading paper dolls.

Scrapie's was not an unpleasant place. The good Doctor was a progressive whose philosphy declared that in life one should always seek something extra (in that card game with Freud he'd had five extra aces in his hand and fifteen more concealed). Instead of padded cells, this bin had playrooms full of toys. Rather than cruel-looking nurses it had dwarves dressed as Disney characters. There were no locks, no bars, and patients who didn't venture far in the grounds were unaware of the fifty-foot high electrified fence and the machine-gun towers, but even those were resplendent with pot-plants and security guards with Rapunzel hair.

Dr Scrapie was the only doctor. He sped benignly along the flower-lined pathways in a motorized wheelchair controlled by his penis.

Cumber was happy. There were, of course, the obvious drawbacks of any institution whose members were all lunatics and who have free range. Cumber was given reminders of Dicks's attacks by being regularly set upon by small gangs of Napoleons, or little gluts of Gods with unconvincing beards. Escaping from a dash of these one day in early spring, having been wandering the corridors weepily for four months, he slammed the door behind him and entered a new world of wonders. It was *Scrapie's* library, one of the best in England. The shelves were so long that they ended in a mist of dust, and went so high they disappeared in a woody numinousish crepeculartude. Cumber took down Morley's *Life of Gladstone* and began to read.

In this beautiful quiet place Cumber spent most of the following eight years, all his teenhood. How he read! Everything! His favourite place was at the top of the stepladders, just where the library's mysterious penumbra began. Taking out a book he could hardly see the title on the spine, but when it was opened the white of the page illuminated its lettering and soon he'd be discovering about Darwin's voyage on the Beagle, Eckermann's conversations with Goëthe, Otway's noble dramas. Looking down in moments of transporting thought he could see the bald head of the only other patient who frequented the library: a broken down academic who was writing an endless experimental novel consisting entirely of the word *thud* written over and over again on page after page after page. The novel was called, unsurprisingly, *THUD*. It was perhaps a revolution in English literature. The pen scratching *thud* was, apart from the occasional distant scream, the only background noise of Cumber's days. He never read the book, but it was a book you could read just by thinking about it, and this he found himself doing at many odd times, and also years later when in yet another attack of the habdabs he scanned thuds in his mind which slowly calmed him down.

One day, with the first heavy snow for years thick on the single thin windowsill, the novelist sat morose before his half-thudded page. Cumber passed with his Thucydides open at the battle of Sybota.

'How's it going?'

'Writer's block.'

'Thud,' said Cumber.

'That's just what I was looking for.'

His pen scratched onward, more silent volumes of thud.

Doctor Scrapie was delighted with Cumber's progress. He was, in his professional opinion, almost totally sane. He didn't even have a fixed grin! There remained only a few little worries. Why, for instance, did Cumber eat of no food but bananas? He tried a Rorschach ink-block test.

'Vot might dis be reminding you of?'

'Two bananas in a coalmine.'

'Unt ziz?'

'Six bananas being run over by a taxi.'

'Unt zis here?'

'A banana swallowed whole by a man subsequently shot in the belly with a double-barrelled shotgun.'

The Doctor detected a residue of violence in Cumber's attitude. Just as the youth was leaving the room, Dr Scrapie tried another of his little shocks: 'Unt how is President Nixon these days?'

'I've really no idea, sir,' he said.

The Doctor's penis doodled on his blotter. Nein . . . Cumber was not yet ready for release.

Shortly thereafter it was Cumber's eighteenth birthday. A Napoleonic party was held for him in the grounds. The machine-gun towers gave an eighteen-gun salute. Somebody strangled the conjurer, but otherwise fun was had by all. The musical chairs was won by a man who claimed to be invisible and who no one had noticed in the game until the last minute.

Afterwards, while Cumber was a spectator at the tennis court, watching a megalomaniac taking on Dr Scrapie (racquet in penis) and losing (it was part of his treatment), a flouncy girl sat beside him and said: 'I enjoyed your party?'

'Thank you,' he said. She was beautiful.

'Can I have a bite of your narna?'

'Sure.'

His narna was well down. Her lips brushed his thumb when she bit.

'You new here, are you?' He had the narna's end.

'Nar. Been here donkeys. I looks different today though, huh?'

Cumber was in love.

His beloved was Leslie-Ann McErrel. He didn't recognize her because, as a split personality, just hours before she'd appeared quite different: a mousey blond hangdogging by the pond, flicking grit at the guppies. Now she was a twittering charmer who'd have broken the heart of all but the strictest homosexual.

Thereafter Thud thudded alone in the library: Cumber spent every minute with Leslie-Ann. After kissing all morning in the laundry room they'd sally forth on afternoons of mischief. They got lots of fun following a certain pop-eyed paranoiacal man everywhere he went.

'I'm being followed,' he told Dr Scrapie.

'No. You are not being followed.'

'Something that giggles is following me, I tell you!'

'No! No! No!'

When they found this man hanging in an old noose in a tree in the shrubbery they laughed till they cried.

The night Cumber lost his virginity came after a long easy day of rolling on the grass together and a tea of banana sandwiches. Suddenly Leslie-Ann dropped her table-tennis bat and said: 'Shall we?'

'Shall we what?'

'You know.'

'You mean . . . ?'

'Yeah.'

They went to the library. At the end of the long table Thud was asleep, his pen dribbling in mid-thud. Cumber gripped his wee-wee thing in his hand the way he had in childhood. He was suddenly very frightened. Leslie-Ann pulled off her knickers, threw up her skirt and lay on the table with her legs spread.

'Get on with it!' she hissed.

But Cumber couldn't. His wee-wee thing was shrivelled. His eyes scanned the friendly shelves: they hadn't prepared him for this. She'd hate him if he couldn't manage it! But then, staring up her wide legs on the polish-smelling table, he remembered his mother flung on tables by Pringle Dicks and his mind twigged to a way out. He pretended he was Pringle Dicks and straightaway his penis went stiff and bigger than he'd ever seen it. He dived on to Leslie-Ann and ravished her like an over-sexed minotaur. She moaned like a masochistic mole dangling on a fence.

'How was it for you? smiled Cumber.

But Leslie-Ann was gone, hiding in an alcove among Kantian epistemology. She was hangdog.

'What's up?'

'She's gone.'

'Who is?'

'Her, the one you poked. I'm in charge now.'

Cumber had lived in a bin long enough to know what was up. He rattled her shoulders.

'Leslie-Ann! Leslie-Ann! Come back to me!'

'I'm Patsy, won't I do?' She slobbered in his ear.

'I want Leslie-Ann!'

She kept coming at him, so he hit her back with a copy of Sewell & Rutty's *History of the Quakers*. How he hated her for taking away Leslie-Ann! He enjoyed hitting her. It was better than the sex he'd just had. This was him! Not Dicks! Him! He hit her over and over and over.

PLETHORA OF GITS

Dr Scrapie wheeled in. He'd been alerted by the censoring devices which told him if sexual intercourse was taking place anywhere on the estate.

'Vat has happened?' he exclaimed, seeing Leslie-Ann's/Patsy's battered body on the floor, stamped with the dates of Quakers.

'I saw the whole thing,' said Cumber. 'I was up the ladders reading. It was him. He did it.'

Thud woke up at last from a deep sleep induced by a hard day's writing.

'Something the matter?' he asked.

He looked at the girl's body and the accusing faces. It was his old trouble.

'I see,' he said firmly, wrote one more *thud* on his page, put five suggestive dots after it, and left the room. An amazingly short time later his shadow fell past the slim window at 120 mph. He'd flung himself from a turret room, landing, it would otherwise have amused him to know, with a thud.

Dr Scrapie was very grateful to Cumber for his help in the aforementioned unfortunateness. He did what he always did to his much-improving patients. He gave him a shopping-list and sent him to Melton-Mowbray with it. Following at a discreet distance on his stumps, disguised as a large dachshund, the good doctor found nothing peculiar in Cumber's behaviour. He released him into the World shortly afterwards.

The hotel in Yarmouth had been sold some years before for £220,000, the money being deposited in a trust fund which profited from a boom in share prices after the election of the government of which Sir Cyril Passey-Wix was a prominent member. Cumber was a wealthy man.

He bought a cottage in his native Suffolk, at a village he found on a long thoughtful drive: Lower Melford near Bury St Edmunds, full of antique shops, retired colonels, jam-making grannies, and a cathedral-sized parish church. He settled down to live a quiet life of simple pleasures, rarely leaving the village except for brief trips to London to buy books for his ever-growing library. After what happened with Leslie-Ann he was scared to go near the sort of girl who turned his head, but sometimes while digging the garden a Pringle Dicksishness would rise in him and he'd speed in his MGBGT to the coast for an evening of passion and bananas with Eva Straight.

To the outside world he was a model citizen.

'What a nice young man,' said a farmer's wife to her friend.

She couldn't have known that the immaculately dressed Cumber was walking past with a mind just filled with a thought that would create other thoughts, resulting in the death of every British comedian.

An articulated lorry had thundered the High Street, making everything shudder . . . Cumber himself shuddered, a few paces ahead the farmer's wife and her friend shuddered . . . just like an orgasm, thought Cumber, amused . . . the world was having an orgasm . . . at the centre of the earth there was a huge sentimental testicle. Just then the lorry stopped, the shuddering stopped, the driver was leaning out of the window . . . he had a big clown's face and was laughing, looking Cumber's way and laughing. If, thought Cumber, there was too much laughter in the world, it would crack with a terrible ejaculation and drown everyone in spunk which would later turn into laughing fishes all with the face of Pringle Dicks which would swim in circles for seven years, then all sink and die. THE END OF THE WORLD IF THERE WAS ANY MORE LAUGHTER!!! He reassured his fizzing brain that wars, famine, pestilence and life's maddening frustrations would keep laughter down to a minimum.

But just as this thought slid between his ears, the truck shuddered again. The farmer's wife laughed. Her friend laughed. The truck wouldn't move: it just stood there shuddering, making people laugh. Cumber hurried on. Quickly passing a butcher's he saw the butcher chopping meat and laughing, laughing. He only saw it for a second but it stayed on his eyes for the rest of his life. Farther on, breathless, he rested in front of an electrical shop. A TV in the window had Frankie Moss and Herman the Goose wowing them on *Pebble Mill at One*. The TV studio was in hysterics. Cumber gripped his wee-wee thing. One more laugh . . . just one more and the world would split open.

'Five hands of bananas, please.'

The fruiterer laughed. 'Got a monkey stayin, has yerh? Harrrrr!!!!!'

Coming out he was hit by chortles like meteors. A pram-pushing mother across the road at the electrical shop was entertained by the sight of Herman Goose attacking a TV presenter. Cumber was about to scream like one of *Scrapie's* worst cases when a fortunate bag of cement fell from the back of that shuddering truck. THUD, it went.

'Thud, thud, thud, thud, thud, thud, thud, thud, thud, thud, thud, thud, thud, thud, thud, thud, thud, testicle, thud, thud, thud, thud, thud, thud, thud, thud, thud, thud, testicle, thud, thud, thud, thud, thud, thud, thud, thud, thud, thud, thud, thud, thud, thud, thud . . .'

He sat mantraizing this in a church pew for hours until his mind calmed down.

The dangerously insane train of thought was derailed. But it was a wonky hand grenade with the pin out rolling around an upturned dustbin-lid in a shut room in his brain. Every day, as he walked about, read Proust, cycled to the shops, it was deep inside ready to make a bang inaudiblizing all possible thuds . . . a moment would surely come when a kindred idea would come salmon-leaping from his stream-of-consciousness to be caught in the bearish claws of an electrical fizz such as make all brain communications . . . opening that aforementioned door to say: 'Here's a funny thing, now here's a funny thing . . .' before the hand grenade exploded in its face, sending out fizzes that would turn on all his lights, making his brain cells like everyone in the World watching the same unswitchoffable TV programme, a show designed to turn them crazy and succeeding.

He had other ideas that had similar potential. One day in Cambridge he was picnicking by the Cam with a recently-released acquaintance from *Scrapie's* when he heard a snatch of conversation from two passing American tourists.

'Say, don't that look like my brother?'
'Which brother?'
'Hoss.'

Cumber glanced at where they had glanced. It was a man riding a horse in a field. But, his mind asked itself without him concentrating on the question, was it the man who looked like the American's brother . . . or the horse? Obviously, the horse. He was alert now. Of course, he fizzed, all Americans are aliens who came to earth in 1884, aliens whose real shape is that of a fat horselike thing.

Punting students slid past, their faces full of high jinks. A hand-trailing girl gave Cumber a slow-lidded wink. Yes, everyone knew, it was common knowledge . . . this realization about Americans came to everyone, but they never told.

He ran after the tourists.

'I know! I know!' he jeered.

'Know what?'

'About Hoss!'

'Hoss? Say, you know Hoss?'

'I knows him.'

'Where from?'

Cumber knocked his stetson off.

'Haw!' went the American, picking it up. 'Hoss was always doing that when we were kids.'

Cumber knocked it off again.

Picking it up, the American gooed with sentiment. 'Yeah, and every time I picked it up, he knocked it off again.'

This might have gone on till dusk had not the American replicated his boyhood treatment of the annoying Hoss. He threw Cumber into the river and whinnied with laughter as he walked away, as happy as a slow draw who'd won a showdown.

Cumber heard the whinny as he came near surface in the olive-green water. When his eyes blinked dry he found himself looking up at a thirsty hummering horse. He swam hippophobicly down river to his picnic and shiveringly peeled bananas without eating them.

His Americans-are-horses-really fixation was mercifully brief, or instead of comedians writhing in his jam-jar, he'd have gotten the Injuns their lands back.

His everyone-is-in-disguise was perhaps his most regular worry. If, he reasoned, everyone is in disguise, then what difference does it make, because everyone is still somewhere. This eased his concern and made perfect sense of life's problems for him: the world was such a mess because everyone was playing a role they weren't ever sure of.

The idea was always a potent one. For instance . . . combining it with the American-horse theory he came up with this: Americans aren't horses because they're other people pretending to be Americans, the horse-people in fact being spread out all over the world . . . in which case some horse-people still might be Americans but at the same time also pretending to be Americans because they're not the same Americans that they're supposed to be. All this just to keep him, Broderick Cumber, confused. Actual proper horsey-type horses, meanwhile, planned the whole thing from a stables in Newmarket. He kept this under surveillance for nearly a year.

Another worry busied him after that. Coming home after a long drive he was stopped at traffic-lights in Sudbury and idly wondered why they were only ever red, orange or green . . . why never blue? But perhaps they did, to please themselves, when there was no one watching. He stood in a bank doorway for a whole winter of wee hours, blinklessly watching, waiting for the three colours to go blue.

A newly recruited police constable on his first beat saw him loitering suspiciously.

'Excuse me, sir. Are you perchance planning to rob this here bank?'

'I'm watching the traffic-lights to see them go blue. They do, you know.'

The copper's lip lifted strangely. 'That's a thing, sir, I must confess, wot I myself always kept a lookout for.'

The copper stood in the doorway with him for an hour or so. His lip kept lifting strangely in anticipation of blue lights, revealing red, orange or green teeth perfect for apple-chomping.

'They'll never do it in front of a horse,' said Cumber.

This remark set the copper's own brain fizzing. He thought better of the project, said an 'evening' and beated it, his boots clip-clopping away on the wet pavement.

Cumber's reading could also unbalance him. A piece in *The Sunday Times* maintained that Hitler was still alive. Sitting in his bath, the comic-killer-to-be held his duck firmly under the suds and fizzed on this idea. If Hitler was still alive and in disguise, and everyone was in disguise, then Hitler could be anybody, anybody at all! He drove all over England, stood on busy streetcorners and shouted: 'ADOLF!'

If anyone turned around, then that was the late Chancellor of Germany caught out in his new guise. It was this project that put extra inches on Cumber's police files, because during an eighteen month period he reported 7,654 people to the police as being Adolf Hitler. It seemed that whenever he shouted 'ADOLF!' someone turned around to see what was up. Cumber only desisted when a postman in Carlisle confessed in barking German and bit on a cyanide-filled tooth in the interview room.

Cumber's only comfort was in the arms of Eva Straight. He discovered her when reading the small print on the sticker of a banana he was eating: it discreetly offered her sexual services and gave a Clacton number. Pringle Dicks tingled in the air some nine inches above his lap: it was where his erection would reach under Eva's sure hand.

Without Eva he would have rampaged years before he did. With her he could indulge fantasies whose trains of thought never left the station. The happiest moments of his life were spent in her red-drenched room.

His favourite game began with them nude, facing each other, sitting on their toes, taking alternate bites from the same banana. It had, for some reason, to be a slightly rotten banana. After her third bite Eva had to say: 'Is it coming?' At which point Cumber would run up and down the aisles of the banana-icky warehouse yelling: 'It's coming! It's coming!'

When he returned he'd be equipped with an erection. Eva, meanwhile, was face down among her red cushions, pretending to be Cumber's poisoned mother.

In the voice of an amateur actor, Cumber: 'What has happened to everybody! Is it possible they have all been poisoned?'

Eva would spit out a mouthful of banana, saying: 'All but me!' and then spin around to receive Cumber's passionate dive which ended with a noise like a hamster being shot into warm honey.

After his hand grenade went off and he killed Frankie Moss, 150 miles away at Basingstoke, he drove immediately all the way back to Eva's. She fried him some bananas.

Shyly he said: 'I am a great man. I have saved the world.'

'Well done, you,' said Eva. She was used to such talk.

He returned to her after every comic-killing, which was often several times a day. Her other customers had to be extremely quick, if not premature. She indulged his every whim and never said an outrightly unkind word to his face. When she died in the fire which destroyed her cosy lovenest Cumber had a complete breakdown and was returned to *Scrapie's* for five years. During that time he didn't speak a word, terrified that if he did he'd tell a joke, someone would laugh and the world would crack open to fill with Pringle Dicks's shark-finned sperms.

He hadn't long been out when he saw Sergeant Petherwick coming up his path with a dandelion clock in her hand. Minutes

PLETHORA OF GITS

later he was delighted to kill her, delighted because he knew of her relationship with Windscale and his hatred of Windscale was greater than the sum of all his lunacies.

He hated him the first time he saw the bloated plod – Cumber was behind trees at Haddock's funeral. The reason was simple enough. Had Pringle Dicks had a giant stooge as gigantic as Windscale then his act would never have failed and he therefore wouldn't have started beating Cumber and his mam, meaning that Cumber wouldn't have had to poison him, in which case his mam wouldn't have been poisoned by mistake and would still be alive for him to adore. Also, his comic killer mentality fretted that if Pringle Dicks was to come to life again (and even yet he saw his bleary eyes at the heart of every shadow and suspected anyone with a lewd grin of being Dicks in disguise) then Windscale might indeed join up with him and create that extra Armageddonish giggle.

But perhaps most hate-making of all: it was Cumber's manic eagerness to finish off Windscale that made him set the fire which killed Eva. Everything was Windscale's fault! He'd make the fat git suffer, play with him like a cat, kill every comic there was . . . and then have Windscale for pudding. He'd risk a laugh of his own then . . . he'd laugh in Windscale's face while he died.

Cumber had to leave his pretty little cottage for good after what he did to Petherwick. He lived in cheap hotels, never more than a few nights in each. Not only was the entire police force after him, but Dr Scrapie was hunting him in his penis-controlled motorized wheelchair.

The excitement of his recent killings had had a physical effect on Cumber. Without the antidotal calm of his visits to Eva's, he became a wheezing mass of insane hatred. His hair stood on end, his face widened, his lips thickened. He looked like an electrocuted clown whose bitter antics would cause people to cover the eyes of their children and empty the circus-tent in silence.

One hand always gripped his wee-wee thing, which was now permanently erect and forever ejaculating inside his trousers. The other hand held a knife, not for killing comedians, but for himself: his belly was full of suppressed laughter. He was ready to stab its deadly bubbles if it dare come out. It jumped up his throat like a sickly meal, making sudden noises like a panda being gut-punched.

One night he checked into the Battenburg Arms, Yarmouth. He was returning there after a twenty-year absence. It was much the same.

With his sudden noises, his rolling eyes and uncontrollably wiggling ears he looked a dreadful sight.

'Are you all right, mister?' asked the youth on reception.

Cumber's face was grinning hugely. He panted like a puppy in a plastic bag. Down his cheeks huge tears rolled, falling on to his fingers where he felt them like Hardy Amies feeling bad cloth.

In the TV room three sleepy reps were watching Snog Duffie doing a stand-up. Duffie was begging Cumber through the screen: 'Please, don't kill me. I'm too young to die.'

Cumber pushed open the dining-room doors. He saw the scene just as it had been two decades before: all the diners face down on their plates. He saw himself cuddling his mother's dead leg, laughing at the wild stranger who stood at the door.

'Dinner's finished, I'm afraid, sir. I could get cook to make a sandwich.'

'A banana sandwich, that would be nice.'

'I'll see what I can do, sir.'

'There's only one left, you know.'

'Banana?'

'Comedian.'

'Oooooo, yeah. Tragic, ain't it?'

These days the aspidistra in the stairwell reached the third floor. Cumber mounted the stairs with a cackle that opened a crack in the wall. Then another cackle! He stabbed its invisible route towards the wall where the first cackle was waiting to take it to the centre of the earth. He must stop! He had to stop! But he couldn't help himself. He was going to kill Snog Duffie tomorrow, then Windscale, then himself.

SEVENTEEN THOUSAND CUSTARD PIES

Windscale had attained his life's ambition. He was the Commissioner of the Metropolitan Police. But he could feel no joy. A world without Petherwick was a bowl of fruit without fruit, cherries especially. He kept remembering things he'd always dreamed of doing when he'd made it to Commissioner, but the non-existent fruit in that fruitbowl went rotten every time he reached for it. Brilliant policing ideas withered on his brain-stem every time he squeezed one from the empty toothpaste tube that was his policemanness. No longer was he a policeman. He was a man who had loved and lost.

His new uniform was as blue as an August dusk over Sorrento, its shiny buttons like stars gone supernova in appreciation of a perfect love. Windscale mused on this image of a better life: himself rowing Petherwick to Capri, bending forward to kiss her after every pull of the oars. He wanted to holiday in this daydream forever. Indeed, in the corner of his eye he could see little seafront bistros opening for business, a sunny morning after a rainwashed night. He was slipping towards a sojourn in *Scrapie's*. But reality intruded into his fantasy: throat-slashed comedians followed his rowboat like dead dolphins still swimming, Petherwick suddenly fell to bits at his side.

His bleak new office immediately sank into his eyes like a grey shirt in a swamp. He found himself stroking Petherwick's pubic hair (the pathologist had slipped a new thatch to him under the table at the inquest) and quickly tucked it away.

'Any messages, Miss Dravitt?'

'Sir Cyril Passey-Wix, sir, would like you to call at his house on the way to the funeral.'

Gordon Twetch, the country's penultimate comedian, was to be buried in Westminster Abbey that morning.

Windscale checked his watch – its tick sounded like rats chewing, and every chew was another mastication with no Petherwick at the end of it.

'I'd better toodle along,' he said.

Words like 'toodle' had been making guest-appearances in his natter since his elevation to Commissioner.

He toodled to the roof of New Scotland Yard and self-flew a helicopter the few brief roofs to Sir Cyril's London residence off Birdcage Walk. The slowing-down rotor-blades knocked his silver-badged hat off eleven times before he reached the safety of the ledge that led into the plush apartments. But two steps later his small cruel mouth looked like an anus gone on strike as he mouthed the smallest of o's in tripping on a shoot of guttering and falling some forty feet on to the balcony of Sir Cyril's bedroom.

The doors were open. Net curtains wafted in and out. A soft voice spoke from within.

'Come in, Commissioner. It's time you knew.'

Knew what? Windscale brushed himself down. The odd lonely raindrop fell from a white sky. He caught these on the end of his pointing finger and rubbed the scuff from his elbows. He walked into the net curtains. They brushed back his hair for him as he entered.

The bedroom was as pink as a rabbit's eye. Dollies embraced teddybears on a frilly bed. At the dressing-table, busy with her face, was a dark-haired woman in a purple dressing-gown whose *Harrods* tags were still dangling from the neck. Ever the gentleman, Windscale tactfully yanked them off.

The woman turned. It was Sir Cyril Passey-Wix, the Home Secretary, Windscale's ideal of manhood, the statesman whose vision of life had long been the greatest inspiration to the bullish man-mountain.

Windscale held his hat in his hands like the steering-wheel of a cliff-bound Lamborghini. He began to gag.

'Excuse me . . . I think I've somefinck stuck in my throat.'

'Can I help?'

Sir Cyril was on his red-toenailed feet using a small womanly implement from a set of such to hook out a hair from the barnacled back of Windscale's tongue. When he'd extracted it he giggled like a schoolgirl playing her first nude scene: he recognized it as a pubic hair (a stray one from Petherwick's thatch). He dropped it daintily into Windscale's hand.

'Erm, I'm here to see Sir Cyril,' said Windscale, these words easing away the last of his throat-tickle.

'But I am Sir Cyril, silly boy,' said Sir Cyril.

His long fingernails reached deep into his scudding quiff and pulled out a pin. Hair fell in inky tresses all down his back. He tossed it, coinciding with a sudden gust of air that lifted it around his petite head like a jagged cutting of night around a statue of a careworn Trojan beauty.

'You never is a woman, is yerh, um?'

Sir Cyril opened his dressing-gown for a moment: the sagging remains of a once pretty body . . . small large-nippled bosoms, pubes like a froth of crows, all unmistakably that of a lifelong feminine dame.

'I had a dangerous moment in the '60s,' he explained, 'When A.J.P. Taylor wrote that book about Asquith being a woman.'

Windscale was poleaxed. He sat on the bed, sinking deeply into it. A tumble of dollies fell into his lap like a pervert's dream come almost true.

Sir Cyril rescued them.

'This is Jermima. Say hello to the Commissioner, Jermima.' Jermima nodded her head. Other introductions followed.

'Look, sir . . . erm, madam . . . miss . . . errr . . .'

'Cerise.'

'Cerise, how nice . . . errr . . . does the Prime Minister know about . . . errr?'

'Nobody knows, not even Loveridge and he's worked for me for thirty years.'

Her fingernails walked on Windscale's chest, making red in the bulges of his silver buttons. She playfully clacked these like an in-season budgie tapping clapperless bells.

'You look very handsome in your new uniform,' she cooed.

'Errrrrr . . .' Windscale mumbled an inaudible thank you. Jermima suddenly opened one eye.

'Now that you know I'm a woman, do you find me at all attractive?'

Windscale was polite. A dry-throated yes came out with a cough. It sent the Home Secretary into a flutter. He was the sort of woman who hadn't existed since 1954.

'All these years I've lived as a man, but I am a woman, with a woman's desires bottled up in a woman's heart.'

'Uh-huh.'

Red fingernails tweaked a silver button. It slipped behind its eye leaving a terrifying length of uninterrupted blue between buttons. Windscale did it up with a twirl of anxious fingers that were suddenly stilled in a ewe's grip.

'I have never seen a policeman naked,' said Sir Cyril with a huge blush. Jermima opened her other eye.

Windscale had received few sexual advances in the thirty-seven years since his testicles dropped and had never refused any. But this time he wasn't keen.

'Look here, sir . . .'

'Sir . . . ise.'

'Cerise, yes . . . you see I'm not up to any nookieing-on if yer gets my drift, see, cos the girl wot I loved has recently . . . well, that were her in that bag, yerh know.'

'Oh you poor, poor boy.'

She kissed him on his chins, missing only three.

'GERROFFF!!!!'

A disgusted Windscale grabbed her by the shoulders and held her at arm's length.

Cerise's eyes pooled like birdbaths with her eyelashes beating in them like chaffinchs on their wedding day. Windscale couldn't help looking into these pretty blue eyes that, though dull with a lifelong hurt were bright with an unquenchable hope. She implored him to love her. Their lips quivered at each other, only Windscale's locked elbows holding them apart.

She was weak and soft in his arms and was suddenly smiling charmfully at the confusion that crusted the pudding that was his face. A moment more and victory was hers . . .

'Darling,' she said in her sweetest voice.

It was the voice from the speeches Windscale had listened to so often on his tape-recorder and her 'darling' was just like the almost-lost words at the end of certain clauses, thrown away in anticipation of a thunderously apt point about to be made. Windscale suddenly wanted her. Ever since he first saw her interviewed on *Panorama* during the height of the three-day week something within him must have realized she was a woman: he had loved her all this time without

realizing it. She licked her lower lip. His elbows unlocked. He lifted her close. She had won! His hot breath dried the pools in her eyes.
  'Darling,' he said.

There had never been such sex. Windscale performed rhinocerously: slow and with grunts. Sir Cyril felt like one of the cups of tea she so often stirred sugar into in the House of Commons tea-room, only now Windscale was doing the stirring, spinning her around and around, filling her with sugar till the spoon stuck hard and melted over her secret parts like all the cold buttons from every policeman's uniform ever made suddenly against an endless nipple who has anticipated nothing but this moment for a million years. Meanwhile Maltesers exploded in Windscale's loins. His every folicle trembled. His ecstatic groan was that of a riot-shield used as a wobble-board.
  Windscale slipped into a post-coital sleepiness awakened by Cerise's sobs. She was cross-legged on the deep-pile carpet, gripping her hammer-toes, crying her eyes out. Windscale knew what to do with an emotional woman. He slapped her face until she desisted.
  'It grieves me so much to say this,' she explained. 'But you were not the first.'
  Windscale was aghast.
  'Loveridge has that honour.'
  'But you said . . .'
  'One night at the Blackpool Conference after too much rum punch. We forgot ourselves under the tower. Oh, it was nothing but a drunken fantasy the next morning. Loveridge remembers nothing. I wouldn't have remembered it myself but . . .' Her voice crackled with shame. '. . . there was a child.'
  'Y'bugger!'
  'My little David grew up to become one of our major comedians. As I speak he is our only surviving comedian. Snog Duffie.'
  The naked Commissioner of Police had never before been more scandalized. A vein on the left side of his nose kicked the bags under his eye.
  'No one noticed I was pregnant. My belly stuck out a mile but no further than most of the other junior ministers. David, bless him, was born during the summer recess in a little nursing home in Bexhill when I was supposedly on an American lecture tour.'
  'Getaway!'

'My constituency agent, Pelham Duffie, brought him up. He thinks I'm David's father, not his mother. David, of course, knows nothing. But, call me a silly foolish woman if you must, I can't bear the idea of anything horrid happening to him and him never knowing the truth. I was preparing myself to tell him when you arrived this morning. He's downstairs now, helping Loveridge bake cakes.'

Windscale went downstairs and ate the first batch of cakes as they came hot from the oven. Snog Duffie got half of one before the big man snatched it from his hand. Windscale dribbed crumbs and grimaced.

'Aren't we a greedy puss!' said Loveridge.

It was an all-mod-cons kitchen. Windscale absent-mindedly played with an electric egg-whisk while beckoning Snog over.

'You feeling okay, lad?'

'I feel much better now. He'll not get me when you're here.'

'Who won't?'

'Him.'

'Oh, him. Naw. Not a chance. Look, you're in for a bit of a shock in a minute.'

Loveridge confiscated the egg-whisk. His madeleines had need of it. Just then there was a shy knock on the kitchen door.

'Ready or not, here I come!'

Sir Cyril Passey-Wix entered a room for the first time as Cerise Passey-Wix. The plunging neckline of his skin-tight policewoman's blouse, the crotch-huggingness of his union-jack-patterned hotpants left no doubt as to his femininity. Loveridge hiccoughed. His thumbs were cooking on the hotplate but he didn't notice.

'What the . . .?' went Duffie.

Windscale put a manly hand on the last comedian's shoulder. 'The Home Secretary is your mother,' he said.

'David!' cried Sir Cyril, and covered the staggered creature with lipsticking kisses. A nipple that had missed its chance at suckling peeped provocatively from the blouse.

Loveridge suddenly screamed at his thumbs. Windscale roughly held them under the tap while Cerise and Snog got acquainted on kitchen stools. Unsure of Loveridge's sex, Windscale carefully felt the front of his trousers. It was the perfect medicine for his stinging digits.

Duffie, meanwhile, feeling the oncoming of an identity crisis, fought out of his mother's affectionate grip and grabbed a bottle of Polish vodka from a trolley. He took a huge viscous swig.

'We'll go away together,' Cerise told him. 'We'll hide somewhere safe until Commissioner Windscale has caught this dreadful man. I hear Corfu is splendid at this time of year and goat's milk is so good for one's complexion.'

Snog stared at the exposed nipple. He took another big queer-tasting swig from a vodka bottle. A drip fell from his lips and hit the formica breakfast-bar with a whipcrack. A tiny mushroom cloud floated to the ceiling, which they all watched with a puzzled interest. In the formica was an inch-wide bubbled devastation.

All four were deadly still. Windscale took the bottle carefully from Duffie's hands and studied it for a long time of silence. In the middle of the label was a comedian's grave overgrown with ivy. The Polish lettering had too many zeds in it, asleep with zeds in fact, obviously faked by someone ignorant of Polish. Finally, the detective took out his fingerprintdustingkit and dusted the bottle's neck. A careful puff and fingerprints showed which he recognized as Broderick Cumber's.

Windscale put the bottle down carefully and mouthed 'nitro-glycerine' to Sir Cyril, who'd chewed the lipstick off his lower lip.

Duffie began to shake with fear.

'Mother!' he yelled.

But she was hiding behind Windscale, Loveridge likewise.

'Erm . . .' Windscale backed towards the door. 'I've just remembered a dental appointment,' he false-grinned with yellow, black, whitish and silver teeth.

Outside in the corridor Windscale, Sir Cyril and a thumb-blowing Loveridge waited with grim patience. When the explosion came they grabbed each other. The boombangabang was followed by a slow sound on the other side of the door like tomatoes being thrown at the sun by a planet sick of orbiting. Windscale swore that in a Renoir over the coathooks a fruit-fleshed girl slipped in her bath.

He peeped with seen-it-all-before eyes around the door. 'Urghhh-hhhhhhhhh!' he went, having not seen anything like this before. He clicked the door gently shut, saying: 'I'm afraid it's a bit of a mess in there.'

'Not to worry,' said Loveridge, regaining his hauteur, 'We have a woman-that-does who comes in twice a week.'

Windscale blinked detectively. 'This woman-that-does, did she come and do this morning?'

'She's got the mumps, apparently. Her third cousin twice removed was good enough to fill in. Leastways, she said she was her third cousin twice removed.'

He was damned clever was Cumber! But at least he'd done in his last comedian . . . there weren't any more left!

Sir Cyril seemed to be taking the tragedy very well. He changed into a stunning dress reminiscent of that in the Winterhaler portrait of the Empress Elizabeth von Habsburg. He was going to Gordon Twetch's funeral in it and he didn't care who saw.

'Do you think it's wise, ducky, after all these years?'

Loveridge's ducky was one reserved only for his closest intimates. Sir Cyril's woman's intuition knew this and was duly moved, more so because she had yet to tell him that the ratatouille plastering the kitchen had been his son also.

One last shock for Windscale that day. His latest bedpartner took his hand and held it over her belly:

'Can you feel it kick?'

Motherless, her grief had compensated her with a phantom pregnancy. Windscale's poke was to blame.

'Does this mean we're engaged?' he queried.

She ran out into the drizzling rain, playing hard to get.

Britain was comedianless!

'It is hoped,' wrote Epping Chowder in his column, 'that a new seriousness will emerge from our hereforeto cultural thrawn whose probity may engender us a camarilla to the greater geophysical sphere.'

Somehow, he was dead right. In a few short months terrible changes were wrought . . .

Young marrieds, weenies in hand on a seaside holiday that summer and wondering what to do with them, would find themselves at an end-of-the-pier show watching club-jugglers followed by two morticianish men chanting Aeschylus. London's Theatreland, meanwhile, was dominated by revivals of Lorca's sorrowful oeuvre. Shakespeare, it was found, played much better without the clowns. Philemon Glase, a dull playwright who'd taken up his pen after a car-crash rendered him blind, deaf, dumb, and senselessly quadriplegic and whose plays people merely endured in more chucklesome times in the sure knowledge they could have a laugh in the bar afterwards, were the surprise vogue. His *Cross*, a depiction of Christ's slow death in real time, filled Drury Lane every night.

'It is finished,' said Hank Lobley as Christ.

'Thank God for that!' said Windscale, sat in a box hand-holding with Cerise Windscale, his new wife, magnificent in her spangled crepe.

'Hallelujah!' went the audience.

Watching television was like chewing spinach with one's eyes. It wasn't simply the absence of sit-coms, jokes, or smile-inducing inanity that palled. It was the lack of the strained flippant levity that had come in a constant pour in the days before Cumber.

A new attitude was born, magnificent for the murderer's purpose: the world would not crack open now! Comedy was frowned upon. When Channel 4 showed *Gimpy* one Sunday afternoon there was a howl of protest. They apologized, promised never to show such a thing again. Next week they showed an opera with a thin soprano (fat ones were considered risable and therefore OUT). The programming was barraged with cheaply-made dramas, mostly using sit-comish sets, depicting failing human relationships in all their monotonous tedium. The shouting on the screen led to discussions in living-rooms which led to shouting in the living-rooms making the shouting on the screen more realistic in the angry eyes of the viewer. Everyone was hooked. Their dull foibles were dramatized, their personal miseries seemed pointful, their tedium was a badge they wore with serious courage.

Channel 3's hit of the season was a game show set in heaven where if a contestant failed to answer a question he had to speak for twenty minutes about his personal failings. Children's TV had *Wuffo*, the moral dilemmas of a basset hound in a one-parent family. The dog died at the end of every episode.

Politics, Lady Cerise found, was now much easier. You could say or do anything you liked if you had no fear of being laughed at. The monthly crime figures meanwhile, plummetted. Obviously, the new mood of self-analysis bred new values of which good behaviour was an essential part. In the opinion polls the government stood at 84%.

Britons returning after years abroad thought the Queen had died when they passed through Customs. The prevalent expression was that of a wronged fish. Within a day or so of having smiles returned by glaring frost, their masks turned fishtragic and they watched cancerous TV dramas mumbling to themselves: 'We're all going to die. All. Going to die. All.'

The few gluts of giggling girls, up in their bedrooms pretending to listen to Berlioz's *Requiem* but in fact making up their own jokes would be dragged downstairs by their hair and made to discuss the fall of Parnell with palsied relatives.

How carefully, how soberly people drove their fully taxed cars! How dopeless were the horses who romped home! And the wall-eyed men who knocked on the old lady's door really did come from the gas company! Policemen sat in their cars, drinking coffee from flasks, discussing their marriages.

Windscale couldn't wholly approve of this new mood. As he slouched finger-drumming at his New Scotland Yard desk, looking at the photo of his wife (she was stretched naked on red velvet), he was zonged with worries. Principal among these was that the mood might decide that chocolate was a levitatious substance and be taken from the shelves. He'd hoarded tons in warehouses and lock-ups all over London but ate every chunk as if it was his last. Even worse than that were the crime figures.

'Anything doing today, Miss Dravitt?'
'A man lost his credit cards in Ponders End.'
Windscale was on his feet.
'But he found them again.'
'Oh.'
Windscale's seat squeaked sadly as he sat.

What chance to bring back hanging if nobody did anything horrible enough! Perhaps, he mused, sneezing could be made a hangable offence. He wrote a memo to his wife on this subject but suddenly sneezed so reluctantly screwed it up. Already in the House of Commons they'd talked of cutting the police force. If things went on this way he'd be the only policeman left!

A depressing morning. Then: *whump*! A Special Branch report landed on his desk describing a sinister group meeting every midnight

PLETHORA OF GITS

in Highgate Cemetery to tell each other jokes. Windscale saw a way of disencumbering things . . .

An airless moonless night at the end of summer. Windscale walked through Highgate in a macintosh and a false beard.

'I say, that beard's a mite frivolous,' said a tough walking his mastiff.

'Bugger off!' said Windscale.

In all the houses he passed by the upper windows had squares of yellow light from which emanated the late-night rows which were so fashionable, never, sadly, descending into domestic violence.

The graves in Highgate Cemetery were blacker than the night, the sickly trees were blackest of all, tangling the few stars in their branches. Windscale walked as quietly as he could along the stony pathways, shoeless, sockless, but still making a noise like a man drowning in an unopened box of muesli.

Shhhhhhhhh! Ghostly whisperings. He leaned on an angelic flourish, his fingernails holding his balance by digging into the mossy dates 1840-1909. Someone was telling "the pig with a wooden leg" joke.

'. . . And HE said: "That's too good a pig to eat all at once."'

Back-of-the-class suppressed laughter.

Someone tugged at his elbow. 'Here, mate, you heard this one.'

Windscale took him by the throat and stepped into the joke-telling hide.

'DON'T NOBODY MOVE. I AM THE POLICE. I HAS YERHS SURROUNDED GOOD AND PROPER.'

Nobody moved. A timid voice: 'Tissent against the law, telling jokes tissent.'

Windscale lit his torch under his chins. He grinned like God with a newly-made World to take everyone to. 'If yerhs wants ter be bloody comedians,' he said. 'I'll gis yerhs yerh chance.'

Windscale placed torches in the trees, pointing on to the twig-cracking ground where his spread-out macintosh made a makeshift stage.

'Panto season's cummin up and us lot's gonna do ourselves a show, gorrit? *Dick Whittington*, see. We'll hire the Palladium and make the buggers laugh like wot they never laughed before. What ya say?'

They couldn't have been keener.

Windscale handed out scripts and costumes. Rehearsals commenced after a brief tussle over the cat costume. The top cop was playing Whittington himself, as himself, convinced, as he always had been, that he possessed an unequalled sense of humour. It didn't fret him that he'd never actually laughed at a comedian before, or even, it must be admitted, a joke. It'd be easy, bloody easy. He'd be a smash. Him and this plethora of gits would have the country wetting itself with plenty enough ha-haas to restore some good-old chaotic normality.

They met to rehearse every night in their cemetery corner. How hard they worked! What a wheeze it all was! But every onceandawhile Windscale would stop the proceedings with a severe shhhhh as he shone his torch into the grave-black darkness. Somewhere out in the graves he thought he heard the sound of a panda being gut-punched and a hand-muffled cackle of most sinister ilk. No one else could hear it. Mebbees it was inside his head, a catchy tune being played on a steam-rollered trombone by a windless Dixielander. OF COURSE! It dawned. His policeman's instinct had sent him a premonition! The comic killer! . . . Their show would bring him out of retirement!

Windscale's lips moved soundlessly. 'Stephanie!' they almost said.

After dispatching Snog Duffie, Cumber had lain low in Gordon Twetch's old apartment in Maida Vale. He seethed on the bed for weeks, grinding his teeth and cackling. He imagined he was a clown in a circus, being horribly abused by children that were all himself. Buckets of water drenched the bed. A flak of pies threw themselves around the room like an intergalactic war not being taken too seriously.

The doorbell rang. *The End* came up over Cumber's reverie. He sat up with the calm unshaven face of a round-the-world yachtsman sailing into a tranquil Punta del Este after a thousand miles of storms. He answered the door. It was Dr Scrapie, his penis just about to press the bell again.

The Doctor whirred into the room in his ball-bearinged chair. Behind him was a phantom Pringle Dicks which Cumber did his best to ignore.

'You are completely INSANE!!!' pronounced the Doctor.

Dicks waved childishly. Cumber averted his eyes.

'We must face zee truth, you unt I,' said Scrapie sadly. 'We hast failed. You vill never be cured. You must be incarcerated forever in ein rubber room.'

Dicks was at Cumber's ear: 'I've a new routine, kid, wait'll yerh hear it. It'll kill yerh.'

'NO! NO!'

'YES! YES!' yelled the Doctor.

'I'se found meself a ginormous giant. We opens in the Palladium tomorrow night. What belters we'll get! We'll have the buggers laughing like wot they never did laugh ever.'

'NO! It's not true. I'm imagining it all!'

He retreated into a recent fantasy, that it was 1493, he was an Italian Prince poisoned by Lucrecia Borgia and had imagined the entire modern world during a poison-sweating fever.

When he came out of this he was lying on a mudbank beside the Thames at Woolwich. He held in his hand what was unmistakeably Dr Scrapie's penis. It was the cruellest thing he'd ever done. In abjectest horror he threw it into the smelly water. It wriggled momentarily before it sank.

Wilfie Windscale
is
Dick Whittington
Tonight 7.30

was what the lights said outside the Palladium. On the poster were a platoon of other names. No Pringle Dicks. Obviously, he'd imagined it. Soditall! There he was, walking straight into the theatre without opening the doors. A bleeding ghost, would you believe!

Cumber shook the locked doors till a sleepy man came up behind them.

'We's sold out for months, mister,' he said.

Cumber ate bananas in a cafe until the theatre crowd began clipping the pavement. They discussed the inadequacies of their relationships, or if this was a first date the inadequacies of past relationships, or if this was their first-ever date the inadequacies of the first few minutes of this first-ever date . . . as they sauntered seriously towards a production of Dick Whittington which they expected would cast new light on the history of local government.

Cumber brained a nun as she stepped out of a taxi. He filched her ticket and seethed into a seat in the Palladium which had expected something different.

'I hope you're not going to do that when the play starts,' said a snooty woman.

Cumber controlled his seethe.

'Perhaps you're having trouble with your relationships. I know I am. Trevor, for instance . . .'

She told him about Trevor, at the same time eating what everyone else was eating: saltless hazelnuts (Windscale had been right about chocolate).

An age passed before the lights went down. A flummery of frivolous music pinged from the orchestra pit. The audience was uneasy, but then they thought: this is obviously an ironic comment on the superficiality of 14th Century political life before Whittington reformed it. Cumber was bleeding from his eyes.

Curtain up. Enter Dick (Windscale) in a pair of loud shorts and a coonskin cap, followed by an upright cat (John Gullybrooke).

DICK: Ho, hum, Pussy, the streets of London are not paved with gold after all.

Obviously this introduced the play's theme: the illusoriness of material possession.

DICK: But I've still got you, hassent I, eh?

Very impressive, this: the playwright was saying that relationships are what really matter in this life. But then the cat wee-weed up his leg and Dick shot it.

DICK: Now I hassent even got a cat.

The lights closed around Windscale and he sang what he hoped would be the show's hit song, *Now I hassent got a Cat*, which may have moved a row or two if the cat hadn't stood up and joined in each chorus, only to be shot again as Dick repeated the refrain. When the cat fetched itself the materials for custard pies, which it mixed angrily on a table while wearing a chef's hat, it was obvious to one and all that the actors were trying to be funny.

PLETHORA OF GITS

They were outraged! Rival critics, Epping Chowder and Habakuk Jones, took their eyes off the stage and watched each other to see which would be the first to stomp out in a cloud of ripped-up programme.

Windscale wiped the first three of a planned seventeen thousand custard pies from his eyes. He was already desperate. Not a titter. Titterless.

Fitzwarren (Henry St Crewn) was finishing his sexual assault on the cook (Deborah Oaks), containing some amusing business with a rolling pin, a bag of flour and some flatulence. They were dying. Not a laugh anywhere. But yes! A definite cackle from seat K21.

It was Cumber. Satisfied that no laughter would disturb the calm of his crackless earth, he'd laughed.

In the play Whittington was about to chuck in his towel, despairing of ever making his fortune. Windscale was equally depressed. Suddenly he stopped in mid-line and stamped to the footlights.

'BLOODY LAUGH, YOU BASTARDS!!!!!' he yelled at the audience.

Not a ha, he or a ho.

'AS COMMISSIONER OF THE METROPOLITAN POLICE I ORDER YOU TO LAUGH!!!!!'

A few hees, a ho here and there.

Windscale loaded his stage gun with real bullets. He shot indiscriminately into the stalls, dislodging several hats. Forced laughter came among the screams. His hands waved come-ons for more. He'd make the buggers remember how to laugh! But when he stepped back to continue the play their faces fell glum again. When the curtain came up for Act II half the audience was gone.

Strange to say, it was the ghost of Pringle Dicks that saved the day. When Whittington came in to spy on Miss Stephanie, his beloved, in the bath, Dicks stood up in the suds in a dripping getup and said: 'What's the weather like up there?'

Epping Chowder guffawed. He couldn't help it.

DICKS: Look, get rid of that cat, what yerh needs is an ostrich.

Windscale didn't remember this bit. 'Errrrrr . . . prompt?'

The prompter was frantic. But it didn't matter. Dicks was leading Windscale aside, rat-tat-tatting quick patter. This was his new sure-fire routine and it was working. Even Windscale got laughs every time he said prompt, especially when he dragged the prompter on stage, stood on his neck and said PROMPT. Dicks, meanwhile, was back in the bath, puffing a cigar during vigorous patter. Then suddenly quiet, over his shoulder to Dick: 'Prompt?'

Windscale scoured the script. 'Look here, you, there tissent nowt about ostriches anywhere in here and I oughta know cos I wrote the bastard!'

The audience was in hysterics.

Cumber was out of his seat, pushing along the row, biting his tongue with all his might. Windscale's head was wobbling smugly with his triumphant laugh.

Dicks, meanwhile, was soaping his comedian's hat when a puppetized ostrich's head came out of the water on a long neck.

DICKS: I wondered where I'd put it.

Huge laugh.

Cumber climbed the steps at the side of the stage, cackling uncontrollably. His eyes were spinning like the fruit in one-armed bandits, stopping every heavy step to reveal a jackpot of two dead Windscales on that very stage. The audience thought this was part of the act. They pointed at Cumber and in hushed expectation dried their smiling eyes.

He faced Windscale across the stage.

WINDSCALE: All right, young fella me lad, it's all over. Yerh nabbed.

Cumber showed his teeth and stepped forward.

WINDSCALE: This is an official warning. One more step and I'll shoot.

Cumber took out a gun of his own, a small pale-grey lunatic of a gun, and stepped forward.

Windscale shot at his feet, splintering the stage. Cumber cackled contemptuously.

But the stage began to move, slowly at first. Windscale's bullet had hit some mechanism under the boards. The stage lurched. Windscale fell backwards just as Cumber fired his first shot: it shaved the hairs between his eyebrows. The stage increased speed, faster and faster. The orchestra played as fast as it could, ran through all the music it had, twice in three minutes. Seventeen thousand custard pies span off the stage, flung relentlessly into the audience . . . by some undiscovered law of physics they all hit the same man. Windscale hung onto the curtain, a boil on the end of a tongue, shooting at Cumber every time he came around. And every time he looked madder, and every time the audience laughed harder at him. He screamed for his mam. He screamed for Dr Scrapie. He screamed for the man he really was to come and save him. Because he knew, for certain, that the laughter was so immense that the world was about to crack, sperm would flood everything and Pringle Dicks would inherit the earth. Trapdoors snapped open and gaped shut. He tripped past them, dodging Windscale's bullets. Then it happened: the earth cracked. Right through the stalls the crack came, up the stage, snapping its spin in two. Screams from all of Cumber's shooting thoughts as the sperm bubbled ankle-high in the stalls. It was the same in Bombay, in Australia and Wisconsin, in Hangchow and Pietermaritzburg. Cumber had visions of it all as the sperm rose giving the flapping fish room to grow and swim. All with Dicks's long lugubrious face, they nipped at his ankles. Each fish, he knew, would eat just one of his bodily cells till there was nothing left of him but one painful cell he could call himself. The theatre was full of sperm now, as high as the Gods, audience and their programmes floating in solution, orchestra and their instruments sunk in the creamy water. Cumber held his breath but he was also screaming. Then Windscale floated out of the fishful mist like a zepellin submarine. He placed his gun to Cumber's forehead and pulled the trigger. Everything was suddenly dry. Ships of dust floated through an air full of light. He was falling forward through a trapdoor to the tumultuous applause of the audience.

In the vast night-time city of Cumber's brain lights went off in all the rooms and all the people in them died suddenly at home, dropped dead doing whatever they were doing. The streets ran with blood and the all-night chemist was slumped over his pestel at a desk of unopened letters.

Windscale was under the stage. He kicked the broken Cumber

on to his back before looking up at the bright lit trapdoor holes. Faces stared down.

'It's him. The comic killer. He's dead.'

'Oops!' said someone.

A rain of saltless hazelnuts plonked the dusty understage.

Laughter came from far away. Pringle Dicks's last night of patter just a murmur to the policeman looking sadly at the murderer's face.

'When I'm gone, there'll never be another,' said Dicks and disappeared during a standing ovation.

Windscale's helicopter swooped out of the air and landed in the begonia patch afront the stately home of Lord St Mawes Godolphin on the Goonhilly Downs in Cornwall.

He ate three Cadbury's Cream Eggs before anyone answered the door. It was Lord Rupert himself, dressed in rusty chainmail and a crusader's hat.

'I'm sorry,' he said. 'It's my time machine. I've lost all the servants in it . . . and this lot won't do anything.'

'This lot' sat in the hall like patients in a timeless dentist's. They were Vikings, Chinese mandarins, Russian serfs, Edward III, numerous paleozoic types and a hot Eskimo.

Windscale was stiff. 'Look, I errrr . . . I thought you should have this.'

He placed Petherwick's pubic hair in Lord Rupert's grubby hand. He recognized his late wife's thatch immediately and wept.

'I've done everything to get her back, but it won't work, dammit, it just won't work.'

He took Windscale downstairs to his workshop.

'Look, I'm sure this is bloody clever, but I've gorra get back to London. There was a wages snatch on Battersea Bridge this morning.'

'Oh, please, I must show you this.'

He poured lemonade into an immense tube. 'Cold fusion from lemonade,' he boasted. Then he twiddled a knob and on an ordinary corner-of-the-living-room-TV with only a smatter of extra knobs there span a rolling picture.

'See if you can get the news. Might be something about the wages snatch.'

PLETHORA OF GITS

Lord Rupert twiddled. The picture span to a standstill. It fizzed with snow. A squinting Windscale could make out the outside of New Scotland Yard. The sign was going around as usual.

'Some sort of villainous surveillance device, is it?' growled Windscale. 'For villains to see wot us coppers is up to.'

'No, really, this is the past, years ago.'

The snow cleared. Petherwick was sitting under the sign in a tight-fitting police tracksuit.

'It's Stephanie!'

'Who?'

Windscale pointed at the thatch poking from the aristo's pen-full pocket.

'Where? I can't see her.'

Snow fell on to the picture again. It began to fade.

'GET HER BACK!!! GET HER BACK!!!'

'Errr . . . oooh, dear, the diffraction's on the wonk, sorry.' Knobs came off in his hands.

Windscale whipped out his truncheon.

'This always works at home,' he sniffed.

'Oooooh, I wouldn't, honestly!' warned Lord Rupert.

But he did.

When the flash cleared from Windscale's eyes he was lying under the turning New Scotland Yard sign. Petherwick was combing magnesium sulphate out of his hair. Burning lemonade dripped from windowsills.

'Stephanie?'

'I've been waiting for you,' she said.

'But it can't be . . .'

It was. He kissed her strawberry-creme lips in a timelost empty-except-for-them London where they could wander hand in hand forever, their first night together lived over and over and over again.

APPENDICES

Appendix One:

A Map of Bulgaria

Appendix Two:

An Extract from *THUD*:

. . . . *thud thud thud thud thud thud thud thud thud thud*
thud thud thud thud thud thud thud thud thud thud
thud thud thud thud thud thud thud thud thud thud
thud thud thud thud thud thud thud thud thud thud
thud thud thud thud thud thud thud thud thud thud
thud thud thud thud thud thud thud thud thud thud
thud thud thud thud thud thud thud thud thud thud
thud thud thud thud thud thud thud thud thud thud
thud thud thud thud thud thud thud thud thud thud
thud thud thud thud thud thud thud thud thud thud
thud thud thud thud thud thud thud thud thud thud
thud thud thud thud thud thud thud thud thud thud
thud thud thud thud thud thud thud thud thud thud
thud thud thud thud thud thud thud thud thud thud
thud thud thud thud thud thud thud thud thud thud
thud thud thud thud thud thud thud thud thud thud
thud thud thud thud thud thud thud thud thud thud
thud thud thud thud thud thud thud thud thud thud
thud thud thud thud thud thud thud thud thud thud
thud thud thud thud thud thud thud thud thud thud
thud thud thud thud thud thud thud thud thud thud
thud thud thud thud thud thud thud thud thud thud
thud thud thud thud thud thud thud thud thud thud
thud thud thud thud thud thud thud thud thud thud
thud thud thud thud thud thud thud thud thud thud
thud thud thud thud thud thud thud thud thud thud
thud thud thud thud thud thud thud thud thud thud
thud thud thud thud thud thud thud thud thud thud

STEVE WALKER

thud thud thud thud thud thud thud thud thud thud
thud thud thud thud thud thud thud thud thud thud
thud thud thud thud thud thud thud thud thud thud
thud thud thud thud thud thud thud thud thud thud
thud thud thud thud thud thud thud thud thud thud
thud thud thud thud thud thud thud thud thud thud
thud thud thud thud thud thud thud thud thud thud
thud thud thud thud thud thud thud thud thud thud
thud thud thud thud thud thud thud thud thud thud
thud thud thud thud thud thud thud thud thud thud
thud thud thud thud thud thud thud thud thud thud
thud thud thud thud thud thud thud thud thud thud
thud thud thud thud thud thud thud thud thud thud
thud thud thud thud thud thud thud thud thud thud
thud thud thud thud thud thud thud thud thud thud
thud thud thud thud thud thud thud thud thud thud
thud thud thud thud thud thud thud thud thud thud
thud thud thud thud thud thud thud thud thud thud
thud thud thud thud thud thud thud thud thud thud
thud thud thud thud thud thud thud thud thud thud
thud thud thud thud thud thud thud thud thud thud
thud thud thud thud thud thud thud thud thud thud
thud thud thud thud thud thud thud thud thud thud
thud thud thud thud thud thud thud thud thud thud
thud thud thud thud thud thud thud thud thud thud
thud thud thud thud thud thud thud thud thud thud
thud thud thud thud thud thud thud thud thud thud
thud thud thud thud thud thud thud thud thud thud
thud thud thud thud thud thud thud thud thud thud
thud thud thud thud thud thud thud thud thud thud
thud thud thud thud thud thud thud thud thud thud
thud thud thud thud thud thud thud thud thud thud
thud thud thud thud thud thud thud thud thud thud
thud thud thud thud thud thud thud thud thud thud
thud thud thud thud thud thud thud thud thud thud
thud thud thud thud thud thud thud thud thud thud
thud thud thud thud thud thud thud thud thud thud
thud thud thud thud thud thud thud thud thud thud

PLETHORA OF GITS

thud   thud   thud   thud   thud   thud   thud   thud   thud   thud
thud   thud   thud   thud   thud   thud   thud   thud   thud   thud
thud   thud   thud   thud   thud   thud   thud   thud   thud   thud
thud   thud   thud   thud   thud   thud   thud   thud   thud   thud
thud   thud   thud   thud   thud . . . . .

Appendix Three:

THE VICTIMS

Pringle Dicks
Freddie Moss
Jerry Muckle
Harry Scouse
Jackey Mills
Jimmy Forrest
Bib & Tucker
Livid & Woebegone
Manny Narna
Stan Leekie
Roy Dibbs
Eddie Haddock
Huey Penzer
Fred Beeves
Curly Nott
Solly Norman
Len Engles
Alf Cooper-Harris
Nifty Orriss
Hu Flout
Minky & Jayne
Barney Fawkes
Sidney Night
Maxwell Drear
Chalky Dookan
Iffy Jocks
Sexton Ballard
Maxwell Drear

Dwight Hepple
Skip Marlow
Nidry & Flint
Elizabeth Kay
George Chowder
W.H. Hook
Sorrage & Porrage
Josie Fain
Marina Coypu
Winston Dukes
Clay Marmion
Fingers Bonar-Law
Dick Shirttail
Fabian Mealy
Pilly & Twit
Jeremy Pascoe
Marcus Bellua
Hilary Penzer
Richard Morton
Bill Freeze
Gavin Dirge
Elvira Carter
Britt Broadbent
Emmeline Armstrong
Emery Placketts
Erica Ware
Don Alexander
Piers Woodwood

STEVE WALKER

Edward G. Fiske
Josh Cummings
Adolf Kirk
Wom
Gobby Gibson
Martina Culver
Ed Butti
Joey Selkirk
Norm Cawber
Morton & Quist
Quackers Mallard
Bernie Higginbotham
Yam and Dammdamm
Gemma Freeman
Yisko (Frank Gray)
Noel Dagg
Debbie Cups
Langley Debenham
Martha Gylchrist
Jamie-Lee Lippinscott
Nonie Griff
Phillip Pears
Iggy Agrippa
Rufus Punter
Phyllis Gifford
The Three Nobbys
Gary Barkis
Horatio Batsie Jr
Will Gemini
Rowena Godsbody
Gunther Carchase
Rita Meek
Harry Barry
Barry Harry
Gummo Browne
Rex Head
Captain Wensley Hope
Ollie Arkle
Achilles Jam

Jim Stocker
Rabbi Aaaron O'Hymill
Ariadne Lurch
Max Conner
Lennie Sprag
Bing Piggywig & Tubby Halliday
Roj Gumm
David Hume
Jack Prince
Chris Tashe
Judy
Hugo Holt
Burt Wellingtons
Ooha Flowers
Lionel Always
Billy Sniffta
Hey Ambrose
Crazy Joe McCormack
Wilson James
Benedict Spinnose
Alf Scott
Gimcrack & Corn
Lennie Penny
Sean Cave
Humpty Prot
Big Bill Towser
Graham Bovering
Chippy Patel
Sidney Klean
Seamus Toole
Lennox & Sadie
Much Bray
Jamie MacPhail
Sir Royston Moes (mistaken for Willie Fowler)
Liam O'Luff
Melanie Legs
Willie Fowler

PLETHORA OF GITS

Maud Claridge
Chester Tree
Barry Barris
Donald Ark
Perc Warbeck
Benny Happuck
Lemuel Niddy
Piggy Volks
Guy Gull
Paul Tarsus
Oscar Locke
Eddie Nasty
Dwain Forrest
Regina Ragga
Francis Court
Ian Act
Tommy Chaucer
John, John & John
Phil Mogs
Lenny Grub
Randolph Longstaff
Silly Burgess
Chrissie MacLean
Barney Thwaite & Renata
Hubert Nixon
Jonah Cornell
Mike Blanchie
Flo Splay
Osric Fyffer
Charlie Balls
George Chiswick
Zoe Wren
Malcolm Lolly
Patience Legget
Alex Munder
Jeff Droon
Ralph Cogswell
Herbert Morrison
Chesney Zit

Joy Oliver
Kitty Armitage & her mother Grace
Art Griswald
Hibbs, Dobbs and Dibbs
Sacheverell O'Blitt
Paul Moffatt
Mack Greer
Jock MacRobinson
Orson Wilt
Amos Dibbler
Witty & Poole-in-Dorset
Jackdaw Daws
Zippy Grafton
Alan Carol
Ivor Bodie
Millicent Murrison
Hutton Mowles
Gordon Card
Mickey Goodlaw
Salome Wellings
Mariebelle Tracy
Jesse Joel
Miles Who
Sampson Clot
Aubrey Bee
Brian Ling
Tich Foxy
Arthur Stanley Laguna
Bart Ditchburn
Carew Blaney
Billy Oi
Mavis Dipple
Septimus Scrivan
Rufus Boxer
Dick Duckie
Absalom Mudhusband
Cora Tharby
Wendy & Jean Minter

Kurt Kruse
Coco Ladbrook
Sneezer Cudworth
Branwell Lubin
Taffy Macbeth
Lena Lovelocks
Bert Crossland
Ronnie Lowe
Crispin Day
Mick Loop
Gus Laffin
Wade Driscoll
Jason House
Kruger & East
Tyrone Lee
Hutch Joel
Rock Marsden
Willie Roper
Charles Pratter
Jilly Beckenthoager-Weevesplatt & her singing cats
Lyle Shaw
Karen Jenner
Ronnie Howath
Salvatore Munke
E. Bygum
Holmes Hare
Mark Usk
Billy Byker
Jules & McGowan
Len Cupnitz
Wally Bradford
Jessup Huntley
Timothy Smiddy
Clark Sussex
Raymond Trumbell
Shakes & Romney
Joey Wafer

Hudson St George
Phutter & Stop
Mandy Patisserie
Higgins Sinatra
Grenville Plum
Mac Kone
Bill Pealaw
Jimjam Blaylock
Curly Purley
Phil & Derek Wardley
Wilma Primrose
Moppy Swinburne
Seb Lushington
Ewart Peel
Havelock Dock
Scouser Shortcake
Prettyboy Manors
Tufty Clancy
Rutherford Hambledon
Zach
Charlton Clough
Herbie Shig
Goldie Gubbins
Mark Mungus
Olaf Snaveley
Ladybird Pritchard
Leon McInnes
Bill & Bigger Bill
The Sharples Sisters
Sherlock Telfer
Henry Zimm
Calthorp Thin
Thomasina Wagner
Silvie Eggerton
Howie Tess
Vinny Frumentius
Stan Whisker
Lothar Gynt
Anita Krummie

PLETHORA OF GITS

Lois Alma
Marco Five
Walter Ajax
Mort Tickatocka
Yolande Clarty
Alan Purvis
Theo Kyan
Curtis Zimber
Trixy Thorne
Micky Millions
Pat Feeny
Lester Dudderson
Clarence Crispie
Buster Bel-Air
Franklin Newcombe
'The Bigteasers' with Jake Bentley
Barnie Ashton
Samuel Posey
Les Athey
Monty Rhombus
Nasse & Crown
Witney Zora
Ballygawley & Whey
Wes Sandy
Zelda Yoxford
Wendel Eccleshall
Chummy Lummy
Edward Dunstable
Drybridge & Si
Judge Jeff
Edie Hills
Dickie Dreer and his seal Wanda
Jasper Ngimbi
Agnes Weeeee
Jacky Yakky
Rich Raven
Jud Prentice

Daigo Frumling
Felix Krantz
Carl Rainbow
Lorne Belding
Stuffy Pozzo
Evans Evans
Ptolemy Rivers
Tomtom Pinkney
Harold Strickland (Ozzy the Clown)
Grover Log
Orville Venus
Silas Binny
Fred Weaver
Bea Raefferty
Noah Huckel
Dick Quick
Stella Rumbold
Vickey Vasey
Sly Robinson
Tancred Floozie
Victor Emmanuel Grass
Gordon Lowther
Birdy MacCool
Ringo Sunday
James Flagg
Pete Ullswater
Bobby Gallup
Darius Figg
Barry Doggler
Xavier Lickmere
Mo de Plessis
Octavius Pope
Darnley Potts
Karl Hall
Christopher Martin Cluck
Ed Minot
Cally Fuchs
Wendell Minto

STEVE WALKER

Tony Ferrano
Frank Dibdin
Larry Lorry
Fidel Cardiff
Jenny Gwynne
Myron Childs
Betty Carp
Henrique Nobbs
Istvan Fenniger
Lloyd Coffin
Vaughan Thomas
Benny Coeurdelion
Mavis Knebworth
Phew Lytton
Henry Beddoes
Aubrey Bugly
Wystan James
Lulu da Silva
Phil Katz
Garath Tinlker
Knuckles MacDoak
Jo Dixon-Nixon
Ethelred Unready
Gay Foy
Willieboy Fragonard
Hugh Cockle
Len Gascoigne
Digger Roos
Francis George
Gabby Mabley
Bertie Audubon
Paul Rooke
Bill Coddrington
The 14 Flying Pinskis
Enoch Jolson
Hedley Roach
Tam Gurvey
Hamilton Plautus
Oz Hart

Wesley Vines
Vince Shrewstring
Pythian Ponders
Florris Hampton
F.U. Two
Dodger Browndog
Tirzah Varney
Penny Churchill
Nev Graf
Gert and Harry Whiting
Horsa Hibbert
Fanny Bloom
Saul Gutteridge
Arfpint Charlie Dinty
Gussy Knowles
Fritz Dingle
Kid Jerry
Geraint Dooley
Jimbo Pinkerton
Hank Abbot
Nippy Richards
Onions
Cosmo Liggy
Brian Royce
John Bucks
Ashby Peabody
Osbert Twaine
John Floage
Billy Mumpness
Hillaire Fields
Percy Street
Mary-Ann Tompkinson
Lilith Dobson
Ninette McNab
Stevie Playfair
Walter Veeks
Philemon Pupplet
Sammy Petrie
Jo Wednesday

PLETHORA OF GITS

Sheila Crowhurst
Little Ma Teacup
Jayne Jayne
Prissie Wilkes
Timmy Floot
Eric Munchie
Sarah Higgins
Brian Jackers
Silas Gint
Perry Londale
Ettie Sharps
Pelham Groome
Erwin Irwin
Hecate Smedley
Hecate Waffen-Smythe
Hecate Dodger
Hecate Wilson
Hank Dean
Davey Buttermere
Dib-Dob Dibley
Hal Jervis
Wiggly Hoop
J. Melvin Sky
Peggy Lewes
Rowland Meese
Queenie Tremayne
Blanco White
Gordon Twetch
Snog Duffie.

Appendix Four:

Two Letters by W.E. Windscale

1. To Sir Cyril Passey-Wix:
(actual size)

2. To Cheryl Petherwick:
(actual size)